Madness in Small Towns

Also by Iza Moreau

The News in Small Towns (2012)
Secrets in Small Towns (2014)
Mysteries in Small Towns (2015)

Madness in Small Towns

Iza Moreau

Black Bay Books

Books for people who like to think about what they read.

Madness in Small Towns

Black Bay Books
1939 Sand Basin Rd.
Grand Ridge, FL 32442

Printed in the USA
First Printing in 2013

ISBN-13: 978-1481929950
Library of Congress Control Number: 2013930541

Cover Images by Edward Deeds
Cover Design by Black Bay Books

First Print Edition

Does this horse go into a trailer without difficulty? If not, you have a deadly serious problem to solve before you can join the cross-country club.

—Bonnie Ledbetter

If he did not load well when you got him, he needs to be trained. There are many good techniques for training horses to load.

—Julie Goodnight

Come on, we're going.

—Cindy McKeown

Chapter 1

I blame the full moon. It was just after 1 a.m. on a cool night in early December. I was lying in bed feeling lousy and wondering whether I should go out and put the blankets on the horses when my phone rang, shattering the first little bit of peace I'd enjoyed for almost a week. I snatched up the receiver before it had a chance to ring again.

"Yes?"

"Hi. Is this Sue-Ann?" The voice was high pitched and whiney, sounding uncomfortable and uncertain, a girlish voice, but one definitely issuing from the mouth of a man.

"Yes it is."

"Sue-Ann McKeown?"

"That's right."

"This is Cletus Donnelly speakin. Clete. We went to hah school together, d'you remember?"

The name was vaguely familiar and I tried to hang a face on it: a gangly, pimply faced boy. A loner? I wasn't certain. Had he been nursing a crush on me for 25 years and finally got brave enough—or drunk enough more likely—to ask me out? Shit. "It was a small high school, Clete. I'm sure I saw you around. Listen, it's the middle of the night and I've been on the road for two days straight. Is this important?"

"Oh, raht. I'm really sorry to bother you. I jist wanted to tell you that ah'm gettin ready to kill mahself."

Brilliant, I thought. Just what I needed. I closed my eyes. "That's great, Cletus," I answered. "I really appreciate you telling me that, but if there's nothing else—"

"Don't ya want to know how ah'm gon do it?" he broke in.

"No, not really. What I really want is a little sleep and—"

"Ah got Mama tied to the bedposts," he said quickly.

I opened my eyes and sat up. "You what?"

"And ah poured gasoline all round her bed. Round the whole house, too. Jist before ah die ah'm goin to torch the whole place." That voice. Almost hysterical, as if Cletus was trapped in a corner by an army of rats. It was the voice more than the words that gave me the whammy jammies.

"Why are you telling me this, Cletus . . . Clete?" I asked. "You need to call a hotline or the police or a mortuary." I threw off the covers and got to my feet, still holding onto the receiver.

"No way, José," he said.

"But why me?"

"You're a reporter."

"And?"

"And ah want you to raht up mah story. An make sure ah get on the first page."

"Your story?"

"Ah have a story."

"Let me get this straight. You're going to kill yourself unless I put a story about you in the paper?"

"No, you don't understand. Ah'm *goin* to kill mahself sure enough. You need to raht about whah ah did it."

Everybody has a story, even though most of us don't have to threaten murder and suicide to get it told. Well, it's not as if I had expected to get any sleep that night. I decided to give him his fifteen minutes. "All right then, Clete," I told him. "Hold on and I'll get my notebook and my pencil. Don't go killing anybody before I get back okay?"

"Yeah, but hurry."

Actually, I had a notebook within reach on my nightstand. What I really needed was in my purse. Placing the phone receiver softly on the bed, I quickly flicked on the light, padded into the living room, and took my cell phone from my purse. I pressed the speed dial number for the Jasper County Sheriff's Department—it was much faster than going through all that 911 rigmarole. A female voice answered, "Jasper County Sheriff, Tequesta speaking. How—"

"Tequesta," I broke in. "This is Sue-Ann McKeown. Listen quick. Some guy named Cletus Donnelly is on my other line. He says he's going to kill himself and his mother."

"Hey, I know Clete. What—"

"Just listen. You need to get somebody to his house and stop him from whatever he's about to do. He's probably armed and he says he's saturated the house with gasoline. You got that? I'll try to keep him talking until you get there."

"Yeah, but where does he live?"

"No idea. Look in the phone book! Who's on duty tonight? Dilly Dollar? Have have him call me at this number when he gets there."

"Right, okay."

I broke the connection, ran back to the bedroom, and grabbed up my notebook. "Okay, got it. You still there Clete?"

"Yeah, raht."

I sat down on my bed with my back against the wall, phone in one hand, pencil in the other. My notebook was on my lap and my cell phone, set on vibrate, was on the bed next to me. "Okay," I told him. "Go ahead."

"Go ahead what?"

"Tell me your story."

The voice that came over the wire was still shriekily unnerving, but more hesitant, more tense than it was previously. "Ah don't, you know, have it written down or nothin. You haveta ask me questions."

I sighed, but not into the phone. "Right. Okay, then, Clete, how are you planning to kill yourself?"

This time he answered without hesitation. "Samurai sword,"

"I'm impressed. Are you going to cut off your own head or what?"

"That's not . . . You're making fun a me, aren't you?"

I spoke quickly. "No, no really. I'm just asking."

"You can't cut off your own head."

"Right, I can see that now."

"Ah mean, think about it." He paused, then resumed, "Ah'm goin ta fall on it."

"Yeah?"

"It's a honorable death," he said. "Samurai guys sometimes had to do it so they wouldn't be disgraced. Even some guy in the bible did it. Ah've thought about it a lot. Ah'm goin to put the tip a the blade against mah chest—raht where mah heart is—and just close mah eyes and fall forward. It'll be just lahk steppin off inta space."

I tried to visualize what he was saying. "Um, what if the handle slips on the floor?" I asked.

"Ah'll, you know, anchor it down some way." Clete's voice was starting to sound a little more frantic if that was possible, so I changed the subject.

"Why are you going to kill your mother?" I asked.

"Well, you know, how could she get along bah herself? She has heart trouble and rheumatism. No, if ah go, she hasta go, too."

"Just a thought here, but are you going to let her burn to death, or are you going to kill her with the sword first?"

"Naw, she'll be dead from the smoke a long time before the fahr gets to her."

"Clete," I began a new train of thought. "Has something bad happened to you recently? Got laid off? Money troubles?"

"Naw, nothin lahk that. Nothin ever happens to me. That's the trouble. Everything is the same day after day. Go to work, come home, give Mama her medicine, cook dinner, go to bed. That's it."

"Where do you work?"

"Ah'm a correctional officer at the prison. A guard."

"Don't you like it there?" I asked. "I mean, you're helping to keep criminals off the street, right?"

"Bullshee-it. Ever one a those convicts should be electrocuted. An ah don't mean tomorrow, neither. Good-for-nothin drug addicts, murderers, an child molesters. An you know what else? The COs are just as bad. Ever damn one of them smugglin drugs inside and takin home a pocketful a money."

"If that's true, then why not tell somebody about it?"

"Tail who? The Captain? He probly knows all about it. The warden? He's a crook, too. Besides, ah just don't give a fuck. Don't even give half a fuck. Let em all rot; at least ah won't be here to see it anymore. Anyway, ah *am* tellin somebody. Ah'm tellin you."

"But Clete, I can't print something like that without proof."

"Who asked you to? Ah want you to raht about *me*." He stopped talking for so long that I was just about to ask if he was still there. But when he started up again, his voice was softer, more wistful. "Ah wanted to be in the army," he said. "But they wouldn't take me. History was mah favorite subject in hah school and ah read about all the wars an battles an generals. Ah wanted to be a general but ah didn't even get to be a prahvate. Ah mean, look at raht now. Ah'd have a chance to be in Afghanistan or Iraq. Ah would love that. Havin on the gear, walkin down the streets of a foreign city raht in the middle of a war zone . . . "

I'd had about enough. "I've been to Iraq, Clete, and believe me, you don't want to go there."

"Ah guess ah know what ah want, all raht," he told me.

"All I've heard out of your mouth so far, Mr. Wannabe Soldier, is a bunch of whining."

"You can't—"

"Shut up. You can't stand to live because nothing good ever happens to you? Your job sucks and your mother's old. So what? Everybody's job sucks sometimes—*most* of the time—and everybody's mother dies sooner or later. At least you still have yours with you, which is more than *I* can say. I mean, how would you feel if maybe your mother got killed and you weren't around? What if you had a disease that forced you to take drugs every fucking day of your life? How would you feel if your girlfriend just up and disappeared without saying fuck-all to anybody?"

Clete's voice now had a confused tone to it. "Ah don't have a girlfriend."

"Maybe if you'd stop whining about what a—"

"Ah don't really lahk women," he interrupted softly.

"You what?"

"Ah think ah'm probly a queer."

"You *think*?"

"Ah mean, ah ain't never done nothin, but sometahms ah get strange feelins when ah look at somma the other COs. Even somma the inmates. Hey, you're not goin to raht that in the paper, are you?"

"You want me to tell people that you're a loser and a murderer, but not that you might be gay?"

"People respect a killer—specially a soldier or somebody on Death Row. But if you're a fag, you're worse than shit."

"Come on, Clete. A lot of great men and women have been gay. James Baldwin, Elton John, Rock Hudson, Sappho . . ." I could have gone on and on.

"Do any of em live in Pine Oak?"

He had me there. Pine Oak could have been a small town in Iran as far as its acceptance of homosexuality went.

"Um, I don't think so—" Just then my cell phone vibrated. I grabbed it up and tried to think of something to keep Clete on the line while I answered it. "Listen," I said. What does your mother think?"

"Mama, well, at least she won't . . . " I lost the thread of his words as I covered the mouthpiece of the land phone and answered the cell. "Sue-Ann," I said both quickly and softly.

"Sue-Ann, it's Bill Dollar. I'm almost there. Sgt. Bickley is backing me up—he lives pretty close to Clete."

Bill Dollar—some of us that had gone to school with him called him Dilly—was one of only a handful of officers who patrolled Pine Oak. He often called in tips for news stories, so we knew each other pretty well.

"Right. What's the address?"

It was a number on Sawdust Street. I wrote it down on my notepad and hung up. I put the big phone back to my ear.

". . . sure hope ah'll be dead bah the tahm the flames hit me cause ah don't lahk fire much."

"Clete," I said. "There's nothing wrong with you that can't be worked out. There are people that can help you, places you can go."

"Ah ain't goin back to Wackoville, no way. No more a that psychology crap for this puppy."

That answered a couple of questions. The state mental hospital was in nearby Waxahatchee—called Wackoville by most of the folks that didn't live there. Clete had obviously had problems before. I was getting really antsy. I knew I had to keep him on the phone until the police were in place, but I also wanted to be there at the scene.

"They keep you drugged twenty-four seven until you feel like you're made outta tar. No bones, no—" I heard a quick intake of breath, then the phone clattered and I heard the rushing of heavy shoes on a wooden floor. I hung up my own phone, threw on a pair of jeans and a blouse, stepped into some Crocs, and rushed out the door. My old Toyota pickup started on the first try and I was soon rushing toward Sawdust Street, cursing the ruts that corrugated the dirt road for the mile before it became blacktop. I buttoned my blouse with one hand and held on to the wheel with the other. I pressed the number Dilly had just called me from, but he didn't answer. I hoped he was all right.

Sawdust Street was only about ten minutes away if I sped, so I sped. And during those ten minutes, all I could think about was Cletus sitting in some room reeking of gasoline with his mother struggling to free her arms from whatever ropes or tape her son had bound her with. And yes, I was already writing the story in my head. It was much like writing the story of a major election. First you write "Republicans in a Landslide," then "Dems in a Squeaker." Add some background that everybody already knows and *voilà*, you are ready to plug in the numbers. In this case it was "Local Man in Tragic Murder-Suicide" vs. "Local Man Captured after Armed Standoff—Hostage Safe."

Better to concentrate on my article than on some of the things Clete had been saying—things that hit a little too close to home. I had reached the third paragraph when I braked heavily for Sawdust Street and turned the corner. It wasn't hard to figure out which was Clete's house. On my left, in the middle of an ordinary residential block, two JCSD cruisers were lined up like spokes toward a hub, their headlights glued to the front door. Two officers crouched behind. One of them—I recognized him by his build and his bullhorn—was Sgt. Joey Bickley, Dilly's superior officer. The other was Dilly himself.

Up and down the block porch lights were on and the eyes of curious neighbors peeped through the blinds. I pulled to a stop next to one of the squad cars and glanced at the besieged house. I caught a brief flash of movement behind one of the living room windows. The bullhorn shouted "Stop!" Almost immediately, I both heard and felt a cold metallic thwack against the car door, then cried out from a sharp pain in my side. My first thought was that I'd been hit by a stray bullet, but when I brought my hand to the pain, I realized that I'd been hit by some type of a shaft. An arrow? I'd been shot by some fucking asshole with a bow and arrow? Whatever it was had pierced the car door and entered my side between a couple of ribs. What now? I didn't dare move because the bulk of the arrow was still embedded in the door. Also, I didn't know how badly I was hurt. Cautiously, I reached down and felt my way along the shaft until I felt—ouch!—the pointed back tip of a broadhead blade. It was a three-bladed hunting arrow, and sharp. I felt along its edge; only the very tip—maybe half an inch—of the broadhead had penetrated into my side. I'd been lucky; if the whole point had gone into me it would have taken surgery to get it out. As it was, I gingerly scooched sideways until I was free, then scrambled out the passenger door and crouched low on the pavement. Almost at once, a dark form materialized beside me: Billy Dollar, gun drawn, riot helmet fitted snugly to his head. "Sue-Ann, what are you—"

"Billy, I said, breathing as hard as if I had run from my house rather than driven. "Is he still in there? Damn it, I didn't know he had a bow."

"Crossbow, yeah. He didn't start shooting until you drove up. What were you—Jeez, Sue-Ann, look at your blouse. Did he hit you?"

I looked at my side. In the light of the full moon I saw a red stain spreading out on my blouse like an out-of-control Rorschach blot. "It's not as bad as it looks," I told him. "What's been happening?"

Billy looked at me carefully, then began, "He's just been doing a lot of yelling about how he's going to burn down the neighborhood. He mentioned your name a couple of times—he figured out that you tipped us off somehow and he's really pissed."

"Yeah, well. What about his mother?" I asked.

"Funny thing about that," Billy said. "One of the neighbors told us that his mother's been dead for years."

"He's just loony, then," I said.

"Yeah, I think so too. But what are we going to do? We just can't just rush in there and shoot him; hell, you and me and Joey, we all went to school with him. It's kind of like he's one of ours, you know."

I did know. However much or little it might have been, we had all gone through it together. "Let me talk to him."

"You look like you need to go to the hospital."

"Damn it, Billy. Let me alone. Come on; I'm the one he called. He trusts me, or at least he did." I started making my way over to where Joey Bickley was standing, being careful to keep down—I wasn't anxious to feel another Muzzy rip into me.

Joey looked down at me—he's about 6 foot 6 and his riot helmet made him seem even taller—and nodded. "You're bleeding," he said, almost admiringly.

The blot was spreading. I could feel blood oozing down my side and into my jeans. "It's not serious," I told him.

"Yeah, but you're bleeding a lot," he said.

As Dilly said earlier, Joey had gone to the same high school we had, although he was a couple of years older. He had been a basketball player, but only because of his height. His bulk made him too slow and he had never learned how to move. But if the coach needed someone to go in and foul someone, Joey was his guy.

"I need to talk to Cletus," I told him. "I think I can convince him to—" But before I could finish my sentence, the front door of Clete's house flew open.

Joey stiffened and stood up. "Looks like it's too late for that," he said.

As we watched, a figure right out of a comic book rushed out the door toward the police vehicles. The man—I would never have recognized him as Cletus Donnelly—had a Mohawk haircut and had black stripes painted down both cheeks. He was wearing baggy camouflage trousers and high combat boots; his upper body was bare and covered with tattoos. As he rushed toward us he held a samurai sword over his head and screeched at the top of his lungs.

"Yiiiiiiiiiii!"

While Dilly and I ducked behind Joey's cruiser, Joey stepped out to meet him. He dropped his bullhorn and stood his ground. Clete stopped yelling and screamed, "Shoot me, you bastard. Shoot me!" but Joey didn't budge. Still running at full speed, Clete brought his sword down toward Joey's head. I heard Dilly gasp, but instead of being cleft to the breastbone, Joey managed to duck out of the way and Clete's sword came down on the hood of the car, snapping the blade like a pencil. Evidently, Officer Training School had replaced some of Joey's dead weight with muscle and quickened his reflexes. I was impressed.

Clete looked uncomprehendingly at the foot or so of blade he had left in his hands. Then he reversed the hilt and tried to commit hara-kiri with the stub, but there was no longer a point and it wouldn't penetrate his chest. Cursing, Clete brought the blade up toward his own jugular, but before he could dispatch himself that way, Joey touched him on the side with a stun gun, and Clete, without a single word or sound, dropped like a brick onto the lawn.

I rushed out from behind the car, but I was suddenly lightheaded, as if some part of the stunning operation had affected me as well. I felt myself falling, felt the cool, damp grass on my skin, felt a pain in my side and a soft squelch of blood. I groaned and looked up at the sky, where the full moon was shining onto my face like a headlight.

Then I passed out.

Chapter 2

Someone was holding open my eyelid and aiming a light at my pupil. I shook my head and pushed the hand away. "Stop it," I mumbled. I opened my eyes of my own volition and saw a young man with wavy brown hair and a trim mustache. He was tucking his penlight into a pocket of his blue lab coat and chewing contentedly on a pencil.

"Dr. Livingston, I presume?" I said, then groaned from a pain in my left side. Oh, right. I remembered now: some joker had shot me with a crossbow.

"Ahhh, Phhssshent Mc—" Seeing my glare, he stopped, took the pencil out of his mouth and began again, smiling. "Ah, Patient McKeown," he said. "I was just wondering if you were dead."

"Not yet."

I knew Dr. Morris well—too well. He had stitched up a gash I'd put on my scalp a few months earlier. In fact, although he was still only an intern at the hospital, he was also the one who had diagnosed my Graves Disease, which is a condition in which the thyroid becomes hyperactive. At the time, I had been getting tired quickly, my heart rate was through the roof, and I was so weak I couldn't even pull a bowstring to my anchor point. So, yeah, I knew the easygoing Will Morris well enough to banter with him.

"How many brushes with death have you had, now?" he asked.

"Does that include my six months in Iraq?"

"Hmm. You'll have to tell me about that sometime."

"Forget it."

"At least this time you didn't damage that wonderful, thick, and shiny head of hair. It is even longer now, I see. Very gorgeous."

"Stop about my hair," I said. I tentatively touched my side and felt sharp pain under a thick bandage. "How sick am I?" I asked.

"Sick? I don't think you're sick at all. You seem to be taking your thyroid meds . . ." His voice trailed off as he glanced at my chart.

"I feel kind of weak."

"You lost most of your blood, so that might explain it. We had to transfuse you—hope you don't mind, but you were unconscious and we couldn't ask."

"My insurance company is going to love me." I struggled to sit up in bed. Dr. Morris helped me with a gentleness I had come to expect from him. He even tucked my pillow comfortably behind my head, then stood back to see if it was satisfactory.

"Maybe Congress will pass that health reform bill before your next encounter with the Grim Reaper," he said.

"I won't hold my breath."

"No."

"What happened to Cletus?" I asked.

"Who?"

"The man who shot me."

"Umm. They brought him in and he was treated for Taser burns."

"Did you see him?"

"I was busy with you, but I understand that after he was treated the police transported him to Wackohatchee."

"Waxahatchee or Wackoville, one or the other," I told him. "Not Wackohatchee. If you're going to work in Jasper County, you have to learn to fit in."

"You're so right."

"You can't say that either," I told him, exasperated. "You can say, 'I know *that's* right,' or just plain "Raht."

"But *you* don't talk that way," he argued.

"I don't have to," I said. "I was born here."

"That makes no sense," he said, but it did in a way. I had consciously lost my accent studying broadcast journalism in college and working in a newsroom for a dozen years. But if you are born in a place, you belong to that place. I knew almost everyone in Jasper County and they knew me, as they had both my mother and father.

I tried to shift my position and winced. "Why does my side hurt so much?" I asked. The point of the arrow only went in a little bit."

"A little bit, maybe, but it also creased two of your ribs. And it's lucky for you that they were there."

"Yeah," I agreed. "If the whole point had gone in, you would have had to cut it out."

"Look at where you were hit," he said, pointing to my side. "If it had gone all the way in, there would have been no need to cut it out. It would be lodged firmly in your left ventricle."

"Yikes."

"Yes, yikes. I have a couple of ibuprofen tablets here if you want them."

"How sophisticated. Did you buy them at Wal-Mart?"

"Do you want them or not?"

"Sure, okay."

Will gave me two of the pills in a paper cup, along with a cup of water. As I swallowed them, he asked, "By the way, where is your wonderful-looking blonde friend today?"

"Gina?"

"If you have others, please introduce me."

I was tired all of a sudden. I struggled back to a lying position and pulled the cover to my chin. "Gina's gone," I said.

"Gone?"

"She quit her job at the paper and left town. She didn't tell anyone where she was going or why. Just an email to the editor."

"I didn't know she worked with you at the paper," he said. "What did she do?"

"She's the office manager." I refused to use the past tense. "She handles phone calls, sells advertising, keeps things organized."

"What are you going to do?"

"Probably kill myself," I said without thinking.

Will Morris' eyebrows went up a notch. "Seems to me you've been trying to do that on a regular basis."

For some reason, I lost my temper and shot back, "You think I *like* getting holes ripped in me?"

Will Morris glanced at me with his usual sangfroid and wrote something on his clipboard. He looked up and opened his mouth, but before he could say anything, one of the last people I would have expected to see peered into the room.

"Joey?"

"Hey, Sue-Ann." Sgt. Joe Bickley clumped into the room holding a small bouquet of flowers—irises, I think, but I'm not sure. This wasn't the self-assured, fast moving police officer I had watched the night before. Without his uniform, and without danger maybe, he looked more like he had in high school. Clumsy, aw-shucksy. His clothes—plain slacks and a white shirt—looked like they came right off the rack of a men's store catering to the big, tall, and unfashionable. "I came to see how you were doing," he said. "Brought these." He held out the flowers. I didn't make a move to pull my hands out from beneath the covers, so he looked around for a place to put them. When he saw that there was no vase in the room, and that the night table was taken up with a lamp and paper cups, he seemed uncertain of what to do.

"Why don't you just put them on that chair, Joey?" I told him.

"Yeah, okay."

It was a stroke of luck that there was only one chair in the room. Now that Joey had placed the bouquet on it, there was nowhere for him to sit. And I didn't want him sitting. Why? Figure it out. I'm a fairly attractive woman in my middle thirties. I'm single and have a good reputation as a newspaper reporter. Joey, as far as I knew, was also single and because he was a man, was probably on the make. His hair was blow dried and combed, he was clean shaven, had on his best clothes, and was in possession of flowers. What else could I have thought? And being courted was absolutely the last thing in the world I wanted.

"Thanks, Joey. They're really pretty, and all-purpose, too. Not gaudy, but not morbid either. I mean, they're just right for a hope-you-get-well-soon hospital visit—like this one. But they would have looked nice on my grave too. I mean, if I had died."

Dr. Morris snickered, but Joey looked confused. "That's not—" he began, then stopped. He glanced at Dr. Morris as if to ask who he was and why he was in the room.

Will took the hint, although my mind and my eyes were trying to rivet him to the spot.

"Well, I have other patients," he said, tucking his clipboard under his arm. Bastard. "Toodle-oo."

When his footsteps died down in the hall, Joey turned his attention back to me. "I think your doctor's a homo," he said.

Anger welled up in my gut and threatened to come vomiting out, but I choked down as much of it as I could. "He's not from around here, Joe," I managed, but my voice was louder than it should have been. "Just because he talks different doesn't mean . . ." I let my words trail off. "Never mind."

The big man fidgeted. He looked confused again, and I knew why. "Well, I just came to see how you were doing," he said.

"Yeah. I appreciate that. I really do. And I'm okay. The point of the arrow didn't quite make my heart."

"Wow, that reminds me!" Joey fished around in his pocket and brought out a muzzy attached to a few inches of shaft. "I brought you this. It's still got your blood on it."

"Cool," I said. And it was. "But isn't this evidence?"

"The man's batty, Sue-Ann. There won't be any trial so we won't need any evidence. Anyway, we're friends, right? If I need it back, I'll ask. We still have the lower end of the shaft. We had to saw it in half it to get it out of the door. You know if you'd a had your window down, the glass would probly have stopped it."

"Yeah, but I was cold."

"Yeah."

I got serious all of a sudden. "What happened to Cletus?" I asked. "What the hell was he thinking, do you know?"

"Um. Clete's kind of been on my radar for a while now, Sue-Ann. More than a while. We grew up in the same neighborhood, so I knew him and his brother."

"He has a brother?"

"Had, yeah. Rufus. I didn't know him too well because he was a lot younger but I saw him around. He was in the army but got killed in Afghanistan or somewhere."

"I talked to Clete on the phone," I told him. "He called me. He said that he tried to get in the army but they wouldn't take him."

"Would *you*?"

"I guess not." In fact, most of the servicemen I had met—and there were hundreds—were fairly normal people. But how could someone from a small town like Pine Oak grow up crazy? Was he just dumber than a cattle egret, or did Cletus, despite his wild, mercenary-like appearance, feel some part of the dark, the unjust, or the fearsome to a degree that he was constitutionally ill-equipped to deal with? What on earth could there be in Pine Oak that could drive someone like Cletus Donnelly over the brink?

Joey's voice broke me out of my reverie. "Know what we found in his house?" Joey asked.

"No one tied to the bed I hope. No gasoline?"

"A collection of nunchucks. There must have been twenty of them. Can you imagine people collecting shit like that? He also had a crossbow, a longbow, some throwing knives—"

"I wonder what the pull weight of one of those things is." I said. It was odd—I probably knew more about archery than anyone in Florida, but I had never even touched a crossbow.

"A crossbow, you mean? Mine pulls about a hundred and seventy five pounds."

"You have a crossbow?"

"I do some hunting every winter. Last year I bagged a twelve-point—"

"What happened to my car?" I interrupted. Archery, yes; hunting no. My own shooting was confined to targets. My mind winced at the thought of having the bolt of a 175-pound crossbow flying at me. My own bows had no higher than a fifty-five pound draw weight and I could still bury an arrow to the nock in a hay roll.

"Your Toyota's down in the parking lot. I had one of the officers drive it over; in fact he's waiting for me downstairs."

"You shouldn't keep him waiting, then," I said.

"One of the benefits of being a sergeant," he smiled.

"Right. But, um, I have to get up to use the bathroom, so maybe I'll see you around. Thanks for the flowers."

"I—I was thinking that maybe we could have dinner sometime. There's a new seafood restaurant out near I-10 that—"

"I'm seeing somebody else, Joey, but it was a nice thought."

"Um. Lucky guy. Anybody I know?" When I didn't answer, he tried a different tack. "You aren't seeing Donny Brassfield again are you?"

"Somebody else," I said. "Donny and Linda C are pretty close to tying the knot, I think. Do you have my car keys?"

"In the car. I told Dollar to put them in the ashtray. And your purse is under the front seat."

"Good, thanks," I said, but what I was thinking was, Shit. One look at Joey's clothes and Dilly would guess that he had come up here to ask me out. Well, it was nothing I could help. I'd just have to take a little ribbing.

"See ya, then," he said. "And try to stay out of trouble."

"Raht."

And then he was gone and I could breathe easier again. I closed my eyes and ran my hands through my hair. I had a headache and my side felt like somebody was trying to drive a train through it. Which reminded me: I had a story to write.

"Boyfriend gone?"

I opened my eyes and saw Dr. Will Morris peering in the room. "You can kiss my grits."

"Do people around here really say that?"

"It was a joke," I said. "When can I get out of here?"

"You're not under arrest," he told me.

"Where are my clothes?"

"Yeah, that's a problem, they're kind of bloody. I can probably rustle up a pair of scrubs for you, though."

"Would you?" I asked gratefully. "I'll bring them back tomorrow."

"You'd better," he told me. "I have a feeling you'll probably need to borrow them again some time."

"You're funny."

Chapter 3

My keys and purse were where Joey Bickley said they would be, so as soon as I was out on the highway, I took out my phone and called the office. I gave my boss a rundown of the night's happenings—including the phone call I had received from Cletus Donnelly that had started the whole episode. "I've got everything in my head, Cal, but I'm going to write the story from home and email it in."

"Is there anything you need?"

"No, I'm fine." I paused, then asked, "Have you heard anything else from Ginette?"

"No. Not a thing."

It took me a good half hour to drive from the hospital in Forester to my farm in Pine Oak. Rather than trying to recount all the things that went through my head during that drive, I'm going to use the time to tell you about Ginette.

A little over a year previously, I had returned to my home town of Pine Oak after my mother's death. I had a then-undiagnosed thyroid condition that was robbing me of most of my strength and will and I was burned out to the max from being posted to Baghdad for half a year. But even with my hair falling out and my clothes several sizes too large, Cal Dent had given me a job at the tiny newspaper while I tried to get myself together. At the time, there were only four employees: Cal, who not only edited and sold ads, but researched and wrote a lot of the stories on finance and real estate; Paul Hughes, who covered the local political scene; Ginette Cartwright, the typesetter; and me. I wrote about any breaking news, and if none broke I wrote up local events such as garden club news, wedding anniversaries, birthdays, and other local trivia.

But I almost refused the job because of Ginette. I had gone to school with her ever since I could remember and during every hour of that time, we were at odds. Although we were both considered attractive, my hair was dark, Ginette's blonde; I was solid, Ginette svelte; I was stronger, but Ginette was taller. I excelled in scholastics, Ginette in social life. Think of two alpha mares locked in the same stall. Then imagine that one of them is a Clydesdale and the other a thoroughbred—well, that's how it was with me and Ginette. While I studied, Ginette flirted and cajoled and snuggled her way to the top. There had even been a time when she had made attempts to steal my boyfriends—and I had done the same to her. The only thing we thought alike on was our love of horses and riding. I thought of her in contradictory terms: a flowering desert, a beautifully carved rock, a dung beetle who was somehow able to speak with the wonderful, lilting southern mellifluence that is unique to Pine Oak. I couldn't wait to get away from her, so when I managed to wrangle a scholarship to University of North Carolina, I jumped free. During the next fifteen years, I didn't think about Ginette much. But when I returned to Pine Oak, like a dog savaged by coyotes, and found out that I would have to work with her, I almost did a U-turn out the office door. And when she was promoted to Office Manager and I found out that she was sleeping with the boss, I almost decided to take the next plane back to Baghdad.

Instead, something strange happened: we became friends. It took me a couple of months to realize that she deserved the promotion. Not only did she have great organizational skills, her folksy yet professional way of dealing with people was directly responsible for a huge increase in circulation and advertising revenue. She may have been fucking Cal's brains out, but she was an outstanding employee—far better than I was. Hell, most of the time I couldn't even roll myself out of bed. Cal was ready to fire me—had even hired young Mark Patterson to assume some of my responsibilities—when Ginette showed up unexpectedly at my house and took over my life for a while. She cleaned my house, visited me at the hospital, and nursed me back to health once my disease was diagnosed, and asked me to call her Gina—a name no one else had ever called her. I found out that, far from being the bimbo I had always thought her to be, she was a down-to-earth, intelligent human being with a talent for music and a deep, if odd, spirituality. In short, she was fun to be around. Over the next few months I taught her to shoot a bow and arrow; she taught me how to trim a horse's hoof. Together, we went on hikes in the woods, we got high, and we became involved in a couple of dangerous investigations that could easily have gotten us both killed.

And somewhere along the way, we fell in love.

Does that shock you?

Well, it shocked me, too. Although sexually, I've never really been a bed-bunny, I've had my share of boyfriends, maybe a couple of other people's share as well. Not only did I not have fantasies about women, I never even had any women friends. Why is that, I wonder? All I know for sure is that the last several months with Gina had been the happiest I had ever spent with anyone.

Cal, of course, didn't know about Gina and me. As far as he was concerned, she was still his girlfriend. Not only was this a good cover for us, but Gina truly liked Cal and owed him a great deal. She had even thought about marrying him but had declined his offer after serious consideration—too serious for my peace of mind. But I hated the secrecy. When you love somebody, you want to be with them, do things together in the open, to flaunt the fact that you have someone very special and have found the kind of happiness that few enjoy. But it couldn't happen—as Cletus Donnelly had reminded me the night before—in Pine Oak.

And now she was gone.

Here's what happened. A week before, Gina and I had planned to drive to Ft. Dodge, Iowa for a horseback archery competition. We had been looking forward to it because it was to be our first real vacation together and because we had been practicing archery from our own horses for a few weeks and wanted to see how it was done by the best. I had another reason, too. I planned to speak to the organizers about petitioning the IOC to make mounted archery an Olympic sport. Having been a member of the 2000 Olympic archery team, my voice would have weight and in fact, the organizers had already set up a meeting and arranged for me to address them. Gina and I were all packed up. We had identified places we wanted to see and reserved rooms in a couple of cities on the way. Then, only hours before we planned to set off, an emergency came up at *The Courier.* Cal's eleven-year-old son had been hit by a drunken motorist while visiting the family of Cal's ex-wife in Louisiana and was in serious condition. Combine that with one of the most important fundraising events in the *Courier*'s history and our vacation was doomed. Only Gina could run the paper if Cal had to take an extended leave, and only Gina could answer questions from potential contributors at the fundraiser.

"I'll stay with you," I said.

"You've made commitments."

"I have a commitment here, too," I told her.

"We'll go together next year," she said. "Mebbe we'll be good enough bah then to take Ahrene and

Alikki." Still, I could see that she was holding back frustrated tears.

I'll pass over the mounted archery competition and the meetings in Iowa, the long drive up and back, and the number of times I stopped for fast food and coffee on the way. I phoned Gina every day and told her what was going on. I was relieved to hear that Cal's son was not as badly hurt as was previously thought—a broken arm and a lot of bruises—and that Cal would be back at the paper a day or two before I was.

But on the Monday following the tournament—the day on which my IOC meetings were scheduled—Gina didn't answer when I phoned her, so I suspected that Cal had gotten back and that she was with him. I was jealous, of course, but whether I liked it or not (I didn't), Cal was part of the deal. On the drive home I tried to call her on the new iPhone she had given me for my birthday a few weeks before, but she didn't answer either at home or on her own cell and when I called the office, Mark told me that Gina had not been in.

"Did she call in sick?" I asked, concerned.

"I don't know. Maybe. Cal just said she wouldn't be in and asked me to answer the phone for a couple of days."

"A couple of days?"

"That's what he said."

"Is Cal there?" I asked, trying to keep the concern from seeping into the transmission. "Can I talk to him?"

"Yeah, sure. Let's see if I can transfer you."

It took longer than it should have but finally Cal was on the phone. "Hey, Sue-Ann," he began. "Are you back?"

"I'm on the road," I told him. "Somewhere in Missouri or Arkansas, it's hard to tell. "Listen, how's your son?"

"James is fine. Carol, my ex-wife, might have gotten a little too excited, but he did get banged up pretty bad. He'll have to learn to be a lefty until he gets his cast off."

"I'm so glad to hear that," I said sincerely. "What about the fundraiser?"

"Better than I expected," he said. "Ginette covered for me like a champ."

"That's good, too," I said. "But speaking of Ginette, Mark told me that she was sick or something."

There was a pause at the other end that lasted so long that I thought I might have driven into a dead zone. Just as I was about to ask if he was still there, Cal's voice came back on the line, but it sounded far away. "Um, Ginette quit, Sue-Ann."

Now I knew I must be in a dead zone, because I couldn't possibly have heard him correctly. "I missed that, Cal. What did you say?"

"I said that Ginette quit her job at *The Courier*."

"But why?" I asked loudly—maybe too loudly. Trying to control my voice, I continued, "You all didn't have a fight, did you?"

"No, nothing like that."

"But what did she say," I persisted.

"I didn't see her. She just sent me an email that said she needed to leave for a while."

"Leave?" I asked.

"She left town."

I remember dropping the iPhone on the seat of my rented car and staring out the window at the long highway. I don't know what was on either side—it could have been skyscrapers or corn fields. It was all I could do to keep the vehicle on the road. If Cal had told me that Gina had crashed her PT Cruiser and died, I could have understood it, but quitting the job she loved and moving away from her home town—away from *me*—was something that just seemed impossible. I felt like a skier on a good run getting buried by an unexpected avalanche. Dark and cold and hurt.

I snatched up the phone again, trying not to run off the interstate in the process, but Cal had hung up. I hit redial and this time, Cal picked up. "Sue-Ann?" he asked.

"Yeah. Sorry about that; we must have gotten cut off. Did you say that Gin—that Ginette had left town?" Occasionally, I forgot that Cal did not know her as Gina.

"Yeah, I did."

"Where did she go, do you know?"

"Not a clue. I thought maybe you might know."

"Me? Ginette and I aren't exactly friends. I mean, she doesn't confide in me."

"I've never really understood that," said Cal.

"Old story," I said. "Yesterday's news."

The truth was, neither Cal nor anyone else at the paper knew that Gina and I had planned to go to Iowa together. My own plans to attend the horseback archery shoot had been firmed up months before. Gina, however, had told Cal that she wanted to fly out and visit her sister in Canada. Subterfuge in small towns.

The rest of the conversation consisted of small talk about the paper. That had been three days ago. Cletus Donnelly had called me the night I got back and you know the rest.

The ruts in the dirt road leading to my house jolted me back into reality, each one like a mallet against my wounded ribs. I stopped and unloaded my bulging mailbox, a task I had forgotten the night before. I dumped the lot on the passenger seat and I was home.

There are some journalists who delight in describing everything in front of them in the minutest detail—the size and shape of my farmhouse, maybe, how many bare azalea bushes and drooping crepe myrtles graced my front yard, the kinds of mail I carried into the house. You'll find that I don't do that unless it somehow relates to what is going on. And when I was walking into the house from the car, I wasn't paying much attention to anything but the pain near my heart and the story I had to write.

So it was a surprise to find that the lights were on in my living room and nasal, Dylanesque folk music was coming from the pirate station I kept my radio tuned to. I was sure that both were off when I had gone out. The house had been burglarized several months before, so I d[illegible]und frantí[illegible] or something. But I don't play baseball or keep flowers, so the only thing I could think of was the broadhead arrow point on the [illegible] or so inches of shaft that I brought home from the hospital. I extracted it from the pocket of my borrowed scrubs and held it ready in case I needed it, then I began—carefully—to search the house. The living room was empty, so was the kitchen, but when I crept into my bedroom, I stopped dead. A form lay huddled under my blankets with only a blonde head of hair exposed to the cold, dim room.

Wouldn't it have cut them?

"Gina!" I cried, dropping the arrowhead on the floor and moving toward the sleeping form, which stirred at the sound of my voice. By the time I reached her, she was raising herself up, shaking her tousled mane of strawberry blonde hair, and blinking. "Hmm?" she mumbled. "What?"

Oh, wait. Gina's hair was near-yellow, not strawberry. And it was rarely tousled. But who—?

"Hey, Sue-Ann."

"Krista!"

The young woman scrambled out of bed, fully dressed in blue jeans, a pink sweater, and white socks. I noticed a pair of boots near the bed, which she took up and crammed her feet into. "Sorry about using your bed,

Sue-Ann, but it was too cold in the living room. I guess I was nodding off."

"Sawing logs is more like it," I said. "But what are you doing here?" I had asked Krista to feed my horses while I was away, but finding her in my bed set off a couple of alarm bells. "Are the horses all right?" I asked anxiously. "Did something happen to your grandfather?"

"Nothing like that. Just got tired of The Compound so I thought I'd hang out here with you for a while. I saw your suitcase on the couch so I knew you were back. I just decided to wait. I've got a message for you."

"A message?"

"Yeah. The Creeper wants to see you."

I hate to do this to you, but it's back-up time again. It's lucky I skipped all that description earlier. Krista was the descendent of the original founder of Pine Oak, which was at that time called Torrington, after her ancestor. She lived with her brother, her grandfather, and a slew of shell-shocked ex-marines on a very secret 1200-acre compound deep in the woods of Jasper County. Krista, a 21-year-old college dropout, served as one of the main DJs of the compound's "pirate" radio station, where she took the handle of Gamma and showed off not only her grandfather's superb taste in 60s and 70s music, but her own wacky poetry and far-fetched recipes to whoever happened to be tuned in. I had discovered the mysterious community—part of which was contiguous to my own 100 acres—while investigating a series of animal mutilations the previous summer, and since then Krista and I—and Gina—had become friends and riding companions. Krista's grandfather, who had been horribly disfigured in the Vietnam War, supervised the activities of the Torrington community from the parlor of his 150-year-old mansion. These activities consisted of farming, broadcasting, craftmaking, and most important of all, healing: for the twenty or so inhabitants of Torrington were all soldiers who had lost something—physically or mentally—in one of the many wars the U. S. had participated in over the last half century. Each resident had the Marine motto stamped on their heart. Semper Fi: no one who left Torrington would ever divulge its secrets.

And Krista's grandfather, Ashley Torrington, was known as The Creeper, both for his creepy physical appearance and for his napalm-scarred voice, which sometimes hissed out short but nightmarish parables rife with macabre images and dark moralizings. And The Creeper wanted to see me.

"When?" I asked.

"When you get a minute."

"What about?"

"He didn't say. He's being mysterious as usual, but he said to tell you to listen to the CD."

"What CD?"

"The one playing in the living room."

"I thought that was the radio," I said.

"Well, we've been playing it on the radio, too."

The CD had gone on to the next song, but it had the same soft sound as the first: a light male voice joined harmonically by a deeper feminine one. Interesting and unusual if not terribly accomplished. "Who is it?" I asked.

"Group called Robin and Marian. They had a single in the early seventies that bubbled under the Hot 100 for a week or two and an album that was dead before it was even released. One or two of the songs are kinda pretty, but the rest are nothing special. I'm not sure why The Creeper is so interested in it. I guess he'll tell you when you see him."

Krista glanced at her image in the mirror over my bureau and tried to smooth out her hair with her fingers. She glanced at my own image and asked, "Why are you wearing scrubs?"

"Long story," I answered.

Krista turned around to face me. She spotted the arrowhead on the carpet and bent over to pick it up. "What's this?"

"That's what the long story is about," I said.

"What happened, did you get shot or something?" She giggled, which was something I expected more from her alter ego Gamma. For some reason she was more flighty on the radio than in person.

"Right," I said. "But if you want me to talk, you have to give me coffee. Come on in the living room and let me know what's been going on for the last week." The truth was, my side was hurting again and I needed to sit down. I rummaged around in my suitcase for a couple of Advil, which I swallowed without water. Then I sat down on the couch. Krista, who was as familiar with the layout of my farm as she was with her own, had gone into the kitchen to turn on the coffee pot. She came back with two full cups and took a seat in the armchair that Gina always chose when she was in the house.

"How did you get here?" I asked her. "Your car's not out front."

"I rode Bob. I gave her some hay and put her in the guest stall."

I was chagrined that I had not thought about the horses the entire morning. "I should have called you and told you I was home, but it was almost midnight when I got here and just after that I got called out on a story."

"No problem. I like coming here." Then she said, "Too bad Gina couldn't go with you to Iowa. She was really bummed out about it."

"You spoke to her?" I asked.

"She was here a couple of times while I was feeding. We rode out to Torrington on Friday and she spent the night."

I sat up straighter. That would have been the night before she had quit *The Courier*. "Gina spent the night in the mansion?"

"Same bed you were in when you were laid up that time. She and Creeper had a long talk."

"About what?"

"No telling. I wasn't invited. And she was gone before I got up in the morning. I haven't seen her for a day or two, though. I guess she's been busy."

"Real busy, from what I hear." I stood up, trying not to wince. "Thanks for feeding. I'll get up with you about paying. Right now I have to write a story about some guy that tried to kill a Jasper County deputy with a sword last night."

"Gina already paid me," Krista said. "What kind of sword?"

"Read the article," I said.

Chapter 4

Local swordsman captured after standoff with police

By Mark Patterson

COURIER STAFF WRITER

Jasper County Sheriff's officers Joseph Bickley and William Dollar got more than they bargained for when they responded to a call at 1:04 a.m. from *Courier* reporter Sue-Ann McKeown, alerting them to a possible murder-suicide attempt at 305 W. Sawdust St., in Pine Oak.

When the two officers arrived at the scene, the suspect—36-year-old Cletus Donnelly—began swearing at them through a front window. "He was out of his mind," remarked Dollar. "Said he was going to kill himself and his mama too."

The incident started when reporter McKeown was awakened by a phone call from Donnelly early Wednesday morning. According to McKeown, the suspect threatened to kill himself with a samurai sword. He also told her that he was holding his mother captive and was going to set the entire house on fire. "Of course I was concerned," said McKeown. "I kept him talking on my land line while I called the sheriff on my cell."

This quick thinking allowed Sgt. Bickley—who also lives on Sawdust St., to arrive on the scene within minutes of McKeown's call. Officer Dollar then arrived, but neither officer was able to convince Donnelly to surrender.

When McKeown arrived a few minutes later, Donnelly became even more irrational. "He just went bonkers when Sue-Ann showed up," Dollar recounted. "She hadn't even stopped her truck before he opened a window and took a shot at her with his crossbow."

The bolt from Donnelly's crossbow pierced McKeown's driver's side door and came within an inch of killing her. "I was hit, but I jumped out the other side of my car and ran over to where the officers were," she said.

That's when Donnelly burst out of his front door screaming and waving a sword. He ran directly toward Sgt. Bickley, who nimbly sidestepped the attempted blow and tasered the suspect, who dropped to the lawn like a brick.

The officers then rushed into the house, but found no sign of Donnelly's mother or any inflammables that could have been used to incinerate the house. What they did find was a bizarre arsenal of swords, arrows, knives, and nunchucks. "The guy must've had like twenty pair of nunchucks—all different kinds," Dollar remarked.

It was later determined by talking to neighbors that Donnelly's mother Betty passed away in 1999.

Both Donnelly and McKeown were taken to Jasper County Medical Center. McKeown was treated for a superficial wound and released the next morning, although, according to Officer Dollar, "Sue-Ann was bleeding like a stuck pig. She lost so much blood that she passed out right next to the suspect. They looked like Raggedy Ann and Raggedy Andy."

Donnelly was treated for a taser burn and transferred to the Regional Mental Health Facility in Waxahatchee for observation.

Sgt. Bickley's squad car suffered $1000 worth of damage from the sword, which pierced the hood before breaking in half. McKeown's vehicle now has a hole through the driver's-side door. She has yet to get an estimate of how much it will cost to replace the door.

Yeah, well. As you can see, I didn't write the article after all. I don't like to write pieces where I have to say things like "This reporter saw this" or "This reporter fainted at the scene." So I gave Mark a chance to do a real crime report, although I gave him a hint or two as to the wording.

I had promised Cletus Donnelly that I would write a story about him and I planned to, but I wasn't yet sure what kind of a story I was going to write. He wanted me to tell *Courier* readers why he was planning to commit suicide, but I didn't know. What he had told me about the sameness of his life was not the whole story. I mean, if people killed themselves just because they were bored, we'd all be dead. I needed to talk to him again, which wouldn't be easy. I assumed that the forensics ward in Waxahatchee was locked down pretty tight. And, of course, if he were found to be mentally incompetent, his case—aggravated assault on an officer of the law with intent to murder—would never come to trial. As Gina used to say, I would probably "fahnd a way," but I had some ideas I wanted to check out before I tried to get to him.

After I started Mark Patterson on the story (he got those quotes from Dilly later), Cal called me into this office and asked me to sit down. "Good to have you back, Sue-Ann," he said.

I murmured something just as banal and looked around the office. Cal Dent was one of the most fastidious men I knew. The pictures of his three kids were hung on the wall with geometric precision and his antique mahogany desk shone with luster. He wore a fashionable blue suit with matching tie over a light coral shirt. His salt and pepper hair was cut in a style more suited to Paris than to a hick town in north Florida. Even so, I noticed an untidy stack of papers next to his computer keyboard and a couple of books lay on the floor near his chair. His tie was just the tiniest part askew—or was that just my imagination? He leaned slightly toward me and asked, "Did you win that tournament you went to?"

"I didn't even compete."

"It was an archery tournament, right?"

"Horseback archery."

"People shoot arrows from horses?"

"The Indians did it for two hundred years." I forestalled a couple of extra questions by adding, "I'm just a novice. I went there to see how it was done."

"Umm. Go ahead and write something up. Maybe you can—"

I cut him off. "Cal, you need to get to the point. What are we going to do without Ginette?"

"Yeah. That's what I wanted to talk to you about."

"Have you heard anything else from her?"

"No." He leaned closer and said in a very soft voice, "Listen, do you think she was seeing someone else?"

I had to think quickly, but the words came. "I've never *seen* her with anyone," I said. "She didn't tell you where she was going? What she was planning to do?"

"Nothing. But I've come to realize that there's so much I didn't know about her. I know her parents are both still alive and living in Texas, but I don't know what city. I don't know if she has any sisters or brothers, I don't know her favorite sport, what grades she got in school. I don't even know if she has any friends."

I knew all those things, but I wasn't saying. "So…?"

"So I want you to find her."

"Me?"

"You're an investigative reporter. I want you to treat this as a disappearance and investigate it."

"Are you saying that you think that there's some funny business? That maybe someone made her leave against her will?"

"Not really, no. I mean, she was pretty clear in her email that it was something she'd been thinking about for a while. But do I think there's something funny about it? Yes I do, and I'd like you to find out what it is."

"And say I find her, and say I find out what's behind it."

"Yeah?"

"Maybe it'll be something you don't want to know."

"Maybe."

"Okay, I'll ask around. Is there anything else?"

"No. Yes. I want you to hire her replacement."

"Forget it."

~ ~ ~

I longed to go home and sleep for ninety hours, but I had one more stop to make. I had to convince myself once and for all that Gina was gone, so I hopped into my pickup (I had no intention of replacing the door, by the way), and drove out of the parking lot. Gina lived on a tiny street in the southeast part of Pine Oak. It was an odd street, because all the houses were small, as if the developers had decided to sell only to singles or childless couples. Although most of them had brick facades, none was exactly the same as its neighbor. It might just be the slant of the roof, or the placement or size of the windows. Or maybe one had a small attic window or a Leyland Cypress in the front yard. Gina's—the last house on the block—had a simple lawn bisected by a series of paving stones to an open porch. There was a box-wood hedge on both sides that she kept well trimmed and I knew that there was a beautiful dogwood in back.

Gina's beige PT Cruise was not in her driveway. I walked up the flagstones to the deck-like porch, where a swing hung on the left, lightly rocking in the cool breeze. I unlocked the door with the key she had given me and walked inside. It was dim in the living room but I didn't bother to turn on the light; I could see everything I needed to see. On my right stood her blue armchair, facing a stone-cold fireplace. A newer version of the same chair stood nearby—one that she had purchased for me. There was a couch against the far wall with a coffee table that held a few music magazines and her laptop. The dining area was to the left, along with doors leading into the kitchen and the only bedroom. Everything, even the dust, was still. The only pictures on the wall were over the couch and there were only two of them. One showed her as a girl alongside her parents and older sister Laurel. All were blonde and stared out of the frame like a bouquet of dandelions. The other picture was more recent, and showed Gina astride her Clydesdale Andalusian cross named Hurricane Irene. The letters of my newly reconstructed dressage ring showed in the background. I thought of the invisible letters that cut the ring into two long halves. G I X L D. Gina had made up a mnemonic to remember them: Gina Is X-cited Learning Dressage. Now it was just Gina Is X. Cal's ex. My ex. Her blue armchair sat empty, but I could easily see her in my mind, the way she sometimes folded her legs and feet under her like a resting fawn.

I went into her kitchen and opened the fridge. It had been cleaned recently; there was nothing inside that was perishable. I glanced at the temperature setting and saw that it had been set to conserve energy. She had been thorough in her planning, meaning that it wasn't just a spur-of-the-moment decision. Yet she obviously didn't plan on staying away forever.

Even though her leaving had struck me nearly dumb, I didn't feel like I was in a trance or anything Zombie-ish like that. In fact, I was more aware than usual, saw her possessions with clearer vision. And they were like me: sturdy, dependable, maybe even expensive, but by no means fashionable. A nook by the kitchen held her CD player and CDs. There were a lot of holes, but I wasn't familiar enough with her filing system to be able to figure out what she had taken, although I know she favored female singer/songwriters like Tracy Chapman, The Wreckers, and The Dixie Chicks.

I moved into her bedroom and just stood there like a plinth in a Greek mural. And, in fact, it was the most Spartan room in the house. It was dominated by a king-sized mattress on the floor, made up neatly with clean sheets, pillows, and comforter with patterns of brown and beige. Aside from that, the room contained only a bare bureau and a nightstand holding an alarm clock, a reading lamp, and Gina's cell phone. The only adornment was a framed photo of a strange, longhaired man with a thick black mustache and hooked nose. Just beneath the photo, in calligraphy, was a framed motto:

DON'T WORRY
BE HAPPY

A year before—the first time I had ever been in Gina's bedroom—I had never heard of Meher Baba, but because of Gina's intense interest, I had studied up on the self-proclaimed Avatar of Mankind and found him to be a benign mystic whose odd personal life demanded more answers than were given by his philosophy. Still, I knew that Gina often sang pieces from Baba's poetry to music of her own composition and that she celebrated the date of his death by keeping silent for twenty-four hours.

I went into the bathroom and noted that Gina's toilet articles were gone. No surprise there. I also noticed that a few towels were missing from a stack in the bathroom cabinet, but it was her closet that had been altered the most. Probably a dozen of her brightest outfits were gone from their hangars. Her suitcase, which we had packed together for our aborted trip to Iowa, was also gone and I suspect that it had never been unpacked. And she had taken both her guitars—her practice Seagull and her clunky Gretsch.

That was it, Gina was gone, but as I passed through the room on my way out, something registered dimly in my brain, like a sound that I couldn't put a direction to. Except that it wasn't a sound, it was a thing. Or things. I looked around: bureau, nightstand, clock, lamp, phone. She had not taken her cell phone. And her laptop was in the living room. Gina had left her only means of communication. Not only was she gone, but she didn't want to be bothered. I have no idea why, but I snatched up the phone and put it in my pocket. I also grabbed up her laptop.

When I left the house, I locked the door and sat on the porch swing for a few minutes. In high school, I had often tried to convince myself that Gina was a bimbo or a Barbie doll clone. Now she was a mysterious runaway. I rocked and rocked. And as I rocked, I thought of images of Gina playing "There's a Heartache Following Me" on her guitar. ("It was Baba's favorite song, didn't ya know?") I remembered her in a farrier's leather apron teaching me the fine points of rasping a horse's hoof ("Don't go messin with the frog; it'll trim itself."). I saw her trying to put on the elaborate Japanese costume we used for practicing Kyodo archery ("These are the aggravatinist things ah ever trahed on."). And on and on. And I thought about something I hadn't told Cal, hadn't told anyone. Gina had left me a goodbye message, too. I had found it in my email when I first returned from Iowa and just before getting the phone call from Cletus Donnelly. It was exactly the same thing she had emailed me when we first realized we were becoming attracted to each other. No words, just an animated symbol, a giffy. It was a small, red, throbbing heart.

Gina was gone, but I was going to find her.

~ ~ ~

The Best Little Bookstore in Pine Oak was the *only* bookstore in Pine Oak. In fact, it was the only one in Jasper County. Located in the same mini-mall as *The Courier* offices, its selection of books was as eccentric as its owner, who was an awkward, gray-haired man in his mid-fifties. In what must have been an attempt to give him the most Catholic name on his block, his parents had named him Dominic Benedict, but he went by Benny. He even looked like a Benny—short, pudgy, and kind of scatterbrained. But after my mother had died, he had purchased her large collection of dressage books from the thief that had stolen them (my father), kept them safe, and gave them to me as a present when I returned from Baghdad. And somehow, despite the tatterdemalion look of his store, Benny always seemed to have what I needed. When I walked in—setting off a small jingle bell over the door—Benny was sitting behind his card-table desk reading two books at the same time, glancing from one hand to the other. A half dozen other books were lined up like soldiers on the desk in front of him.

At the sound of the bell, Benny looked up, smiled a crooked smile, and let out a hearty "Ho ho ho." It was only then that I saw that he had put Christmas decorations up. There was a plastic tree in the corner that might have been decorated by a child, plus a few tinsel-like streamers festooning the doorway and windows, looking more like something that vandals would do using streamers of toilet paper.

"Your Christmas stuff is up early this year, Benny."

"Sooner the better, heh heh. Moola boola."

"I know I shouldn't ask this, but why are you reading two books at the same time? Have you invented a new type of double reading technique?" Benny, aside from his bookstore persona, was also an inventor of sorts. He had, for instance, discovered that Chinese gongs, used as yardage markers on driving ranges, increased a golfer's accuracy by about 30 percent. People were so anxious to produce that long, lingering, cymbally crash that they practiced longer and with more dedication. The only reason it failed to make him rich was because any country club that used his gongs on their driving range had 33 percent fewer golfers actually playing the course. And as for my wariness about asking him a question, that was always true; his answers often came from a realm not many of us have ever visited.

"Naw. I'm turning Japanese."

Well, you can't say I hadn't asked for it. "Come again?"

"I started, you know, reading this novel by Murakami. Japanese guy." He pointed vaguely to one of the books on the desk. "But the introduction said that Oe, another Jap chap, thought he was just a poseur, so I got a couple of Oe's books so I could compare. Turns out, though, that Oe influenced that guy that wrote *Remains of the Day*—another product of the Land of the Rising Sun, so I wanted to check that out. I just go from one thing to another, hmmm."

"So those two books you are holding are Japanese novels?"

"Naw. German."

"But there's a reason, right, for saying all that about the Japanese?"

"Maybe. I mean, the Murakami novel I started reading was called *Kafka on the Shore*, so—"

"You had to start reading Kafka."

"In the original." He indicated the two books he held by nodding at them. "One's in German the other in English. Learned a little German in the Army. *Arous mit der schweinhundt*! Heh heh."

"So why didn't you learn Japanese for the others?"

"Ah. Umm. "Yikes. Never thought of that."

"Any new inventions for real?" I asked.

"Naw. The ole noggin be quiet as the grave. Wife had one, though."

"Yeah?" No one I know had ever seen Benny's wife, although it was a rare conversation in which he didn't mention her.

"Um hmmm. Christmas cats."

"I know I shouldn't ask," I said, and didn't.

"She wants to take some of our cats, the ones she can't sell—which is all of them, heh heh—and paint them green, then glue decorations on them."

"She wants to paint cats?"

"Spray paint. Yuk yuk. Thinks that people might like to have little reminders of Christmas scampering around their abodes."

I wasn't really sure how I could respond to something that silly without being ugly toward his wife, so I just asked, "And your response?"

"Arrrrr. Hmm. Told the little woman that we didn't need the lucre any more. Told her I'd just sold a novel for megabucks."

"Benny!" I cried. "That's great! I didn't even know you'd—"

Benny held up his hand for me to stop. He had an abashed expression on his face. "Little white lie," he said. "Couldn't let her paint me kitties."

"But what if she asks to see some of those megabucks?" I asked.

"No problemo, señorita. Ever heard of production delays? Heh heh. It'll be in production for years. First this and then that." He spread out his arms and smiled. "Whoo."

"And if she asks to see the novel?"

"Didn't make any copies. Anyway, not sure she can read. At least, I've never seen her."

I just shook my head. "Listen, Benny," I asked. "Was there a reason I came in here?"

Benny just clucked his tongue a few times and said, "Could be."

"Right. Have you got anything about Meher Baba?"

"Baba, baba," he said in a chanting voice. "Whoops, zip!" he pretended to be closing a zipper across his mouth. Right. Gina had told me that Meher Baba maintained a vow of silence for over forty years. Didn't ya know?

"Just point, then."

"Nah, I'm not one of those strong, silent types." Benny put his books down and led me to a biography section against a far wall. "Lessee, Babababababababa, hah, here we go." He handed me a much dog-eared copy of *Modern Avatar*, by somebody or other (look it up). We small-talked for a minute or two more, then I gave him five bucks and walked toward the door. Yet something made me stop in my tracks and look back at him with a fondness that had grown over the years. Benny was looking with dismay at the two books he had put down on the desk. He had failed to mark his pages. He picked one up, then the other, then put both down, shrugged just the tiniest bit, and went off searching the shelves for something completely new and different. Then everything would start all over again.

Driving home, I turned the radio on for news, then realized it was tuned in to the pirate station, which was located on the Torrington compound and run by Krista and her brother Smokey. I reached for the dial, then stopped. The tune that was playing was vaguely familiar—almost like something I had heard in a deep dream. Soft, lilting, and very softly masculine.

Pay the moon to stay bright,
Monsters travel at night.

Then a deep female harmony came in and I knew: it was a song from the CD that Krista had brought me.

Pay the moon to make me smile
'The distance widens every mile

I hadn't really been listening to the song before; I had been too busy looking for a weapon. In fact, I wasn't even sure that it was one of the several songs I had heard earlier, but it was certainly the same singers. Robin and Marian. And this song, rough as it was, had something indescribably beautiful about it. A very rare innocence and haunting lyrics.

Then a thought hit me in the gut. The Creeper. He wanted to see me.

Sleep? I wasn't sure I remembered what it was.

on to

It was getting onto dusk when I finished feeding the horses and I was resting on one of the cold metal picnic chairs in the barnyard. I was bundled up pretty good, though, and listening to the radio I had set up out there. Smokey was deejaying another unusual set of tunes. First there was "The Batman Theme," followed by something called "I was Kaiser Bill's Batman." Weirder and weirder, but not as weird as what came on next. It was the ghosty, raspy voice of The Creeper, the alter-ego of Ashley Torrington. It was rare for The Creeper to come on the air, but when he did, it usually had a purpose. Then, too, The Creeper loved telling scary stories.

"When I look up at the sky at night, do you know what I see, hmm?," he began. "I see bats. Tiny little flying mammals that I could eat up in a gulp, yas I could. But bats is not for eating, no. Bats is to keep the mosquitoes away, bats is for living in caves and belfries—do you have bats in *your* belfry, hmm? I do. Bats is what reminds us that we're all a little crazy. The Creeper, of course, is crazier than all you little babies listening tonight; The Creeper knows what he is talking about. The Creeper can see things other people can't and he knows what other people don't. The Creeper has watched bats for hours flying with their wings looking like canvas painted black, has watched them dive and swoop and shudder and watched them fly way way up into the night sky. But if you think I'm going to say that they fly up so high that they turn into the stars, you are wrong. The bats are everything in between."

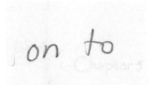

~ ~ ~

How can I describe Ashley Torrington? Well, think of a handsome American officer—an educated man with a good upbringing—lost in the jungles of Vietnam in the early 1970s. Then imagine that this soldier was caught in a napalm attack, killed, buried, and then dug up again a week later. That's not exactly what happened, but that's what it *looked* like happened. Horribly burned along one side, Lt. Torrington's right arm, eye, and ear were no longer part of his body and that side of his face was scarred almost to the melting point. Yet he survived and, in a way, flourished. Despite his ghoulish appearance, he now almost single-handedly ran the sprawling camp that for over a hundred years had provided homes for soldiers whose minds or bodies had been disorganized by combat. And the rest of Jasper County didn't have the slightest clue that Ashley Torrington or his little enclave even existed. I had discovered the place by accident and become friends with Mr. Torrington and his grandchildren Krista and Smokey.

Surrounded by miles of dense forest in all four directions, there were three ways to get to Torrington. One of these was a horse trail that began behind my own barn. Although the temperature was dropping rapidly and darkness was coming on, I saddled Alikki, my young Oldenburg mare, and set out through the woods. I carried a Scythian horsebow made for me out of horn by Lukas Novotny. Only 46 inches long with a 35-pound draw weight, it was short enough to carry easily and powerful enough to pin a rattlesnake to an oak tree at 30 meters. I had a hip quiver with half a dozen arrows and a small fanny pack holding a flashlight and various pieces of archery tackle, such as a bowstringer and broadhead points. Don't laugh; my bows and arrows had already saved my life more than once.

The other two horses, my filly Enemy Hunter and Gina's mare Irene, whinnied at us as we passed through the far gate of my pasture and disappeared into the trees. Alikki responded briefly without taking her eyes from the trail in front of her. I stroked her neck. Good girl. My side still hurt where I had been shot and I was riding kind of gingerly, but I soon relaxed and enjoyed the ride. Alikki had not been ridden in over a week and she gave me a big walk as she trod the familiar trail. She knew, too, that there were horses at the trail's end, including Krista's gray gelding Trigger, who she had winked at more than once on previous trips.

It was a circuitous route, dark and cold, under massive canopy oaks and through a long stand of pines, coming out into paths so small they could have been deer paths. Although I kept my arrows in their quiver, I was alert for signs of humans, although Alikki would have sensed anything long before I did. I liked The Creeper, Krista, and Smokey, but was not quite convinced that the ex-soldiers, in various states of disconnect, were harmless. It was silent in the trees except for Alikki's hooves striking the leaves below, but on previous trips I had often heard the firing of weapons—pistols, rifles, even machine guns—as some of these soldiers got their ya yas out on deer, squirrels, or just the broad flanks of giant oaks. I had also become aware that one of the several state prisons in the area was within a dozen miles of the back of my property, and although I had never heard of an escapee heading for these woods, the possibility existed.

A barred owl in the distance gave off its distinctive "hoo hoo ha *hoo*," and we came through the last of the forest. Just beyond, a high chain-link fence stretched in both directions as far as the eye could see. I dismounted and led Alikki to a padlocked gate. Inside were several cross-fenced fields and half a dozen horses trotting in our direction, their ears turned forward like tiny radar dishes. Krista had given me a key to the gate, so we went inside.

As I put Alikki in a spare stall, checked the water bucket, and gave her a little hay from a nearby roll, I could see through the dusk the outline of the mansion and the three large guest buildings. I also caught the gleam of the radio tower nearby, sending out waves of invisible music to all corners. The compound itself seemed deserted. Still carrying my bow and arrows, I walked toward the mansion, but halfway there, a shadow jumped out from behind a tree and barked out, "Stop!" I did, but my heart almost jumped out through my mouth.

The shadow stepped closer and I recognized an ex-soldier I had seen once or twice before—a fairly handsome but haunted-looking man in his thirties dressed in thick camouflage. He held an army-issue rifle level with the wound in my chest. Jeremy, his name was. I had even heard his voice on the radio several times when he filled in as disc jockey for Krista and Smokey. It was like listening to a hypochondriac. Even the songs he chose were usually downers, like the anti-war song "I Feel Like I'm Fixin To Die Rag," and "Timothy," where a group of boys eats their companion. It makes me depressed just to list them.

"Give me a break, Jeremy," I said.

He took another step forward and looked at me closely. "Oh, it's Bow-Babe," he said, lowering his rifle to the level of my crotch. "Shot anybody with that thing lately?" In fact, I had almost shish-kabobed his head from a hundred yards the first time I had visited the place.

"You know that was an accident," I told him. "I was sick. I was hardly even conscious."

"Yeah, yeah. When we carried you inside the big house it was like carrying a rug."

"I'm better now," I told him.

"Wish I could say the same."

I had no answer, so I changed the subject. "Is The Creeper in?"

"Creeper's always in, Dumb-o."

"He wants to see me."

"Lucky you." Jeremy lowered the rifle the rest of the way and stepped aside. As I walked the final fifty yards to the house, I was thinking about how Jeremy reminded me of Cletus Donnelly. They were about the same size and shape and even had similar psyches. One had been addled in combat, the other longed for it, went crazy without it.

Over the edge of the house, the moon—not quite as full as the night before—was rising like a balloon floating on a slow tide. I pressed the bell and looked back, but Jeremy had already disappeared into the shadows.

"Hey Sue-Ann. What's shakin?" The door had opened silently and Smokey Torrington stood in the doorway, holding what appeared to be a half-eaten Big Mac. Smokey was the handsome twenty-three-year-old grandson of Ashley Torrington . Or maybe the adjective should be cute instead of handsome because he was a small man—no taller than five and a half feet. His hair was dark and smooth and reached almost to his shoulders. His laughing green eyes told anyone who cared to look that he found fun in everything he did. A rare gift. He was dressed casually—blue jeans, Nikes, and a T-shirt advertising an AC/DC album. "Come on in," he said. "It's cold out there!"

I stepped in and closed the door. It was warm inside and I caught the whiff of wood smoke from a fireplace. "Since when did you start posting a guard outside?" I asked.

"Guard?"

"Jeremy's prowling around outside with an M16."

"Jeremy's wacko," Smokey replied nonchalantly. "He's afraid that someone is going to break in here and try to make him re-enlist."

"A scary thought," I said and walked through the hall and into the kitchen. I took off my quiver and lay my bow on the table alongside a couple of wrappers and a paper bag from McDonald's. Smokey was right behind me. "Listen," I told him. "I need to see The Creeper."

"I thought it was the other way around."

"It's both."

"He's in the drawing room. Go on in. Here—take this. He handed me the bag off the table. "I bought this for Krista, but she got something from the mess hall."

I took the bag—I wasn't sure if I had eaten that day or not—and walked through another wood-paneled hall and into a spacious but dimly lit room. The high, thick wooden door stood open as it usually did, revealing the furnishings within: six shell-backed chairs upholstered in red linen which matched the patterned carpet, a roll-top desk, a single bookcase, dozens of portraits in antique walnut frames. In a corner near a blazing fireplace, Ashley Torrington—The Creeper—sat in an armchair that matched the others, but which dominated them in a way that a stallion dominates a herd. Although the chair dwarfed him, Mr. Torrington looked regal with his lightweight dashiki and matching drawstring pants, both in light pastels and embroidered in gold thread. He looked regal, that is, until you looked at his ruined face. Even his scalp was mostly scar tissue, with occasional clumps of jet-black hair that fell down past his shoulders. The Creeper was a good name for him; a better one was what Krista called him behind his back: The Zombie. He was sitting in shadow, his better side facing the doorway. Incongruously, he was bent over a small cardboard container that held most of a McDonald's fish filet sandwich.

"Not you, too," I greeted him, smiling and holding out the fast food bag Smokey had given me.

"Um, yas," he responded in a voice made ghastly by inhaling napalm fumes, almost a gasping and hissing. He swallowed. "How do you do, my dear?"

"I'm a little hungry, to tell the truth," I answered, dragging one of the other chairs around to face him and feeling the kind warmth of the fire. "But what's the story? You have your own cooks and your nephew Clarence owns a food market, yet you sit here eating fast food."

"A blind man longs to see," The Creeper replied. "And one without hands wishes to grasp something. I am stuck here in these woods, alas, and in this house day after day, year after year, so from time to time, I send Smokey out for a taste of the forbidden. If I can't visit a place, at least I can sometimes taste its essence. And besides, Clarence is a vegetarian."

"Yeah, I know." We ate our sandwiches in silence for a minute, then I said, "Krista told me you wanted to see me. Is it about Gina?"

"Eh? About Gina?"

"You know that she left town, right? I mean, from what I can piece together, you were probably the last person she talked to before she left."

"Um, yas. Perhaps I was." The Creeper turned his attention to the rest of his filet, then crumpled the box and put it in the bag.

"Well, what did she say? What did you two talk about?"

"We talked about music."

"Music?"

"Yas. She asked me for a list of all my favorite female singers, so I asked Smokey to burn her some CDs for her trip."

"Like what?"

"Oh, Keely Smith, Billy Holliday, Nina Gordon, Juliana Hatfield. People like that."

"So, what, she just wanted some traveling music?" I asked, exasperated at his coolness.

"I think that maybe she wanted to talk about life, yas. She is very confused, but can a dead man advise anyone about life? No, I don't think so. I gave her the music instead."

"But what did she want?" I cried.

"You mean, don't you, why did she leave?"

I nodded slowly and bowed my head. The brief silence that followed was broken by the sound of a burning log falling into the embers of the fireplace.

"But you already know why."

"Because I was stifling her?"

"You're not foolish enough to believe that. You were bringing out everything that was good and true in her."

"But Cal was doing that, too. Do you know who Cal is?"

"Yas, we talked about all that. But your editor gave her a job and a sense of self-worth. What you gave her was life. She is running away for much the same reason that I ran away."

"You?" I asked, surprised.

"You can't be a monster in a small town, no."

"And what Gina and I feel for each other is monstrous?" In fact, Ashley, his two grandchildren, and nephew Clarence were the only ones who knew about my true relationship to Gina.

"It is in a small town. But it is more than that. She was brought up here and has lived here almost all her life—not so with you and I, is that not so? She is still figuring things out, and I think she needs to do it away from you and from the man in her life."

"Did she tell you where she was going?" I asked hopefully.

"She did not. She did not because she knew that you would ask and that I would want to tell you and want to keep her secret at the same time. We all have our little conundrums."

"I guess," I said lamely, and groped for the armrest to get up.

"But that's not why I wanted to see you," he hissed.

Halfway up from my chair, I looked down at him. "It's not?"

"No. I brought you here to tell you a story."

"A story about Gina?" I asked, bewildered.

"Not about her, no. A story about me."

"Um, okay." I tried not to be uneasy about the fact that the last person who wanted to tell me their story ended up trying to murder me with a crossbow. But the fire was warm and the room pleasant. I settled back in my chair to listen.

"Once back in time, I was a man," The Creeper gasped. "A young man with wavy black hair and a mustache. I was nineteen when I left Tucson and came to Florida to go to college in Tallahassee. Do you know why that school was the one I chose, hmm? It was because it was the closest to Torrington. Yas, I knew about this little city even then, and I wanted to see it for myself, much like Dorothy wanted to see the Emerald City.

"But that was the middle of the Sixties and I didn't know that study would take up so much of my time. And I had girlfriends, yas, sometimes, and that took up more time. There was beer and movies and dope, too, yas, and I had a part-time job at a department store selling records. So one whole semester went by and then it was two and I had not come out to Torrington even once." The Creeper opened his eye and gave me what, on someone else's face, would have been a sad smile. "What it took was a broken heart and the end of another semester before I finally made my way here to this secret place and its soldiers and its horses."

He spoke for a long time. If I had been doing an interview, I would have had a tape recorder between us and a notepad on my lap. But all I had was my ears and my memory and I can't remember the exact words The Creeper used. With apologies, then, here is the gist of his story.

Chapter 6

It's a 45-minute drive, tops, to Pine Oak from the university, but driving a borrowed [illegible] hand-drawn map, it took Ashley [illegible] part of two hours before he finally [illegible] the shiny Quonset hut that formed [illegible] Market. The front of the building [illegible] doorway was strewn with bales of pine straw, atop of which teetered crates of melons, stands of windchimes, and pots of various kinds of flowers he didn't know the names of. A white slab of plywood had been painted in garish red letters: "APALACH OYSTERS." Two pick-ups were parked in the lot and Ashley noticed a couple of old timers with straw hats standing and shooting the shit with the proprietor just inside the door. It was a hot day in July and thick dust from the parking lot gave a reddish tint to straw, melon, and leaf alike. The young man walked in, avoiding the eyes of the two customers and the counterman, all of whom had gone silent at his approach. He thought he might have heard a muttered remark about damn hippies, but it could have been his imagination. It didn't matter; he hadn't come there to make friends.

The inside of the market was dim, but Ashley could easily make out rows and rows of rough wooden shelves topped with crates tilted up toward the shopper. They were crates of apples, peaches, oranges, cabbages, cucumbers, and fat, juicy tomatoes. But it was what was beyond the produce that really caught his attention. There were crates of old license plates, used Army-issue boots, coconuts painted to look like monkey heads, horseshoes from small hooves, combat service medals from World War II. There were boxes of nails and screws of odd sizes and one crate filled with nothing but different-sized hex wrenches. Ashley was bent over a container of 78 rpm blues records when he became aware of footsteps coming toward him. He looked up to see a balding man in his fifties giving him the eye over a thin pair of spectacles.

"Anythin I kin do fer ye?"

Ashley took a step toward the speaker. "Are you Mr. Clayton Meekins?" he asked.

"That's raht. And you?"

"My name is Ashley Torrington."

"Hmmmph. Thought you maht be."

"Why?"

"Cause ye don't look lahk yer from around here. Don't talk lahk it neither. Still, ye kind of favor The Caretaker—even though The Caretaker don't wear no beads."

Ashley smiled. "You mean my uncle? Is that what he's called around here, The Caretaker?"

Meekins gave him a hard look. "Not around here, son, no, he's not. Ye need to be dead certain positive that me and my son Clancy are the only two people in Pine Oak that even know that yer uncle exists. Are ye straight on that?"

"Right. Of course, I forgot."

"And that's the one thing ye *caint* forgit. Ye kin forgit yer own name and where yer family jewels is hid, but ye got to remember that Torrington is top secret. The people inside depend on that."

"I understand."

"Wars take things outta people. Sometimes they jist need ta disappear."

"There's a war going on now," Ashley said. "People my age are fighting in it. Maybe they'll need to disappear, too, someday."

The geezer looked the young man up and down, his eyes flickering over the strand of beads Ashley wore around his neck and the picture of Frank Zappa on his garish purple t-shirt. "Ye don't look like no soldier to me," he told [illegible]

"Maybe [illegible] 'But in exactly a year I'll graduate [illegible] ond lieutenant in the Marines."

"Hmm. [illegible] oy?"

"Right. If "The Caretaker" can survive on Okinawa, I can probably survive Vietnam. How do I get to Torrington?"

"Normally, I'd have my son take ye," said old man Meekins, "But his wife Gladys jist had her first baby—my grandson. They call him Clarence. So I'll just have to draw ye a map."

It was an unusual map, drawn on a brown piece of paper torn from a grocery bag. It called for Ashley Torrington to enter the woods in back of the market on foot and make his way slowly down what looked like a deer path, threatened on both sides with scrub oak and blackberry brambles and overshadowed by cedars, live oaks, and an occasional pine. It brought to mind descriptions he had read in R.O.T.C. class of some of the jungles in Vietnam. It was dark, too, and thick with the calls of crows and woodpeckers. Some of the identifying features included a clearing, which he was instructed to go straight through, and a snaky S-curve through high grass. Similar instructions referenced a giant dead oak, the skull of a cow, and a nearly hidden plank road that had been constructed a century and a half earlier. Wiping the sweat from his eyes and watching carefully for rattlesnakes, he followed the planks until he came to a high wire fence nearly hidden behind a long row of thick cedar trees. Peering through the branches, his sopping t-shirt torn in three places and his shoelaces untied by low brambles, he saw the compound. The trip had taken him well over an hour, and he had no idea how far he had actually walked. A mile? Ten?

He had found Torrington, but where was the entrance? The map didn't say. He was agile and athletic, but he had no intention of climbing a ten-foot high fence and being shot as an intruder by some screwball before he could identify himself. He decided to follow the fence to the left. As it happened, this took him to the same gate that I had entered with Alikki an hour before he began telling me this story, but it was a trip that took him another hot half hour. The gate was padlocked, but Ashley peered through and saw several acres of lush pasture. A path veered slightly left from the gate to a small set of stables with a paddock on each side. The stables were a couple of hundred yards away, but he could still make out the forms of two horses—Quarterhorses they looked like, with maybe some Arabian mixed in. As he watched, a young woman with two blonde pigtails came out of one of the stalls with a halter and approached one of the horses. She looked to be about his age and pretty tall. Ashley thought it odd that there were any young women in Torrington at all, but what made it stranger was that she was wearing the kind of clothes he would have expected to see at a protest rally: bell-bottomed jeans, sandals, and a loose, frilly off-white blouse. But it wasn't just the sandals that told him that she was a novice around horses; she kept trying to put the halter on backwards and seemed confused when the ring ended up on top of the horse's nose.

"Hey!" he shouted through the mesh, which was a bad mistake and he knew better, because when the horses heard his voice booming out of nowhere, they very nearly bolted, tensing their bodies and flicking their ears toward him as they tried to locate the source of the sound. The horse the woman was trying to halter whipped it out of her hand and flung it five yards away into the dirt. The girl skipped away a few steps and stared at the gate until she saw Ashley waving.

"Shit!" she cried. "You almost killed me."

"Sorry about that, I—"

"What do you want?" she called out. "There's no trespassing here."

"I'm here to see my uncle," he said loudly. The horses must have been trained well, because they remained rooted to their few square feet of paddock, faces and ears radared in his direction.

"What?"

"I said I . . . Come closer so I won't have to shout!"

Reluctantly, the girl walked forward, leaving the halter—and the two horses—where they were. When she was close enough she asked in a softer voice, "What do you want?"

"My uncle is The Caretaker," Ashley replied.

"Really?"

"Really. My name is Ashley Torrington. Can you let me in?"

"I don't have a key."

She was almost to the gate by then and Ashley was able to loo ... y. She was even taller than he hac ... lose to 5' 10", and her pigtails—ex ... at straw—hung down beyond her ... lid; if she didn't have an ounce o ... ave an ounce of thin either. From what he would see of her shape under the flouncy shirt, her breasts were slightly on the small side. She wore no make up and no nail polish. She had straight white teeth and kind of a long face—almost horsey—but it was an intriguing face nonetheless, a face that morphed from plain to pretty in the time it took her to blink one of her blue eyes.

"You, um, you shouldn't wear sandals around horses," he told her.

"What are you, an expert?" she asked, looking at his beads and his torn clothing.

"I've been riding all my life," he told her. "I'm from Arizona," he explained, but she just looked at him. "I live on a ranch with half a dozen Arabians. I do some reining and a little roping." When she didn't respond, he changed tactics. "What are you doing here?"

"Visiting my dad," she said.

"He was a soldier?" Ashley asked.

"World War II," she said. "It made him kind of freaky. Mickey and I wanted to see him before we went to New York."

"Mickey?"

"Mickey's my younger brother. He's a folksinger and songwriter like Bob Dylan. Sometimes he lets me sing harmony."

"And you're going to New York?"

"He wants to play some coffee houses and get a record deal."

"Cool," rejoined Ashley. "Maybe you can meet Phil Ochs or Tom Paxon or Eric Anderson or somebody."

"I don't know who they are," she admitted.

"I don't know who *you* are," said Ashley.

"Oh, right. "I'm Maryanne. Maryanne Simmons."

"I'd shake your hand, but, you know . . ."

"Oh, right. Shit. Let me go and get The Caretaker."

"Okay."

"I'll be right back."

"I'll be here."

Ashley Torrington watched her hurrying away in the direction of a large white wooden house—almost a mansion. Two stories with gabled windows and a tin roof. A well-kept green lawn fronted the house, surrounded by what looked like a picket fence. Beyond this he could make out the shapes of two other houses—both pretty large, but not as commanding as the first. He saw a few men walking languidly from one house to the other. To the left stretched acres and acres of greenery—mostly fields of growing vegetables. It was astonishing that such a place could be hidden in the middle of the woods so completely.

He stood by the gate and waited and looked. He wondered who owned the horses and what they were used for. Who took care of them when Maryanne was not around. He thought of many things—school, the war in Vietnam, "Sad-Eyed Lady of the Lowlands," Maryanne. He stood by the gate for more than twenty minutes before he saw Maryanne returning with a white-haired man he recognized as his uncle. He would have waited a lot longer, because in the few minutes he had stood across the fence from Maryanne, Ashley Torrington had fallen in love with her—heart, stock, and barrel. Yas, he had.

~ ~ ~

Capt. Tony Torrington, the older brother of Ashley's father, was in his early fifties, yet his hair was the color of an octogenarian's. It was as if he had passed through one of those frightening experiences that you hear about from time to time where your hair turns white overnight. And maybe he had. Certainly being on Okinawa for 82 days would have been enough to turn anyone's hair white. I did a little research on it later: over 100,000 *civilians* dead. Mass suicides, rapes of villagers by both American and Japanese soldiers, corpses rotting in every street. I had seen a lot during my stint in Iraq, but nothing like that. Despite this, Capt. Torrington stood steadfast among the walking wounded. There was nothing wrong with The Caretaker—not wrong like The Creeper was wrong outside or like most of the men in the compound were wrong inside. In fact, he was a surprisingly jovial little man who just wanted peace and quiet and the opportunity to help those he could help in a small setting. He had been a medic in the Army and had later gotten his MD, but the real world did not suit him. When he learned that the current Caretaker of Torrington had become too ill to continue, he had quit his job in the Army hospital and moved to Torrington with his wife. Over the next few years, he managed to relocate a few other soldiers from his company—people whose ailments he was familiar with—and they got on as best they could with their pensions and their little gardens.

Back in 1968, the compound of Torrington was less populated than it is today. Less space was cleared for growing fruit and vegetables, the two smaller houses were more ramshackle, and, of course, there was no radio tower. It took The Caretaker only an hour or so to familiarize his nephew with the compound. And throughout the tour, Maryanne Simmons stayed with them, as if she were interested in the workings of Torrington for reasons of her own.

Dinner was served in what was then—as now—called the mess hall—a large room in one of the smaller buildings. There, he met most of the inhabitants of Torrington. Some of them were suspicious of him, but as his uncle later told him, they were suspicious of most people. They were a varied lot, just like they are today, with ages ranging from 25 to about 75—veterans of both world wars, the Korean War, and even Vietnam. Some were missing limbs, some missing parts of their brains, but in Torrington, at least, they were safe.

The only real downer was when, halfway through the meal, Maryanne's brother Mickey stormed into the room like someone had just scratched his new guitar. He was puffing furiously on a cigarette.

"What's wrong, Mickey?" Maryanne asked. She was sitting at the long table between me and her dad, a broken man who was barely functional enough to hold his fork steady.

"Why does something have to be wrong?" Mickey retorted. Several inches shorter than his sister, he wore his hair in a high perm, almost as if he had gone to a hairdresser with a copy of *Highway 61 Revisited* and said, "I want to look like that." Ashley could see the resemblance to Maryanne in his blue eyes, though, and in his button nose. It was cute on her, but made him look kind of mousy. He stared directly at Ashley and said, without preamble, "Who are you?"

"Ashley Torrington."

"What, another one?" said the young man, sitting down heavily at the table and looking suspiciously at the dishes of food.

"Ashley is Capt. Torrington's nephew," Maryanne explained.

Mickey just grunted.

"Your sister has been telling me about your music," said Ashley.

"Yeah?"

"Yes she has. I've always wanted to be a musician but I never had the talent. I'm a good listener, though. Anyway, you look the part." It was an innocent comment, but Mickey took umbrage.

"What's that supposed to mean?" He crushed out his cigarette in a saucer like he was crushing a bug.

"Come on, Mickey," begged his sister. "He only meant—" But before she could complete her sentence, her father suddenly straightened up in his chair, dropped his fork onto his plate, and stood up. "He meant that you look like a fairy," he barked, and the other men around the table, with the exception of The Caretaker, snickered. With that, Mickey pushed his chair back, glared at his father across the table, and stalked from the room. As soon as his form passed through the doorway, his father slumped back into his chair and stared at his spaghetti. "That boy needs to eat more," he muttered.

There was a lot more to The Creeper's story, but much of it isn't relevant. He ended up staying at the compound that night. In fact, he passed a full week there, spending as much time with Maryanne as he could. He was able to listen to her and her brother rehearse and was impressed, if not by the quality of the songs they sang, then by the energy and time they put into them. Unlike many of the topical folksingers of the day, Mickey's songs were soft and dreamy. Love songs or songs about beauty and nature or traveling to new and unknown places. His voice was soft and kind of nasal, and it was difficult to make out the words he was singing. His guitar playing ("He taught himself," Maryanne said) was rudimentary but effective and Ashley appreciated it as only a non-musician could. But what he liked most about their music was—you guessed it—Maryanne's harmony. Unlike her brother's soft tenor, her alto was clear and sultry, and the intertwining of the two added a complexity to songs that otherwise would have been pretty ordinary. Ashley enjoyed these musical evenings, which took place on the lawn in front of the big house with most of the inhabitants in attendance. Despite his outward distain for everyone in the compound, Mickey was no idiot—he knew that if he could get a grudging respect from this audience of wacked-out infantrymen, he had a chance in New York.

Another thing Ashley enjoyed was the time he was able to spend alone with Maryanne. Almost every day that week he gave Maryanne a riding lesson—first on a lunge line, and then walking beside her through the pastures and even through the compound. It gave them a chance to talk. Ashley found out that Maryanne's family was from Pensacola. Her mother was a high-school teacher who had divorced Maryanne's father when Maryanne was in her early teens, then married a man who taught in the same school. They had been comfortable enough. Her stepfather was a good man—better than her father—but Mickey had never accepted him, hardly spoke to him and was always running away from home. Maryanne had become her brother's intermediary, his protector. She had bought him his guitar with money she earned from waiting tables. She wanted him to go to college, but all he was interested in was music. And now he felt that he was ready. He was only 19—a year younger than Ashley and two years younger than Maryanne.

That Friday—the day before she and Mickey were to take the bus to New York—she and Ashley sat together in one of the pastures after a ride in which he taught her how to post the trot. The two horses were grazing contentedly nearby and the sun was just beginning to set.

"I was never around horses before," she told him unnecessarily. "I never knew how wonderful they were until I came here. They make me feel so calm when I'm with them—I don't know how to describe it."

"There's a ranch in Arizona where they bring problem kids," Ashley began. "Children with disabilities, juvenile delinquents, kids that need help. The horses can sense what they're feeling and the kids really take to them."

Maryanne was silent for a while, then looked at Ashley and said, "My father wasn't in Okinawa with The Caretaker. He didn't even fight."

"Where was he stationed, then?" Ashley asked.

"Here, stateside," she answered. "He was unfit for combat."

"How so?"

Maryanne lay back in the tall grass and stared up at the darkening sky. Ashley imitated her. "Our family has an unstable gene or something," she began. "Like a hereditary craziness. My grandfather died in Waxahatchee."

"What's that?"

"It's a small city in the next county over. There's a big mental hospital there. We used to visit him sometimes, before my father got worse."

Ashley turned his face toward hers just as she turned toward him. There was a question in her eyes. He answered it by moving the few inches from her lips to his, and they kissed for the first time. Ashley felt like he was floating, felt like if he were to rise up above the earth, no matter how far, all he would be able to see would be the two of them lying there together in a tiny glow of starlight.

Maryanne pulled away suddenly. "Ashley, I'm afraid."

"I won't—"

"I'm my father's daughter. I have the gene," she said. "I can feel it in me like a presence, so that every time I get depressed, or angry, or tired, I think 'This is it, this is when it starts."

"Maryanne, there's nothing wrong with you. There's not. Everybody gets depressed sometimes."

"Everybody except you, you mean," she smiled.

"Me?"

"You're always happy."

"I'm happy when I'm with you," he said.

"Shit, Ashley. You have a rich family, you have horses; pretty soon you'll have a college degree . . ." Her voice trailed off wistfully.

Ashley was silent for a moment, staring at the pin-pricks of stars that had begun to be visible in the night sky. "Families can be hard," he said finally. "About six generations ago, one of my ancestors was the first settler in this area. He got into the lumber business and made bundles of money so that not only this compound, but the entire town of Pine Oak was called Torrington. But a couple of generations later, the Civil War came, and two of that man's sons were killed. Ever since then, all of the Torrington men—and some of the women—have been soldiers. I'm expected to be one, too. When I graduate, I'm going to be a Second Lieutenant in the Marines. You know what they call Second Lieutenants in the Marines in Vietnam? Fertilizer."

"You don't want to go." It was not a question.

"No. I don't. I don't even want to be in R.O.T.C. I don't even believe that the war is right. People who look just like me have been picketing the R.O.T.C. building for months, but I'm going to go through with it because my family expects it and because I've been brainwashed into thinking it's my duty." He stopped and looked back at her. "So you think I'm not depressed sometimes?"

She took his head in her hands and kissed him for a long time. During a short break, she asked, "Do you think we'll ever see each other again?"

"I don't know," he responded.

~ ~ ~

"And *did* you see her again?" I asked The Creeper in his study that night.

"I never did, no," he sighed. "She and her tiny brother went to New York and they called themselves Robin and Marian and yas, they did get a record deal, and put out a single that was touching and sad, then an album that wasn't."

"And you?" I asked.

"Me, I got a degree and went home. While I was waiting for the orders to go get caught in a napalm attack, I became foolish enough to marry a girl I barely knew and get her pregnant. I ended up here, as you know. I don't know what happened to Maryanne."

"I'm glad you had someone to love," I told him sincerely.

"Yas."

"But you generally don't tell stories that don't have points," I pointed out.

"Yas, um hmm, as you say. I want you to locate her."

Chapter 7

My radio alarm clock woke me up the next morning much too early to the tune of Patsy Cline singing "Crazy" in a voice that would have melted the ice hanging off a Siberian peasant's beard. I wasn't paying much attention because my wound was stiff after six hours of sleep. I took off the bandage and stepped into the shower as the Patsy Cline tune segued awkwardly into Heart's "Crazy on You," which I had heard way too much of on Freedom Radio in Iraq. My wound was still puckered and angry looking. I washed it carefully and patted it dry. As I waited for my skin to be dry enough to put on another bandage, I walked naked back into the bedroom, where a demented-sounding voice was coming out of the radio speakers:

They're coming to take me away, ha ha
They're coming to take me away,
ho ho hee hee ha ha
To the happy home
With trees and flowers and chirping birds
And basket weavers who sit and smile
And twiddle their thumbs and toes
And they're coming to take me away, ha-haaa!

After a minute more of this, Krista's voice came on the air. "Hey hey hey, all you nuts out there. That was Napoleon the Fourteenth from 1966, I'm Gamma, and this is WMAD, your crazy-ass pirate radio station. Listen, do you sometimes feel like you've fallen off your proverbial rocker? Felt a bevy of bats beating their wings somewhere up in that dusty belfry of yours? Every once in a while do you feel like you are out of your *freakin mind*? Well, this is the station for you. And hey, I've just written a poem that you'd have to be loony tunes to like. It's called, "Rabid Squirrel Soup."

I don't have a copy of the poem and I've never asked Krista for one, but I remember that she mentioned egg nog in conjunction with breaking into the governor's mansion to steal candlesticks. I decided I needed to have a talk with her sometime. I mean, let's face it, Torrington wasn't the best place for a good-looking young woman to be cooped up in. The last few words of poem were cleverly overlaid with the intro to an old Donovan song, that began:

Mad John came down from Birmingham
Very carefully.
And from Borstal he had ran
He made it down to Torquay.
Good boy, Mad John.

After I gingerly applied a new bandage, I put on a pair of blue jeans—just washed and neatly pressed—along with a fresh red pullover sweater and comfortable step-ins. In the living room I slipped on the pile of mail I had dropped the morning before and almost fell on my face. Wincing with the pain in my side, I picked up the mail and stacked it on the couch right next to where my black shorthair cat, Kitty Amin, napped. I switched on the radio in the living room, then walked outside to get the morning paper.

Eventually I settled on the couch with a monster-sized cup of coffee. I took my thyroid pill and opened the paper. Mark's article on my shooting was the lead story, along with a picture of my Toyota with the arrow vanes still sticking out from the door. It was what I saw underneath the story, though, that would have set me to gnashing my teeth if people really did that. Cal had made Betty set it off in a heavy box so that it would stand out.

Courier seeking office manager

The Pine Oak Courier is looking for a full-time Office Manager. Interested applicants should come by *The Courier* offices and fill out an application before Friday, December 11. Experience in answering telephones, selling advertising, and using computers is preferred. Excellent people skills are required. Completed applications and resumes should be given to Sue-Ann McKeown between the hours of 9 a.m. and 4 p.m.

No way! I was no personnel manager and the idea of having to interview a bunch of clunkheads made me wince. Cal had sold me down the proverbial river. I looked at my watch—already 9 a.m. I should have been at the office already, but I decided to postpone things for a while and try to figure out what direction my seemingly useless life was taking now. It seemed that I hadn't had a moment's rest from worry, disappointment, and confoundedness in weeks.

But first the mail, which mostly consisted of catalogs from various equine supply stores: Jeffers, Dover, Dressage Extensions, and the like. I put them aside to browse through later. There were also the normal amount of bills and life insurance offers. I put the former in my purse and tossed the latter. Then there were two personal letters. The first was from my father, who I hadn't heard from in, shit, who knows? Six months? It was postmarked Florence, Italy. I opened it against my better judgment.

Susie:
You have a new baby brother. His name is

That was enough. I stuffed the letter back in the envelope and threw it on the coffee table. Fuck. Why couldn't Cletus Donnelly have used a stronger bow? Or maybe I could just get one of my own arrows and fall on it. Where the hell was Gina? I opened the other envelope. The letterhead was of a well-known publishing house specializing in books about photography. *My* publisher, in fact. Several months before, they had agreed to publish a book of photographs assembled by Jack Stafford, an award-winning photojournalist who just happened to have been my live-in boyfriend when I worked for the *Richmond Times-Dispatch.* The photographs showed sites and scenes of historical significance in Iraq before and after the U. S. invasion. He had sought out the "before" photos and had taken—at much risk to his life—the "after" shots himself. The al Shiraz mosque, for instance, was shown glittering in the morning sunlight in 1955, its minaret lifting straight into the blue and cloudless sky. Jack's photo showed a pile of rubble that seemed imbedded with facets resembling nothing less than tiny fallen stars. A 1924 photo of the Iraqi National Herd filled a two- page spread—a valley full of galloping Arabian horses whose purebred line went back almost five thousand years. Jack's "after" picture, taken after the U. S. had bombed Baghdad and destroyed most things of value, showed a little over a dozen dazed and penned animals.

My part in the book was to write a brief paragraph or two about some of the photographs and edit other descriptions contributed by people Jack met in Iraq. Written under a punishing deadline—the publisher had been afraid that the war in Iraq might end—it had been both difficult and painful, but I had done a good job for all that. I could never do the photographs justice, but neither did I cheapen them. Jack's reputation had led to us both getting a nice advance—even though the book would not be out for several months yet. I had used my share for the Scythian horn bow I had taken to Torrington the night before and which now hung securely in my archery room in the barn. Jack was another problem, always hinting in his emails that it would be nice if we would get back together. It was a problem I had no problem putting off.

On the radio, Buffalo Springfield was playing "Out of My Mind." The lunatic theme was no coincidence, of course. The Creeper had obviously read the newspaper story about me and Cletus Donnelly. He had already been dwelling on madness, so the mention of Cletus being sent to Waxahatchee had set him off on one of his extended musical themes, giving Gamma full rein to extemporize as she saw fit.

Right. The letter from my father was still on the table, but I chose to browse through the Dover catalog, idly looking at different types of snaffles while my memories were cooking under a slow heat. Two years earlier, my mother Cindy had fallen off a green-broke mare and smashed her skull on one of the railroad ties that defined her dressage ring. I had missed her funeral when my flight from Baghdad—where I had been working as a war correspondent—was delayed. Cindy's will left my father several thousand dollars in cash as well as a few small properties she had accumulated. The house I was sitting in—along with the barn and about 100 adjacent acres—were left to me. She had even allowed for inheritance taxes to be paid. Baghdad had been tough for me. I didn't want to go back, so I quit my job and planned to move back to Pine Oak. But while I was tying up my affairs in Richmond—and breaking up with Jack in the process—my father had liquidated the properties Cindy had left him. And not satisfied with that, he went ahead and sold all my mother's books, her Ford F-250 pickup, and her three wonderful, incredibly well-bred Hanovarian horses to whoever would take them quickly. He was in Italy before I returned. The problem was this: the horses, the truck, and the large collection of dressage manuals were not his to sell and the sneaky, underhanded, weaselly way he sidled out of Pine Oak before I got back to confront him had been gnawing on me ever since.

It's odd, because before I left Pine Oak for college, I kind of liked my father. Although he was dominated by Cindy, he was always good natured about it. He was, I suppose, an average father who enjoyed an occasional fishing trip and a beer or two with friends during Super Bowl season. He ate what was put in front of him and generally stayed in the background of our family. But after Cindy died, Mike had shed his old personality the way a snake sheds its skin. The last I had heard, he was trying to make a living in Florence as a street artist as well as giving an occasional drawing lesson. I liked the idea of my father scratching his traveling itch at long last, but the idea of seeing him in a red beret and sporting a goatee made me squirm with embarrassment. I snatched up his letter again and read it through.

> *Susie:*
>
> *You have a new baby brother. His name is Salvatore Antonio McKeown. We might call him Sal or Tory. I like just calling him Sam, like his initials, or maybe Tony. But I guess this is coming out of the blue, huh? Maybe I should*

start by saying that I'm married again. Her name is Maria and she is a 34-year-old art student. I was attracted to her from the first day we met in the Uffizi. She used to work as a guard in Room 33, which has some of the sexiest paintings, by the way. When I found out she was a novice painter, I told her I would give her lessons if she helped me improve my Italian. Well, as they say, one thing led to another, ha ha.

Having an Italian wife and child means I'll be getting my Italian citizenship almost by the time you get this letter. Also, your dear mother left me fairly well off, so we've decided to buy a small villa just outside Florence. The economy is just as bad here as it is there and property is going for a song. All in all, I guess we'll be okay financially, although Maria will have to go back to work eventually.

I'm sorry I haven't been in touch, but Cindy's death tore a hole in me emotionally. I feel that I'm finally getting back to normal. And, yes, I've been drawing some. Nothing serious, just copying some of the old masters, trying to get my hand in again. They say that them that can't do, teach. But does that mean that if I'm not teaching, I can do? Ha ha.

I hope you're doing well at the paper and that you feel better after your thyroid surgery. Are you still doing archery? How about boyfriends—any progress on that front? Anyway, Susie, think about your old man sometimes. Maybe when things have settled down we can get together somewhere. I'm anxious for you to meet your little brother.

Ciao, mia figlia,
M.M.

I crumpled up the letter and threw it across the room like a newspaper article begun badly. So Cindy had left him well off, had she? He hoped my thyroid condition had stabilized, did he? If I hadn't been at death's door, I would have noticed that he was a lot more well off than Cindy had left him. Boyfriends? Give me a break. His girlfriend was younger than me. And as for that reference to the "sexiest paintings" in Room 33: gag me with a spoon. The whole letter, even the news about his new son, was inexpressively repulsive to me. Ha fucking ha.

Gina, you bitch, where are you?

On impulse, I got out my cell phone and looked up the number of Myra Van Hesse, my mother's favorite riding buddy. It was she who had purchased one of my mother's horses and was instrumental in getting another placed at a good equestrian facility in DeLand. She had also let me know where Mike had sold Alikki, the three-year-old filly that had bucked Cindy to her death, and I had purchased her back. Alikki was now coming five and had a filly of her own. I had been riding her without incident for over a month now. Myra answered on the third ring.

"Hello?"

"Myra. It's Sue-Ann McKeown."

"Sue-Ann, why what a nice surprise."

"How are you doing, Myra? Are you riding?"

"Now and then, when my back is well enough. When are you going to come out and see Facilitator?"

I had quit smoking over a year before, but even so, I involuntarily glanced around for a cigarette. "That's why I called. Do you think I might come out for a lesson?"

"My land, Sue-Ann. I haven't given a lesson in years. Have you been riding at all?"

"A lot, yeah. I, um, bought Alikki back from that backyard cowboy and I've been doing a lot of work with her. I have a couple of friends that ride, too, and they've been helping me."

"My goodness, Sue-Ann, is it safe?"

"Alikki is a dream, Myra. She's everything that Cindy thought she'd be. But I can't take her anywhere until I get some help. That's why I thought you might give me a seat lesson or something on Facilitator."

"Well, sure, Sue-Ann. Sure. When would you like to come out?"

I wanted to come out that second, but I knew I had other responsibilities. "Would tomorrow be too soon?" I asked.

"I'm happy to have you, Sue-Ann."

"Thanks, Myra. And there's also a couple of things I need to talk to you about. Are you still working at the hospital?"

"I have another 22 months until I retire," she said.

"Counting down the days, huh?"

"You got that right, honey. What's it all about?"

"I'll tell you when I see you. Is, what, 10:00 all right?"

"That's fine. You remember the way?"

"Couldn't forget it. Bye now."

I hung up the phone, stubbed out my imaginary cigarette, and went into the bedroom for my jacket. It was cold outside and I still had to feed up before I drove to the office. That's a given, by the way. Just because I don't mention feeding every morning and evening doesn't mean that I don't do it. I soak beet pulp in warm water and top it with a rich rice bran and alfalfa cubes. I also talk to all three horses and put my hands on them and let them know that I'm there for them. But as I was just about to go out the back door toward the barn, I caught the lyrics of another song on the radio, this time it was the song by Robin and Marian that had impressed me earlier.

Pay the moon to stay bright.
Monsters travel at night.
I've got my chains but you've got my light.
I'm not so sure where I am.

Was I born just for breeding?
Was I brought here because I'm bleeding?
Pay the moon to make me smile,
the distance widens every mile
that I'm receding.

Listening to the song this time, I was struck by the fact that Maryanne Simmons' voice was dominant throughout the song. It was almost as if the producers of the record realized that her brother's lyrics were better suited for a woman and that his own voice was, in this song at least, better suited as accompaniment. Mickey's voice was soft but effective, even rising in the chorus to a perceptive emotion. After what The Creeper had told me about him, I could see him trying to do his best, but seething with anger all the while.

There was something that disturbed me about the song, but at the time I just didn't have the time to figure out what it was. I grabbed up the Robin and Marian CD Krista had brought over to listen to in the car.

Chapter 8

"A little more outside rein, Sue Ann," Myra called out from E, where she sat comfortably in a chair while I was trying to canter 20-meter circles on her 17-hand Hanovarian gelding. "That's right—not too much bend. Bring his shoulder around," she shouted. "Okay, now half-halt and back to trot. Goooood, now let him stretch—don't throw him away, just ease your reins out as he reaches down. Good, now walk and pet him. Don't let him quit on you, tell him to walk on . . ."

It was easy for her to say. She was resting while I was using muscles I hadn't thought of in years. Sure, I'd been riding a lot with Krista and Gina, but it was mostly trail riding, with a few sprints thrown in when we decided to take up horseback archery. But dressage made you use almost your entire body and after about 40 minutes on Facilitator, I was beat and my arrow wound throbbed menacingly. It might be mid-December, but sweat poured from my body and my helmet felt like an oven slowly broiling the top of my head.

"All right, I think that's enough for today." I looked over and saw that Myra was getting up from her seat. She looked happy and relaxed. I dismounted and hugged Facilitator. He looked around and nibbled the pocket of my riding breeches. I released him from my hug and said, "Okay, okay," and extracted my last sugar cube. He crunched it.

Facilitator had been my mother's schoolmaster and he had taught her a lot of what she knew about classical riding. But he was past his prime and when Cindy bought her next horse—imported directly from

Europe—Facilitator had been given a smaller role. In fact, I had often ridden Facilitator when I came home on holiday visits. When Cindy died, Myra had bought Facilitator from my father, but back problems made her a sporadic rider. Still, Cindy had been convinced that horses remember everything they are taught. I supposed that Facilitator could have piaffed if I knew how to ask properly—which I very definitely did not. I looked him over with pleasure, then stuck out my tongue at him. "You're not even breathing hard." Myra had walked up to us and I turned to her and said, "He doesn't have a bit of lather on him."

"He's still in good shape for a 20-something," she said fondly. "It brought back a lot of good memories when I saw you dismount."

I thought for a few seconds, then remembered. "You mean dismounting on the off side?"

"Mount on one side, dismount on the other. Everything Cindy did was balanced."

"It's so ingrained in me, I never even think about it," I said. I hitched up the stirrups and loosened the girth, and we headed for the barn. "You know, I've been thinking of making a book out of her sayings. When I was going through her papers, I found that little notebook she used to carry around in her back pocket. It had all kinds of little sayings like, um, 'Horses need shoes as much as cows do.' And how she was convinced she could tell a horse's breed from its poop."

Myra laughed softly. "I remember that little notebook, and I think that's a fine idea." She pronounced it "fahn " like Gina would have.

"She used to write things in the margins of her books, too," I added. "I've been copying them out—making a file out of them on my computer. When I get finished, I wonder if you would look them over and maybe add any that you can remember. And catch anything that she might just have been quoting from somewhere."

"I'll do my best."

We reached the wash rack. I took off the saddle and blanket and put them in the tack room, while Myra rubbed invisible sweat from Facilitator. As I was helping her put his cooler on, she said, "Go ahead and walk him for a few minutes, then put him out with his buddies. I'll go in and make us some snacks. Coffee?"

"Always," I smiled.

Facilitator's halter had a purple lead rope. I took the end of it and led him up and down the driveway—I was going to cool him off whether he needed it or not. I watched as he sniffed old piles of poop and nibbled at a few weeds, and I spoke softly to him about Cindy and Alikki. He glanced up from time to time and seemed to say, "I know, yes." Then I led him out toward the paddock, where Myra's three other horses were standing around a new roll of hay. I opened the gate, removed his halter, and watched him trot very collectedly—very proudly—toward them, as if saying, I got ridden and you didn't. He had always been like that, had been the dominant horse in whatever group I had seen him in. Although in summer, his coat had a brownish tinge, now it shone like black ice. In a single weekend, Cindy had gotten her third-level scores on him, and with them, her USDF Bronze Medal. Watching Facilitator in his paddock, I was flooded with memories.

I had been home the weekend of that show and she was so nervous that she insisted that I trailer to the show with her and call out the tests. It was a two-day competition and she had signed up for one test on each day. The Third Level 1 test was on Saturday morning, and Cindy was concentrating so fully that she barely acknowledged my presence until she entered the ring, and even then I wasn't sure she heard me. I stood at E with my test booklet and called out, "A: enter collected trot. X: halt, salute. Proceed collected trot." Cindy was too stiff and I could feel it. The halt was not only off line but Facilitator's right hind trailed behind. Not a good start, but the pair seemed to get better as the test went along. The first flying change was clean with a nice jump—at least a 7. She was making up points, but then Facilitator stumbled and almost completely missed the second change and I knew that the judge would slam her. Somehow, though, they recovered again and the final halt was almost a perfect four-square. It was a fine ride overall, but the bobbles would hurt. I waited by the office for the scores to be posted—it had to be over 60 for it to do her any good— while Cindy walked Facilitator back to his stall. I knew she was disappointed with the ride, but I couldn't tell it from her walk—every ride was a learning process. The score was 60.35—just enough. I ran back to the stall and almost shouted, "You did it!" We hugged each other and gave Facilitator a whole carrot to crunch. That was only the first test, but it broke the ice; the next day they nailed the more difficult Third Level 3 for a 73.5 and the high-score point award for the competition.

That was the last time I ever saw Cindy perform at a show, and it was Facilitator's final performance in a show ring. I stood outside Myra's barn for a long time just watching him munch hay. I had to will myself to turn away and head back to the house.

It was very warm in Myra's ranch-style house and I took off my jacket and hung it over a chair in the kitchen, where Myra had some tuna sandwiches ready. I could smell coffee brewing. I took a seat at the large wooden table, bare except for salt and pepper shakers shaped like mustangs. It was a comfortable kitchen, a place I could go to sleep in and not have to worry about friends or jobs or people trying to shoot me.

"Where's Phil today?" I asked. Her husband was an English teacher at the local community college.

"He's out playing golf with a couple of his friends. Seems like he's always—my land, Sue-Ann! Is that blood?"

I looked down at my blouse. She was right and I felt like an idiot for not wearing a darker colored shirt.

"Is it yours? Are you hurt?" she asked anxiously, putting the tray of sandwiches on the table.

Instead of answering, I began crying, which surprised her only a little less than it surprised me. And it wasn't just a few tears, either—it was a drawn-out jag racked with sobs, although I was able to keep the blubbering to a minimum. It was the first time I had cried about Cindy's death. Myra put her arm around my shoulders to comfort me—and it did—although I know it hurt her back to bend over me like that. When I could control myself, I wiped my eyes with a napkin. "Sorry, Myra," I managed.

"But what's happened, Sue-Ann?" she asked.

I smiled ruefully. "If you want me to talk, you have to give me coffee," I said.

With a cup in front of me and Myra sitting across from me at the table, I began talking, but what came out of my mouth was another total surprise. "I miss her so much, Myra." I took a sip of coffee, then another. "Sometimes when I'm cleaning I'll see one of her handprints on the wall. There's part of her in all her books and papers. I sit on her furniture and muck out her stalls. I think of her every time I ride Alikki. I want to talk to her but she's not there."

"I think about her too, honey," Myra said. "She was a wonderful friend and a fantastic rider. I think that if she were still with us she might be riding Trifecta at Grand Prix by now."

"You taught her everything she knew," I said.

"No, honey, that's not right. I taught her everything *I* knew, but it didn't take her any time at all before she had gone way past what I could teach her. She had a feel for riding that only the top riders have, and a mind to go with it. And what a reader! I think she studied every riding master who ever put words to paper. But unless I'm mistaken, that bloodstain is getting larger." She looked at me with a question in her eyes.

But did I give her a straight answer? No, I just started crying again—not so heavily this time, but still with considerable emotion. And when I stopped the waterworks, I told her all about the nut-case who had taken a potshot at me with his crossbow. Then I ranted in great detail about my father and his doings over the last couple of years. I ranted about his selling off Cindy's things, about his moving to Italy and wearing a red beret, about his screwing the first bimbo he meets and making her pregnant. About his wanting us to "get together." My thyroid medicine came in for its share of abuse. Then I told her about having to hire a replacement for *The Courier's* office manager position—how I'd gotten to work on Friday and had to fight off a crowd of about a dozen people thrusting applications in my face and talking about their hungry families, how the next week was just going to be more of the same, if not worse, and that Mark Patterson was going to get to write all my stories because I would be busy interviewing all week.

"And if all that's not bad enough," I finished, "The editor wants me to find his girlfriend."

"My goodness. Is she lost?"

"She just ran away, I think."

"She probably doesn't want to be found, then. Do you even know this woman?"

"We went to high school together," I answered. "But we weren't close."

"Well, Sue-Ann, just treat all this like Cindy used to train a horse."

"What do you mean?" I asked.

"Just concentrate on one small step at a time. When that's done, then go on to the next."

"You're right, Myra."

"And she'd say that the first thing for you to do is to get better. If I'da known about that side of yours I'da never let you on that horse. Now let's go into the bathroom and take a look at it. We'll get a new bandage and something to clean the wound. Go ahead and take that shirt off."

Luckily, the wound didn't look nearly as bad as I thought it would, and while we were changing the bandage, I remembered the real reason I had come—or the reason I *thought* I'd come.

"Listen, Myra. I need to ask you a question and maybe even ask you to do me a favor."

"What is it, Sue-Ann?"

"The guy that shot me. His name is Cletus Donnelly. Have you heard the name before?"

"Not that I can recall."

"He called me on the phone that night. He was talking a bunch of foolishness."

"You mean he's a friend of yours?"

"No, not at all. He just wanted me to write a newspaper story about him. He gave me this line about how he was going to kill himself and set his house on fire. He even told me that he had his mother tied up and was going to kill her, too."

"My gracious, Sue-Ann. Sounds like he should be in Waxahatchee."

"That's exactly where they sent him. I was wondering whether there was any way I could visit him."

Myra gave me a glance that seemed to ask, "Why on earth would you want to do that?" Instead, she just handed me a t-shirt that obviously belonged to her husband and said, "Here, put this on."

"I think the only reason he shot at me was because he thought I had betrayed his trust—which, of course I did when I called the police. It may have been just a wild shot. I mean, how could he have seen that it was me in that car at that time of night?"

"Even if you're right, Sue-Ann, I don't see any reason . . ."

"Because I promised. I told him I would write that story. Sure, the guy is bonkers, but, you know, he grew up in Pine Oak just like I did. He went to the same high school, knew a lot of the same people, played basketball in the same gym. What happened that made him so different that he cracked?"

"Baby, when you've worked in a mental hospital as long as I have you realize that it could be a thousand reasons. Or it could be none—leastways none that you ever find out about. We have a young Asian woman in one of my wards. She's smart, talented, and pretty. Inside the hospital she's just as normal as a pin—can talk a blue streak about anything under the sun—but whenever she goes back outside, she's like someone without a skin. It's the same air outside, but she says it breathes different. Outside, she hears noises differently and couldn't cluck at a duck even if it came up and asked her the time of day. But she has a nice family—both her parents are college professors. They have money."

"Another thing Cindy used to tell me, though, Myra. If a horse is skittish, nine times out of ten it's because someone beat on it. What I want to know is what happened to Cletus Donnelly that made him want to stab himself with the broken-off hilt of a sword."

"So how can I help?"

"First of all, give me an idea of what you do at the hospital."

"I'm what they call a WBS—a Ward Block Supervisor. That means that I'm in charge of the administration of a building of about 150 residents. There are nine other buildings just like mine. Each one has its own clerical staff, janitorial staff, and medical staff. My job is to keep everyone happy."

"What is the difference between the ten buildings?"

"Okay, one is for geriatric residents. A couple are for mentally retarded, one is forensics—for the criminally insane who aren't competent to stand trial. A couple are halfway houses for residents who are getting ready to go back out into the world, and the others are for everyone else. I'm guessing that your shooter was taken to the forensic block."

"How can I get in to see him?"

"Well, Sue-Ann, the hospital isn't run like a prison. You don't have to go through security to get on the grounds or anything like that. Even though I'm not a doctor, I have access to everyone's records. I can do a search for this Cletus Donnelly and find out which block he's in. Then I'll talk to his WBS and see if he can have visitors. If so, I'll let you know and we can set something up."

"That's great, Myra. You won't get in trouble or anything will you?"

"I deal with things like this every day, honey. Now how about one of those sandwiches before the bread gets all stale?"

"I'm starved," I admitted, following Myra back into the kitchen. "Got any more coffee?"

"Coming right up. Now tell me something happy."

"Happy?" I was at a loss.

"Your riding, your boyfriends, stuff you're writing—anything not so depressing as what we've been talking about so far."

"Hmm." And so I told her about the book Jack and I were putting together and some of the stories I had written for the paper in the last few months. I didn't tell her about Gina, of course, and the subject of Torrington was off limits, too, but that didn't mean I couldn't refer to them obliquely. "Me and a couple of my friends have been learning horseback archery."

"I'm glad you've been keeping up with your archery, Sue-Ann, but on a horse? You don't shoot arrows off Alikki, do you?"

"She's used to it now, although we're taking everything very slow. She and I just walk the course. My friends' horses are more advanced. But why don't you come out and watch. I have a course set up in the dressage ring."

"I'm curious enough that I just might."

"And you can give me another lesson—this time on Alikki."

"I don't . . ."

"I want you to get to know Alikki, Myra. She's not a killer. What happened to Cindy was an accident."

"I try to tell myself that, Sue-Ann, but it's not easy. I've been around a lot of falls and I've been bucked off more times myself than I care to count. I've felt guilty ever since I let your father sell Alikki to that Horse Heaven man, but . . ."

"She has a filly, you know," I told her.

Myra looked at me in surprise. "You never told me you bred her, Sue-Ann."

"It was Mr. Moon—the guy at Horse Heaven—that did it. Bred her to a Quarterhorse, if you can believe it. When I bought her back from him Alikki looked like she'd swallowed a wrecking ball, but Emmy's a pretty little girl—she's a bay with a blaze that looks just like a capital T."

"All right, Sue-Ann, you know I have a soft spot for babies. And this horseback archery stuff does intrigue me. When can I come out?"

We finished our sandwiches and our coffee and Myra walked me out to my car. As I was getting in, something popped into my head. I rolled down the window. "Listen, Myra. I hate to ask, but I wonder if you could do me another favor."

"If I can, I will."

"I've been thinking about doing an article about a couple of folksingers that had their fifteen minutes of fame back in the Seventies. It was a brother and sister act from North Florida that called themselves Robin and Marian. Their music was interesting and original and for a while they were performing in the same clubs as people like Bob Dylan and Judy Collins. They don't really figure in any history of American folk music, but I think they deserve at least a footnote. I'd like to find them."

"But how can I help?"

"It's a real long shot, but it's possible that the girl had a hereditary mental illness. I know that the two of them grew up in the Pensacola area and it just struck me that if she had become, you know, incompetent, she might have been sent to Waxahatchee. In fact, her grandfather died in Waxahatchee, but that would have been long ago." I took a couple of breaths while I was thinking this idea out. "The woman's name is Maryanne Simmons. I don't know if Maryanne is one word or two; I don't even know how she spelled it, but when you're checking the records, could you see if she has ever been committed? Both Maryanne and her brother disappeared more than thirty years ago and they may both be dead by now, but I'd really like to know for sure what happened to her."

"I'll do what I can, Sue-Ann, and I'll let you know if I find out anything."

Chapter 9

The mental hospital, along with a couple of state prisons and a home for delinquent boys, provided hundreds of jobs to Jasper County residents. But with the whole country trying to recover from a hard recession, people responded to Cal's ad for an office manager like termites respond to a new load of raw lumber. In all, I received over 150 applications, some of them legible. I sat at my desk for four days straight, greeting the applicants and thanking them for their interest in *The Pine Oak Courier*. When there was a lull in activity, I worked crossword puzzles, edited news items about upcoming Xmas activities, and answered the phone. I experienced the true meaning of champing at the bit.

The whole week had been miserable. It had turned not only cold but rainy, and I had to work hard just to keep the horses' stalls clean and their water buckets filled. Short winter hours and the wet weather made it impossible for me to ride, and I missed it dreadfully. I spent most of my evenings reading thick fantasy novels—one after the other—that I purchased from Benny's used bookstore. It was a bad habit I had picked up from a former boyfriend, who read nothing else. Don't get me wrong, I completely lost myself in each of these thrilling adventures of princesses and soothsayers and gnomes, but loathed myself each time I finished one for all the time I had wasted.

By Thursday evening I had narrowed the hopefuls to five and scheduled interviews. On Friday morning I sat with Cal and Mark Patterson in our small conference room waiting for the first applicant. *The Courier's* photography intern, Becky Colley, was relishing her job as temporary receptionist. Still a high-school student, Becky had until recently dressed entirely in Goth clothing and had run around with a bad crowd. Ironically, it had been another of my old boyfriends, Jack Stafford (who had never heard of thick fantasies), who had given her an interest in photography and, almost literally, a new outlook on life.

Our first interview was with Betty Dickson, our typesetting and paste-up specialist. She had worked for *The Courier* for almost two years, having been hired when Gina was promoted to Office Manager. I'm afraid I didn't share Betty's idea that being the typesetter made her next in line for Office Manager, but I had scheduled an interview to avoid hard feelings. And after all, she did have intimate knowledge of *The Courier.*

The four of us sat around a newly purchased conference table of real oak, stained with just the lightest touch of honeyed pine. In fact, the entire room had been newly refurbished with lightweight, ergonomic chairs, a flat-screen TV on one wall, and attractively framed photos depicting important events, people, or buildings in Pine Oak history. Cal, Mark, and I each had an interview question to ask, but the actual answers to the questions were not as important as the applicant's personality and way with words, although we didn't tell them that.

Cal Dent, who was dressed even nattier than usual in a green, warm-looking tweed suit, opened the interview. "Okay, Betty. Each of us has a question to ask you about a different aspect of being an office manager. We are all going to be making notes, so don't let that bother you. Take as long as you need to answer, and don't be nervous. Are you ready to start?"

"Yes."

"All right then." Cal put on his glasses and glanced down at his question sheet. "If a new business moved into Pine Oak, say next to the Piggly Wiggly, what steps would you take to get them to advertise in *The Courier*?"

We had given Betty a copy of the question sheet and she studied it carefully, or seemed to. "There's no room next to the Piggly Wiggly," she pointed out.

"Let's pretend there is," said Cal patiently.

You might want me to go on with this kind of tedium, but I wasn't really listening to her answers. I had dealt with Betty Dickson long enough to know that her monosyllabic way with words and generally sour disposition were the exact opposite of what was needed for the job. Instead, I was thinking about the way she looked. She had on a mauve blouse with dark gray slacks and matching vest. Her hair, always cut fairly short and looking like she had used a bowl and a mirror, had been teased and tinted professionally. I suddenly realized that she looked like the stereotype of a lesbian. Odd that I could have been around her so long without that thought ever entering my head. The truth is that, aside from the information she had put on her application, I knew nothing about Betty's private life and I had never encountered her outside the office.

I looked from her to Cal. Before I knew he was sleeping with Gina, I had actually asked him out for a drink. His looks, personality, and drive made him one of the best catches in Pine Oak. Although by now my feelings toward him were so mixed that I doubted I would ever be able to come to terms with them, I found that I was almost as attracted to him as I was when I first met him. My eyes moved across the table to Mark, who was asking his interview question, and studied him closely. Despite his many personality flaws, Mark was a good-looking young man and if I had been 19 I wouldn't have minded jumping his bones.

But I felt absolutely no attraction for Betty. I had no interest in what was under her slacks and the idea of even hugging her was fairly repulsive.

This was interesting. I thought of famous women who had come out as lesbians. Ellen DeGeneres did not appeal to me except for her wonderful sense of humor. I think, on the other hand, I could have been tight with her girlfriend Portia de Rossi, but maybe that was because she was so involved with horses and because her tall, blonde, confident demeanor reminded me more than a little of Gina. I conjured up in my mind a bevy of famous men: Johnny Depp, Matt Damon, Colin Firth, yum. I wouldn't have minded hopping in bed with any of them, so I still wasn't a total lesbian. Yet hopping in bed with someone wasn't the same thing as loving them, and I loved Gina. I wondered—and not for the first time—if I was truly bisexual or had I just happened to come into contact with the one woman—the one *person*—I could give my whole heart and soul to.

"Your turn, Sue-Ann." Cal's voice startled me out of my reverie, and I hastily looked at my question sheet.

"Um, what would you do if a subscriber called the office and started cursing you out because *The Courier* ran a news story that they didn't like?"

Betty looked at her own question sheet again and began in a hedging voice, "What, uh, I mean, which story?" And I tuned her out again. I had just remembered that Portia de Rossi was now Ellen DeGeneres' wife. Her *wife*. Wow, what a strange concept. I had always disliked the word wife; certainly I never wanted to be referred to as one. But would I like to be Gina's wife? Would I like her to be mine? In a world without small towns, the answer—yikes—was yes. But Pine Oak existed, and I existed within it. What to do? Well, the first thing was to find Gina. And then? I looked guiltily at Cal, who was scribbling on his question sheet. I would do whatever it took and use any means necessary.

"Thank you, Betty. We'll let you know when we've made our decision." We had half an hour before our next interview, so Cal stood up and went to his own office. He had told Betty to take the morning off while the rest of the interviews were going on. I looked out the window and saw her get into her car and drive away. Mark was doodling on his question sheet and I was still pondering my sexuality when Cal poked his head back into the conference room. "Sue-Ann, can you come to my office?"

Mark raised his eyebrows, but I just shrugged and got up from my seat. Cal was waiting for me at the door, which he closed before taking the seat behind his desk. He obviously had something on his mind and I was pretty sure I knew what it was. When I was seated across from him, he asked, "Well, what do you think?"

"About what?" I answered.

"About Betty."

"Oh. You mean seriously?"

"She didn't exactly ace the interview, did she?" he asked.

"It told us what we wanted to know," I said.

"But here's the thing," he continued. "Betty is really good at what she does now. How many people in Jasper County know how to use PageMaker and Photoshop and all of the rest of the design programs that she uses?"

"What you're really asking is what we'll do if she decides to quit because you don't give her the Office Manager job?"

"Right."

"Give her a raise," I said.

"Yeah?"

"Give her the same as the office manager and tell her that we can't give her that job because she's so good in the one she already has. Tell her we're proud to have her. And by the way, I haven't found Ginette yet."

Cal looked up and took off his glasses, which he had just recently begun using for reading and which made him look more studious and refined. "Um," he said.

"I've called her parents in Texas and her sister in Canada and none of them knows where she is. She *has* been in contact with her mother, though."

"And?"

"And she doesn't know any more than we do. Just that her daughter quit her job and decided to travel for a while."

"Travel?" Cal asked. Like where? You mean to Ireland or Cambodia or somewhere, or just in the U.S.?"

"She didn't know, Cal."

"How did you find out where they lived?" he asked.

"There are ways, Cal. That's why you pay me more than an office manager." I smiled at him over the desk. "But I'm not going to quit. If we ever get through these interviews, maybe I'll have time to do some *real* research."

Outside, I heard Mark talking to Randy Rivas, who was the newest member of the reporting staff. He was an ex-Auburn baseball player who also happened to have a degree in English, and had been hired to write up local sports events. Another recent hire, Annie Gillespie, was attending a County Commission meeting. More on these two when they have something to say.

"Let's get to it, then," he said brightly. Who's the next applicant?"

"I'm not sure. Dick somebody."

Cal opened a folder that contained copies of the five applications. He sorted through them and said, "Richard L. Smerk. Fifty years old or thereabouts. Graduated from Jasper County High School, no college. Present occupation, produce worker at Food World. Geez."

We were in the conference room again when the applicant, a short, plump man with hair implants and a string tie, walked in with a big smile. "Howdy, howdy," he said as Cal introduced each of us to him. "Sorry I'm a mite late, but a boocoodle a cabbages just got delivered and I hadta count heads, ha ha."

"Mr. Smerk . . . Dick," Cal began. "Why don't you tell us a little about yourself."

"Glad to, glad to," said the little man. "As I guess ya'll know, I work at Food World—in vegetables. Now Mama don't like Food World no way ever since she bought a bad can of pork and beans, but I don't mind the work—been there goin on three years now. I was waitin on a customer earlier this week—turns out that he used to coach my son in softball but he'd got cancer and changed so that I didn't know him from Adam's house cat. Anyway, this guy told me about this job—said his wife was gonna apply for it—so I just thought, hey. I'm a people person, ha ha. And it wasn't ten minutes later that my boss came up to me and told me she was thinkin about taking me away from vegetables and puttin me in fish. And I thought fish my Aunt Gussie. The only fish I eat are fish sticks, ha ha. And when I went home and told Mama I'd be lookin for another job she was so tickled she almost strangled." And he smiled his big wide smile.

But I wasn't thinking about Dick Smerk or his mama either. I was thinking about love.

I was pretty much a loner in high school. I had a few dates and what you might even call a boyfriend or two, but they only lasted for a couple of weeks at most. The most thrilling part was the anticipation of being with someone. Thinking about someone all the time until you finally met and touched and maybe even kissed. It was incredibly exciting but not very rewarding. The kisses were hot but messy and my desire never seemed to reach further than letting a boy touch one of my breasts through a sweater. I was curious about the bulge I felt on occasion when I was pressed in a tight embrace, but never enough to touch it. Maybe if I had been with someone a little more exciting or mature I could have achieved a greater emotion. But even then, would it have been love?

I thought I felt love for the first man I dated in college. His name was Lars Erickson and he was an engineering student I met in the library, where I often went to study. He had blonde hair and dreamy blue eyes and more than a hint of a Swedish accent. His kisses were soft and gentle and when I went to his apartment, he peeled off my clothes tenderly, like they were bandages, and brought me to orgasm before he even undressed. Yes, I thought that was love, and when he left me and married his old flame back in Sweden, I pined for weeks and months. Even after I graduated I couldn't hear the name Lars without a hitch in my heartbeat. But how often do you hear the name Lars? Pretty soon I completely forgot about him and met someone else who became my boyfriend for a while. There were, in fact, others too—all gleaming with love's scintilla.

I was approaching 30 when I met—and fell in love with, so I thought—Jack Stafford. He was just making a name for himself as a photojournalist and I had recently moved to Richmond to accept a job on *The Times-Dispatch*. Handsome and brilliant, Jack was truly a great artist, but was never sure why. There was something about the angle of his vision—I don't mean that he was squint-eyed or anything, just that he was able to grasp the important features of a scene and shoot it at just the right moment and from exactly the right vantage point. And he did it so intuitively that it was only after he developed the photos that he realized why he had made the shot at all. When *Times-Dispatch* readers saw one of Jack's photos, they not only witnessed news, but understood it. He had once told Becky Colley (who was probably fantasizing about him at the reception desk) that he didn't shoot nudes; rather he shot portraits that made his subjects seem to be naked without them having to take off their clothes. It was true for breaking news as well.

The National Press Photographers Association Prize Committee agreed, and soon after he won his first national award, I agreed to marry him and I thought that was what I wanted. Instead, I volunteered (Jack still doesn't know this) to go to Iraq for six months. It was there that I realized that not only did I not want to be with Jack for life, but that I didn't love him. Respect, reverence, awe, admiration, fondness—all these I felt and much, much more. But love? Uh uh. This became even more apparent as I began to slide off the edge of normality. The scenes in Iraq sickened me, but there were other sicknesses taking hold as well. The first was my thyroid condition, which I've spoken about before, but the other was my growing dissatisfaction with my life as a whole. I had several one-night lovers in Baghdad, including a Crow Indian lieutenant, who I was in bed with the day my mother was killed. Did I love any of them? Of course not. Except for Lt. Enemy Hunter, if I saw any of them today I doubt I'd know them from Adam's house cat.

So what did that say about love? That it was fleeting? Maybe. If Lars hadn't left me, would I still love him? If I hadn't grown dissatisfied with Jack's neediness and naiveté, would I still love him? More to the point, if I just decided to let Gina go, would the love I felt for her fade? I supposed it would, but I wasn't willing to let it go so easily. The only fear I had was that she was no longer in love with me.

When Dick Smerk with the hair implants had gotten in his car and departed, I went out into the main office and sat down next to Becky at the reception desk. Today she was dressed in worn but clean-looking blue jeans, high-cut pink sneakers, cranberry ankle warmers, and an oversized red sweatshirt. Her hair was cut short and dyed blonde and she had a small ring in her nose.

"Shouldn't you be in school?" I asked her.

"Got a pass from my OJT teacher until we get somebody to replace Ginette."

"Better tell him not to hold his breath," I said.

"Nothing yet, huh?"

"Two down, three to go," I told her.

"Who are the others?" she asked.

"Um, one is Linda C. She was in Ginette's crowd in high school. Another is a substitute teacher who's been working at Waxahatchee Elementary. Young guy," I looked at her, "but not very cute. The third one is a thirty-something woman I don't know much about—she mailed in her application so I didn't see her. But she has a college degree and has some experience in—"

But Becky was no longer listening. Instead, she was staring at the door, where the very woman I was talking about was coming in for her interview. I must say I was pretty impressed at first sight. She was dressed very fashionably in a light-colored pantsuit and faux-suede coat. Dark, pretty, about my size or a little shorter, with feathered hair that cascaded down her neck and just missed her left eye. The woman blinked and glanced at the reception desk.

"Hey, Bec," she said. "Shouldn't you be in school?"

"What are you doing here, Mama?" Becky said.

The woman shook her brown feathers as if she were shaking off the cold outside. "I'm here for my interview," she smiled.

"No fucking way," Becky moaned.

Chapter 10

Let me tell you a little about Becky Colley's mother, Linsey. First of all, she was the wife of County Commissioner and part-time goat farmer Ray Colley. And Ray Colley was one of Cal Dent's regular golf partners. Favoritism? Not so. Linsey was an educated, fashionable woman about my own age. Because she had attended a rival high school in Forester, I didn't know her; had never even seen her, in fact. She had a B.A. in Marketing and had interned in the advertising department of Bealls before returning to Jasper County and marrying Ray. She was attractive, outspoken, and tenacious and she was our unanimous choice to fill Gina's position.

Betty Dickson, of course, hated Linsey right away but her new raise kept her muttering to a minimum. I didn't get a raise, but Cal gave me an attagirl for a recruiting job well done. As for Cal, he was so tickled that we hadn't had to hire Dick Smerk that he almost strangled. Becky was suicidal and threatened to go back to being All-Goth-All-The-Time unless we promised not to hire Linsey. She even emailed Jack Stafford. I know because Jack blind copied me on his reply.

> *Rebecca:*
>
> *Thanks for sending the photograph of your mother. Although cell phones do not take pictures of very high quality, we sometimes have to take them when we see them—with whatever is at hand. You have framed her well and caught more than a spark of the attitude you mentioned. There is a danger, though, of believing our preconceptions rather than our eyes. I think that you*

will remember that you introduced me to her when I was in Pine Oak, and I remember her well. In the expression you describe as "the haughty arrogance of a Red Lobster cook ordering at McDonalds," I see more than a hint of self-assurance and competence. Using the gleaming iPhone "surgically attached" to her hip as the focal point to the photo was a very nice touch on your part, but I suspect that carrying such a phone impressed the interviewers by pointing out her accessibility to a client-filled world.

No, I don't think I would like to work for my mother either. But I don't think I would dislike it as much as all that. In fact, it would be great to see her finally leaving that awful housewifey world and actually having a life. Getting this new job seems to be something that is very important for Linsey so why not give it a chance? Maybe her happiness and fulfillment will lead to better relations between the two of you. And remember that the Office Manager does not assign your work—Mr. Dent does.

Rebecca—Bec—I don't think it's cool for you to hack into your mother's cell and download those nude pictures you claim she sends to her boyfriends. "Sexting" is a widespread phenomenon and not limited to Linsey. And no, I do not want to see them. And although I am honored by your suggestion that you would like to send me some of your own, I beg you not to if you want me to remain a free man.

I have had word from Mr. Dent that you are doing an outstanding job there at The Courier. We can both hope that it leads to other opportunities and a first-class education. I am proud of you, by the way, for organizing the new darkroom for The Courier. I'm glad I was able to convince Mr. Dent that a darkroom was long-needed. I take it that the paper is growing steadily, and you are part of the reason.

Attached is a photograph taken by one of my own interns of a single-engine plane crash just south of Richmond last week. Your assignment is to critique the photo. I want to know what is good about it—and what is not. No hints from me this time.

Thank you for asking my advice. You're an important friend to me and it makes me happy if I can help you to work stuff out. And btw, I'm thinking no on the back-to-black impulse. You've moved on from that now and besides, you're so much more attractive without licorice-colored lipstick and hobnailed boots.

Okay, then,
Jack

Sigh. Jack was surely special, but I doubted whether he was blind-copying Becky on emails he sent to *me*, otherwise I would probably find razor blades sticking up out of my computer keyboard. Phrases like, "I've been losing weight," or "I forgot to renew my driver's license" were Jack's way of whining that he wasn't as good at taking care of himself as I was. He was right, of course, but that's why I had burnt out on the relationship in the first place. I couldn't simply be needed without needing in return. I had very firmly disabused him of any reunion possibilities, but either he didn't read what I was writing or he just ignored it. If only Becky were 30 years old—or even 20—I would buy her a ticket to Richmond and drive her to the airport.

But in the meantime, things went along surprisingly smoothly at *The Courier*. Because it was the Xmas season and because Linsey was brand new, all of us at the paper except Betty were out selling or taking advertisements on the phone. Although Becky spent most of her time ignoring Linsey, Cal spent a lot of time with his newest employee in his office, letting her know exactly how Gina had done this or done that. I didn't envy her, but Linsey seemed to take it with good grace.

The paper had recently gone from a two-day-a-week publication, to a three-day, so we now came out on Tuesday, Thursday, and Sunday. Our new local sports section was a big hit with our readers, and Randy Rivas always had a slew of phone calls, emails, and letters about upcoming sports events or the results of the bowling leagues at Jasper County's only bowling alley.

It was right around this time that there was a spike in the circulation and Cal racked his brains to know the reason for it. Was it the local color stories I was writing? The smart, funny, political stories our new columnist Annie Gillespie was posting? The high school football coverage? Advertising circulars for Piggly Wiggly? Cal printed out the names of the new subscribers and read them aloud in the office, trying to find a connection. It was Betty Dickson that came up with the answer. She simply raised her head up from her work and said, "They bowl." It turned out that a large percentage of Jasper County's population spent time at Hi-Score Lanes on the eastern outskirts of Forester—and they all liked to see their names in print if they bowled well. Randy himself bowled in one of the leagues and, surprisingly, Betty bowled in two. Who knew? But it is things like this—the unexpected little quirks—that made newspaper work so much fun at times.

And of course, I was writing. I wrote a story about an elderly couple who always rode their Shires in the Pine Oak Xmas Parade. The huge draft horses were probably the only Shires in Jasper County and everyone knew they were coming by the sound of the thick necklace of jingle bells they wore around their necks. Gina, Krista, and I had talked of riding in the parade this year dressed as cowgirls, but now that wouldn't happen.

Although I often wrote my stories at home, during Linsey's transition time I spent most of my time in the office. From my desk, I could see two city workers putting up the battered tinsel and paper mache reindeer. It made me feel kind of melancholy, but it would be just as bad at home. And being in a bustling newspaper office—even a small one—inspired me, and I turned out story after story. One was about a new children's playground that was ready to open in Forester, one described a new biodiesel company that had made enquiries into relocating to nearby Hanson's Quarry, a third reported on how several small businesses—including Benny's bookstore—were faring in the slow economy. There were a lot more—enough for two weeks' worth of future issues. The origin of holly and mistletoe as Xmas plants? Yep, I wrote about that. I wrote about Salvation Army drives for the needy and a human interest story about a family whose house had burned to the ground because of a faulty wood stove. But my favorite piece was about a recently deceased resident that had been a volunteer Santa Claus for as long as anyone could remember. The quirk was that he had a repulsive, mole-like growth on his face that was completely covered by his Santa whiskers. Except during the Xmas season, the man never left his small farmhouse just outside Forester. But why the flurry of writing? It's almost like I planned to take a vacation.

I hadn't yet been able to begin the story I really wanted to write—the story of Cletus Donnelly and his attempted suicide, so in the midst of editing birthday notices, taking phone calls, and soliciting ads, I called Myra. It took five rings for her to answer.

"This is Myra."

"Hey, Myra, it's Sue-Ann. Listen, have you thought any more about coming out to the farm and giving me a lesson on Alikki?"

"I'd love to, Sue-Ann. To tell you the truth, I've been shut up in this house since Monday and I'm goin as crazy as a betsy bug."

"Have you been sick?"

"Oh, it's this back of mine went out again. It's not real bad, but as long as I have sick leave I might as well be careful."

"Maybe we should put it off, then," I told her.

"No, really, Sue-Ann, I'll come. But I had better sit down again while you ride. I'll bring my bullhorn. Will Saturday afternoon be all right? I have some errands in the morning."

"Perfect. I'll have a comfy chair waiting for you at B."

"That'll be nice. And listen, Sue-Ann I haven't been back to work since I talked to you, so I haven't been able to check on your friend."

"That's okay, Myra. Whenever. I'll look forward to seeing you Saturday."

"Bye, then."

And so the week went by.

On Friday afternoon, I gathered my stuff from the office and was walking out to my Toyota when Benny Benedict came hopstepping out of his bookstore toward me, the door banging closed behind him. "Gotcha," he said.

"You've been waiting for me to get off?" I asked. There was no point in asking him why he hadn't just come into *The Courier* office, because his answer would have confused me.

"Yah," he said, huffing a little. "Got something for you."

"A new invention, Benny?"

"Naw, Xmas present, heh heh." He handed me a smallish booklet of maybe 50 pages with a plain red cover containing only these words in a bold black type:

The Gritty Goatherd
A play by
Dominic Benedict

"Benny" I exclaimed. "You finished your play!" I knew he had been writing a play for over a year, but usually his personal quirks prevented him from writing more than a page or two before either starting again from scratch or going on to something different altogether.

"Finally, whew!" he answered.

"You wrote a play about a herd of goats?" I asked.

"Naw, ha ha. A goatherd is a guy—or gal, heh heh—that tends goats. A shepherd for goats."

"I knew that," I said, and I did; at least I had at one time. "And thanks; it's a great present."

"Do you, ah, do you think you might be able to . . ." He stopped talking and cut his eyes toward the newspaper office. It took me a few seconds, but I got his meaning.

"Write a review?"

"Umm."

"We don't usually do book reviews, Benny," I began, but seeing the disappointed look beginning to form on his features, I added, "but I'll see what I can do."

"That'd be great, little lady, thanks. Well, gotta go," and he waddled toward his red jeep.

"Are you closing up?" I shouted at him.

"Yep. Gonna quaff a few at Eat Now on the way home. Glug."

"You think you might want to lock up first?" I asked.

"Oh. Umm. Where's my mind at?"

"See you, Benny."

As I drove out of the parking lot, I just happened to notice a dark Ford F-150 pickup pull out after me. I didn't pay much attention until I realized that it seemed to be following me. The driver had the visor of his cap pulled down so that I couldn't see his face, but it was obviously a big man. I noticed that the front of the truck had one of those license plates showing deer antlers—advertising that said driver was a dues-paying member of the hunting community. Normally I wouldn't be so jumpy, but the little incident with Cletus Donnelly had worn on my nerves. I told myself I was being silly—the driver probably lived in the same part of the county I did—but I cautiously passed the street I usually turned down to go home and pulled in at Meekins' Market a mile down the road. When the truck pulled in behind me I thought, okay, he was going vegetable shopping. What's the big deal? Still, I hurried toward the entrance—Gladys would probably be behind the desk reading a romance novel. Before I quite got inside, though, I heard, "Wait up, Sue-Ann," so I stopped and looked back.

"Joey!" The big policeman was dressed in the same street clothes he had on when he had visited me in the hospital. This time, though, he was wearing a baseball hat with a green alligator emblem. The relief I felt at recognizing him immediately gave way to irritation. I took a few steps back toward his truck, fully intending to ask him why the hell he was following me all over town. But something was wrong. I don't believe in a sixth sense, but I have noticed that people who have seen combat or who hang around horses have an increased sensitivity to their surroundings. I fell into both categories and I sensed something about Joey that unnerved me. Then I saw it; it was his eyes—it was as if he were sighting me through a scope. I stopped a few yards from his truck and put on a smile. "What brings you out this way, Mister Sergeant?"

"Oh, you know, just getting off work."

An obvious lie, since he had been waiting for me in *The Courier* parking lot—which was exactly in the opposite direction from his own office in Forester. But what was his game? I tried telling myself that this was the same old shit—he wanted a date—but my crawly skin wasn't buying it. Was he stalking me, and if so, why? The police aspect had me worried. A maniac like Cletus Donnelly wasn't nearly as dangerous as a sane cop with some kind of weird agenda.

"I saw you pull in here," he said with a sly smile. "Thought I'd ask how you're doing."

"That's great, Joey. Thanks a lot. That hole in my chest is almost completely healed. Most of the time I don't even think about it. Thanks for asking, though. Well, I'm in kind of a hurry, so I hope you'll. . ." I turned to go into the market, but I only got to the doorway when I felt his hand on my arm. It was all I could do not to ratchet my arm free and bolt through the door. As it is, I could feel my body go rigid.

"I was wonderin whether you'd reconsidered my offer to take you to dinner." The fact that there wasn't a question mark after what should have been a question gave me an inward shiver.

I shook off his hand—gently—but replied firmly. "I told you before, Joey, no."

"Why not?" His eyes still had me in his sights, and I didn't like it at all. He may have been over a head taller than me, but I suddenly didn't care.

"I'm just not interested in you," I said very deliberately. "I wasn't two weeks ago and I'm certainly not now."

"What's that supposed to mean?"

"What are you doing, Joey? You were waiting for me in the parking lot back at *The Courier*. You followed me here. That's a pretty creepy way to get a date, don't you think? In fact, in some places they call that stalking."

"Shut the fuck up, Sue-Ann," he interrupted brusquely. "Stalking, shit. There's lots worse things than stalking."

"Like what, Joey?" I tried to stop myself from trembling, or at least to tell myself that the trembling was from the cold. But I felt like I'd just heard a hammer cock at close range. "Why don't you just say what you came to say."

"I heard a little story that I'm beginning to think is true."

"What kind of story?" I wanted to flee into the store and let Gladys see what was going on, or to at least hide myself among the shelves of goods, but something—in his voice this time—kept me just outside the doorway.

"A little story Clete told me when I was taking him to Waxahatchee," he smiled.

"And what story was that, Joey?" Frightened or not, I was getting angrier and angrier at this cat-and-mouse game that seemed to be Joey's idea of courtship.

"That he'd seen you and that bitch Ginette Cartwright down by the Okachokeme River being real cozy with each other. You a homo, Sue-Ann? Clete says you are."

I have to admit that I hadn't seen that one coming, and for a moment, the world seemed to stop turning. I was like Betty Dickson when she had absolutely no idea how to respond to an interview question so just sat there, staring at her sheet of paper. On one hand I was devastated that, despite all our caution, someone had found out about Gina and me; on the other, I was furious at the idea that he could control me with that knowledge. Still, I managed to lift my chin and look into his malicious eyes. "Clete is in Waxahatchee, Joey."

He actually chuckled. "Yeah, I thought he was crazy, too at first, but then I started thinkin. Why do I never see you on dates at Eat Now or Hi-Score? Why would you not want to go out with *me*, when you obviously don't have a boyfriend?"

"I told you before," I began. But I was running out of ideas and the panic was rising. I had absolutely no idea how I was going to convince him I wasn't what he thought I was. And what was he going to do to make me prove otherwise? Demand sex? That seemed most likely, and revulsion crawled through me like a plague of worms. He could expose me if I refused and there are some people who would believe him.

He interrupted me again. "Right, right, you said you were "seeing" somebody. Well, where is he?"

I was ready for this to end and I decided to end it the only way I could, which was to bluff. "Who I date is none of your fucking business," I said, but when I whirled to go through the door, I almost bumped into Clarence Meekins, who was having to stoop a little to get his tall, lanky self under the doorframe.

"It's okay, Sue-Ann," Clarence said. "Joey's one of us. You can tell him."

Joey's eyes seemed to get bigger as he watched Clarence stop beside me and place his large paw softly on my shoulder.

"Clarence," Joey began, but I could tell he was bumfoozled. The two men were about the same height and weight, but there was something about Clarence that said granite while Joey seemed more the consistency of hardened paste. "Don't, ah, don't tell me that *you're* Sue-Ann's boyfriend?"

"We're seein each other, Joe, if that's what you're askin."

"Yeah?"

"That's right. Is there something I should know about her?" He looked from Joey to me with a question in his eyes. A question and a little bit of a smile.

"No, Clarence. Nothin. Why should there be? A lotta people would say you were a lucky guy."

"That's the way I feel every day," Clarence said. "Why don't you come on in and see this new shipment of butter beans I just got in."

"Naw. I gotta be goin. Just wanted to see if Sue-Ann had recovered from, you know, that shooting awhile back."

"Well, then, it was nice to see you. Drop in again soon." And with that, Clarence ushered me inside to the desk. We watched as Joey Bickley walked back to his vehicle, being careful to keep his spine straight—kind of the way my mother used to teach her riding students to sit in the saddle. A crunch of gravel and he was off down the highway. But then I was really in for it. Clarence stepped behind his counter, bent down, and looked me squarely in the face.

"God's balls, Sue-Ann, who have you been blabbing to?"

"Nobody, Clarence, I swear. I thought that you were the only person outside of Torrington who knew about me and Gina." I sank into a chair by the counter. The adrenaline was draining away like blood from an embalming table and my knees were beginning to shake.

"But?" The big man waited.

"But evidently Cletus Donnelly saw the two of us together sometime." I said weakly. "It must have been the first time we ever got together down at Cypress Lake Lodge. He told Joey what he saw and . . . shit, Clarence, Joey's probably been watching me ever since."

"That man Joe Bickley isn't all good, Sue-Ann. I don't like to think what might have happened if I hadn't been here."

Me neither. I thought of all the times I had come to the market looking for Clarence and finding only his mom. I thought of all the men I knew who wouldn't be intimidated by Joey Bickley and could think of only Clarence. Clarence, who had been a marine and seen heavy combat while Joey had to settle for the Department of Corrections before moving on to the Sheriff's Department. Clarence had been there for me when I was sick and had even pulled me out of the woods when I recoiled from a rattlesnake and knocked myself unconscious against an oak stump. He was a not-so-distant relative of The Creeper and, like him, knew how to keep a secret.

"But Sue-Ann," Clarence said seriously, "you can't dodge that particular bullet forever. Either Joey will find out that I lied to him or someone else will find out, somehow, some way. And you know that after what just happened, he might tell one of his friends, and the story will go around."

"I know, Clarence," I said. "I know."

It looked like I was going to have to make a decision. Somehow, some way.

Chapter 11

Okay, think of a football field.

On one sideline, right at the 50-yard line and at both 15-yard lines, there are poles on which are mounted large bull's-eye targets. The one in the center faces the opposite stands while the other two face the goal posts. You are on a horse in the end zone. In your left hand is a bow and two arrows, in your right, you are nocking a third arrow on the string. A whistle sounds and you touch your heels to the horse's flank, urging her into a canter. Ten yards in bounds you fire at the first target, which is facing toward you as you approach it. You have had time to prepare, and you shoot just to the left of your horse's head, hitting near the center of the target. But you can't think about the score, only the necessity of taking a second arrow from your bow hand, fitting the nock to the string, and trying to balance above the four pounding hooves using just your seat and legs. The second target is on you before you are ready but you manage to get off your shot before you pass and you think you see the arrow plock in somewhere toward the outer part of the target. Your horse is well-trained. You have spent hours and days shooting from the ground while she grazed nearby, getting her used to the sound of the twanging string. Then more weeks sitting on her bareback—first just standing still, then at a walk—shooting one arrow after another at a nearby target. When you added a saddle and got used to shooting from a trot and—finally—a canter, you thought you might be ready for your first competition. Now you are two thirds of the way home, struggling to transfer the last arrow from your bow hand

and get it ready to shoot. The last target is tilted toward the far goalpost, requiring that you twist your body like a spring and fire at the colored circles behind you. There is no chance to see if you hit the target because you are whipping back around, snatching up the reins from the safety strap to rein your horse in before she flies past the goalposts and leaps into the stands. The buzzer sounds; you made it within the time limit. You look up at the scoreboard, waiting for the numbers to appear. . . .

You don't like the football field analogy? Well, if it were written in the form of a dressage test, it might look something like this:

A: Enter working canter

A—C: Working canter. At D, X, and G, loose arrows at targets located at V, E, and S respectively.

Short and sweet. No time to think. No judge at C, no scribe, no X: Halt, salute. Whoever scores the most points within the time limit wins.

I had set up my own horseback archery course inside my dressage ring, and I was explaining the rules to Myra as I trotted the course with Alikki. I was good enough at that speed to at least be able to get my arrows transferred from hand to hand and get off a shot, but the scores were usually low and we would have been penalized for taking longer than the time limit.

At the end of the course, I halted Alikki and petted her with my free hand. I had spent months training her not to spook from the sound of the bowstring and for the last few months she had been as calm in the mounted archery course as she was when the arena was clear and we were practicing our half halts and shoulder-ins—as we had been doing for the better part of the last hour under Myra's watchful eyes. Kitty Amin, curled up atop a hay bale near Stall #4, had been watching, too, but with much less interest.

I heard Myra clapping and I rode back to a chair near the stables where she had been watching. "Sue-Ann, that's just marvelous. Such wonderful balance."

"But think of this, Myra," I told her, dismounting from the off side. "At actual competitions, some of the riders are shooting more than one arrow at each target." I took three more arrows out of my quiver and positioned them alongside my bow in my left hand.

"My land, Sue-Ann. Is that fair?"

"It's in the rules. The faster you can get off an arrow, the more chance you have to win. And you should see some of these Hungarians kicking up the dust! I've seen one man shoot eight arrows on a single run. I watched him do it in person, but I still don't see how it was possible. You just saw the limit of what I'm capable of right now."

"And do they all use bows like yours?" she asked, giving my bow a quizzical look. I didn't blame her. At only 48 inches long, it was shorter than most bows and very colorful, with deep shades of blue and gold on white. Gina had once described it as an "elegantly desahned and beautifully decorated pretzel." I smiled at the thought.

"Well, similar bows anyway. This one's a reproduction of a bow used in Eastern Europe somewhere around the Fourth Century. It's made in layers: wood, ram's horn, sinew, leather, and a touch of fiberglass. Light and efficient, but if William Tell had a ream of paper on his head. I could pin it to a tree from twenty meters."

Which led to a basic discussion of the history of horseback archery. I'm not going to waste time here talking about the Huns, Magyars, Scythians, Mongols, and other people of the horse, but there are a lot of references on line if you are interested. I'm not sure Myra was, but she was courteous enough to listen and even ask follow-up questions. I didn't run the course again as I had planned. Instead, I just lounged by Myra's chair, holding my bow and arrows in one hand and Alikki's reins in the other. After a while, the topic moved from archery to dressage.

"Have you thought about riding Alikki in a rated show?" she asked.

"What, me ride in a dressage show? Hell, Myra, I don't even have the test booklets." I *had* thought about it, though; I'm not going to lie.

"I have copies I can give you," she said. "Or you can order them off the USDF website."

"But what level should I start at? Introductory? Training? I mean, assuming I really wanted to do it."

"I'm not real high on Intro tests, Sue-Ann, but without a consistent training routine, it's hard to say. You've got her doing second-level lateral work, but she's not steady in the bridle and she needs to get stronger and more through her back."

I agreed, but I had noticed that Alikki's ears had cocked toward the barn, which was located on the other side of the arena and beyond the target I had been shooting at. In the pasture, the other two horses stood erect, both facing the same direction as Alikki's ears. Amin jumped down from her perch and ran into the barn.

"What is it, Sue-Ann?" Myra asked.

"I'm not sure. Maybe a deer."

Alikki snorted. She wouldn't have snorted at a deer, which were almost as common as wrens. "Is anyone there?" I called out. Beyond the barn was a forest of oak and pine. In fact, the property had been carved out of it: barn to the south, stalls to the north and acres of pasture to the west. I was trying to see into the trees beyond the barn when I heard a noise.

"Wooooooooo! Woooooooo!" A cartoonish imitation of a ghost.

"Krista, is that you? That's not funny."

A dark figure darted from a clump of brush and disappeared behind an oak tree. Not Krista, then. "Who's there?" I called out, getting concerned.

The voice came out of the trees like out of tin can: disguised but definitely male and redolent with menace. "Ah'm the ghost of Christmas past, ha ha." The voice was familiar, but not familiar enough to identify.

As a horsewoman, I knew not to tense my body when I sensed danger. Still, my pulse kicked up a notch and my hand tightened around my bow. Myra struggled to a standing position and faced the trees. As we stared, the figure made a dash from the tree and disappeared around the side of the barn. I saw him more clearly this time and believe it or not, he was dressed all in black and wearing a ninja mask. And, oh yeah, he carried what looked like a sword. The sword and that voice. It couldn't be a coincidence. I silently handed Alikki's reins to Myra and nocked an arrow.

"Cletus?"

"Ah ain't Cletus." But this time any attempt at disguise was gone and the high, shrilly whine gave him away.

"Cletus, how did you get out of the hospital?"

"Hah. Wouldn't you lahk ta know?" I saw his head peep out from behind the side of the barn.

"What do you want?"

"Ta finish what ah started las tahm." He slowly stepped out from behind the barn.

"Don't come any closer!" I shouted, and raised the bow to chest level.

"What the hell's that shahny little thing?" he laughed. "You gonna shoot me with a toy bow?"

"I wouldn't risk it if I were you," I said evenly, but it didn't stop him.

He walked steadily toward us. "Got suction cups on them arrows?" He laughed and I looked closer at the sword he carried by his side. A samurai. What the fuck? Hadn't Joey and Dilly confiscated all his weapons? A movement just in back of me made me remember Alikki. And Myra. I turned to her and whispered, "Run in the house and call 911. Take Alikki with you—just throw her reins over the gate post."

"But—"

"Just do it, Myra."

But as Myra started toward the house, Cletus yelled. "No ya don't, bitch!" He raised the sword and started running toward her. I had been doing instinctive shooting for the last two years, almost every day. It's kind of like shooting from the hip; there is no ready-aim-fire, you just raise your bow and shoot. When Cletus had gotten inside the dressage ring, about 25 yards away from Myra, I raised my bow and shot. That's how quick it was: I raised my bow and shot.

This is a really bad time to digress, I know, but I have to tell you something about horsebows because it might save your life.

I hadn't done a great deal of research before I bought my first horsebow. In fact, there wasn't much information to find, so I ended up buying a couple of fancy-looking bows—one for me and one for Gina—made by a company in Hungary, or at least that's what they said. The bows turned out to be made out of fiberglass with cheap wooden handles and syahs and covered with brightly colored leather to disguise the poor construction. The first time I tried to string Gina's, it responded with a loud crack. Whoops. I managed to get the string on the other one and was amazed to find that it consistently fired an arrow low and to the left of the target. Say your target consisted of three men sitting together on a couch. At twenty meters, if you aimed at the head of the man in the middle, you would hit the man on the left in the balls. This wasn't acceptable, so I shopped and shopped, buying—and almost immediately selling on eBay—half a dozen bows. I finally traveled to Michigan and worked with a famous bowyer to construct the one I had fired at Cletus Donnelly.

I would have liked to just knock the sword out of Cletus' hand, but I couldn't guarantee that he wouldn't move his arm and cause me to miss high. And I also didn't particularly want to shoot him in the head or the balls so I fired at his wrist, which was exposed when the billowy black sleeves of his robe slipped down his raised arm. As it happened, Cletus raised the sword a few inches just before I shot so that the arrow pierced his right arm between the radius and ulna. Cletus screamed, stopped in his tracks, and looked at his arm in shock. My arrow had gone almost all the way through his arm—shaft on one side and feathers on the other. The sword was on the ground and forgotten.

"You shot me," he screamed. "You shot the shit out of me!" I could see tears of pain or rage or sadness in his eyes as he stumbled forward a few steps.

I already had another arrow nocked. "And I'll do it again," I told him.

"How can you just shoot someone like that?" he screamed.

"It's just like shooting a rattlesnake," I told him.

He looked up at me through his silly black mask. "And you never even wrote mah story." His mood had changed from rage to sadness in only a few seconds.

I looked behind me and was glad to see that Myra had disappeared into the house. "Now I need you to get into one of those stalls," I told him. "We'll talk about your story while we wait for the police."

"Fuck that," Cletus said, straightening up. His left sleeve hung down over his wrist; his right was hung up by the arrow sticking through his arm. He was holding the arm at an odd angle and blood had started trickling down into the dressage ring. Without another word he took off running toward the back of the stables. I yelled for him to stop but he only speeded up. I raised the bow, thinking to maybe shoot him in the leg or something, but what was the use? He couldn't get very far in the woods with an arrow sticking through him. The sheriff would be here soon and . . .

. . . and shit! What if Cletus was able to run a mile? Two? He might stumble on the Torrington compound, and if the police followed him there . . . I didn't want to think about what would happen if the police learned that Torrington existed. Or what would happen to Cletus if he managed to break into the compound. I rushed to the back of the stables, but Cletus had disappeared into the woods.

I ran back to the house, almost knocking down poor Myra, who was making her way back outside. "Sue-Ann," she cried out as I passed. "What—?"

"Just a sec, Myra," I said in as calm a voice as I could manage. "I need to call somebody." I threw my bow on the couch, grabbed my cell from my purse, and went into the bedroom. I hit a number on speed dial and waited an eternity until I heard a voice.

"Yas?"

"Creeper, I mean Ashley. Listen!" I quickly told him about Cletus, his escape from the mental hospital, the arrow in his arm, his ninja costume, and the fact that he may have been heading directly toward Torrington—especially if he came upon the horse paths that ran from my farm to the compound.

"We know what to do," he said, and rang off. I remembered another young man who had accidentally discovered Torrington a year or so ago and who met a tragic end when a horse kicked him to death. His body was discovered the next morning in a pasture on the other side of town. I didn't know what Ashley's plans were, but I knew that he had some.

Back in the living room, Myra was seated on the couch. I sat in the armchair beside her. "Was that the man you were telling me about?" she asked.

"Cletus Donnelly, yeah."

"Where is he? You didn't shoot him again, did you?"

"No. He just ran off. I thought about following him on Alikki, but the woods are too thick. Somehow he escaped from the hospital." I looked at her. "Does that happen often?"

"Very rarely."

"Wouldn't the hospital have notified the police?"

"The hospital has its own security, Sue-Ann. And they like to think they can take care of everything themselves." She paused. "If I would have been at work I probably would have gotten an email that he was missing, but that's all we ever see. Sue-Ann, that man would have killed me if you hadn't stopped him. Why did he come here? How did he even know where you live?"

"I'm in the phone book, Myra."

"Oh."

"And I don't know why he came here. I don't even know the man—I spoke to him on the telephone for fifteen minutes, that's all. The whole thing is ridiculous. How's your back, by the way?"

"Pretty good, really," Myra smiled. "Adrenalin will do that."

"What did the sheriff say when you called?"

"Just that they'd send someone out as soon as they could."

I was thinking hard. "And what did *you* tell *them*?"

"That I was at such and such address and that a man had attacked us with a sword and that you shot him with your bow and arrow and, my land, Sue-Ann, you live a dangerous life."

"I need to take Alikki's saddle off and let her out. Wanna come?"

We were outside when I heard the sheriff's car arrive and I hurried inside to open the front door. I had hoped it would be Dilly Dollar, but instead, the large form of Sgt. Joey Bickley loomed in the doorway. From the look on his face, I was the last person he had expected to answer the door. "What are you doing here?" he asked.

"This is where I live."

"Someone named Hess called 911 and gave this address."

"*Van* Hesse," I said. "Myra Van Hesse. She's my dressage instructor."

"What kind of instructor?"

"Riding coach," I explained.

"Right, your riding coach. And she lives here, too?" I didn't have to look into his eyes to know what he was thinking. Didn't want to either.

"She's just visiting for the afternoon," I explained.

"Yeah, well, let's go inside and you can tell me what happened here."

No way was I letting Joey in my house. "Let's go around to the back," I told him. I closed the front door behind us and led him back to where Myra was just returning from the pasture carrying Alikki's halter. It was just beginning to get dark and the temperature was falling like a rock off a table as I explained the situation to Joey as quickly as I could. As I spoke, I noticed Joey giving Myra the once-over and frowning. When I finished, he turned to her.

"You the woman who put in the call?" he asked her.

"That's raht, officer."

"You're Sue-Ann's riding coach?"

"Maybe you could just call me her mentor," she smiled. "Sue-Ann's mother was my best friend for donkey's years."

"Is that right? Well let me ask you, Miz Van Hesse, did you see this man Sue-Ann has been telling me about?"

"Sure I saw him! He ran at me with that sword." She pointed to the spot in the dressage ring where the sword still lay.

Joey put on a pair of rubber gloves and picked it up gingerly. He looked at the handle, where a price tag was still attached with string. "Here's one mystery solved, anyway," he said.

"What mystery?"

"The Chinese restaurant in Waxahatchee sells these on the side. They called this morning to report that someone had broken in and stolen money, food, and this sword." He shook his head. "The Chinese call to report a little theft, yet hospital security can't let us know they've got a homicidal maniac loose on the streets. Can you beat that with a stick?"

"Not really," I said.

"So okay, Miz Van Hesse, this guy ran at you with the sword. I believe it because he ran at me with one just like it last week. But are you saying that Sue-Ann shot him with a bow and arrow?" He was obviously skeptical, but that didn't surprise me. I think I would have been skeptical, too, but Myra came to the rescue.

She pointed to a place on her arm a few inches down from her wrist. "She shot him right there, Sergeant. The arrow went almost all the way through."

Joey looked at me. "How could you possibly be that lucky? And what were you doing with a bow and arrow anyway?"

Again, Myra. "There wasn't any luck to it, Sergeant. "Didn't you know that Sue-Ann shot archery? She won the National Championship once."

Joey looked at me in disbelief. "That was years ago," I told him. "You're right. I was lucky."

Joey shook his head and looked at me in a way that made me feel uncomfortable. It was as if he was adding this little bit of information to his dossier on McKeown, Sue-Ann, and was looking forward to studying it later and seeing what good he might get from it. "All right then, which way did Clete go?"

Without any hesitation, I pointed to the trees where Myra and I had first seen him. "He went into the forest right there. Then he made his way back to the street because I heard a car start up pretty soon after that and squeal off towards the highway."

"Squeal off?"

"Right."

"You didn't see the car?"

I shook my head.

"All right then," he said. "I'll put out an all-points bulletin for him. Then I'll make sure that some of the "security" at Wackoville get themselves some new assholes reamed out. If I think of any more questions, I'll come back. Lock your doors."

Yep, that sounded like a good reason to lock my doors all right. So I did.

Chapter 12

Mark Patterson was pissed off about being rousted out of bed early on a Sunday morning, but there you are.

"Sue-Ann, goddamit, leave me alone," he mumbled. Still in his mid-twenties, Mark liked to troll for girls at Eat Now or the Karaoke Bar in Forester and had been known to quaff a pitcher or two in the process. I knew how he felt; in Iraq, hangovers and I had been on a first-name basis even when some of the men I went home with had not.

"Shake that booty out of bed," I told him

"But you can't just bump the lead story at the last minute," he whined.

"Yes I can." I was the newly appointed Bureau Chief, small as our bureau was, and I could do pretty much anything I liked.

"What about the boss?"

"I called Cal and left him a message."

"But—"

"Come on, big boy," I said in a coaxing voice. "One-nighters come and go, but this is the kind of story you can put on your résumé."

"What makes you think I—?"

"Leave her a note and be here in half an hour," I told him.

"But I don't—"

I hung up. I may not have been the boss, but I was *his* boss, and I needed him to come in. Once again, I felt like I was too close to the story to do the actual writing myself, but wanted to be able to shape and guide it along. And make no mistake; this was a breaking story that might get statewide coverage. The public had no desire to find mental patients lurking like alligators in their back yards. And as far as I knew, Cletus Donnelly was still wandering around in the woods. I had tried to call Torrington several times, but no one picked up and I didn't want to call the sheriff's office because Joey Bickley might be there and want to ask more questions. In fact, one of the reasons I had driven to the office was because I didn't want to be home if Joey called or came over.

Mark arrived looking disheveled with two-day stubble and scruffy looking hair, but he was sober enough and ready to work.

"Listen," he said, sitting down at his hand-me-down desk. "If I'm going to be getting all your stories, I think I should have your office."

"Dream on, young man." In renovating *The Courier*, Cal had an office built next to his just for me. Everyone else still had to use cubicles. I wasn't about to give it up either.

He fired up his computer and we talked over the story while I looked around for some coffee to put in the machine. There was none, and I cursed Linsey for not making sure that we were well stocked with the best. I gave it up and went back to Mark's desk, where we were able to get a good start on the story quickly. I gave him the general outline while he came up with the construction and most of the words. Mark was a quick study, and even though I knew that he had left the university before receiving his journalism degree, I had a healthy respect for his intellect and his ability to use the written word.

But I'm a huge coffee freak, and we were only able to work for about 45 minutes before I started Jonesing. "I can't think any more without coffcc," I told him. The only cup I'd had all morning was a reheated one made the night before, gulped down while I was feeding the horses and forking hay into their pasture. "Do you think you can pop over to the Burger King and get us some?"

Mark frowned and looked up from his screen. "Why don't *you* go?"

"I have to review a play," I said.

"What play?"

"Never mind. Just go and get us some breakfast. I buy, you fly." I scrounged a crumpled tenner from my purse and handed it to him.

"I suppose I can use a break. What do you want?"

I told him to get me two large coffees and some kind of breakfast croissant, then watched him bundle up into a heavy coat and scarf and venture out into the winter air.

With at least 20 minutes to kill, I went into my office and took Benny's play out of my desk. But before I could even open it, the phone rang.

"*Courier* office, Sue-Ann McKeown speaking.

"Sue-Ann, this is Bill Dollar. I've got some news."

"Is it about Cletus Donnelly?"

"Sure is. And it's weird."

"Tell me."

"Not on the phone. I'm just getting off duty and I can swing by the office on my way home."

"Perfect." I hung up. Weird, huh? Well, what else was new?

It would take him at least half an hour to drive in from Forester, so I took up Benny's play again and opened it to the first page. I had tried to read it carefully a few days before but just hadn't been able to get through it. It was such a mishmash of times and cultures and characters that I wasn't even sure what it was about.

It began in Ireland back in what seemed like prehistory. The main character, whose name is Fearghal, is tending his herd of goats in a balmy dell when he notices that one of his kids is missing. A search reveals a group of feral human teenagers who have killed the young goat and are eating it raw.

In the next scene Fearghal, who (like Benny) is in his fifties, is sitting cross-legged under a giant yew tree. He is naked, as is the young woman sitting across from him. This young woman, whose name is Aoife, is one of the teenagers who had appeared in the first scene with fresh blood smeared on her face and lips. A jar of mead and a platter of goat cheese lie on the grass between them.

> **FEARGHAL**: Eat and drink well, lass. Who knows when the noose may find ye?
> **AOIFE**: I do, old man, for on the day I was born, it was carved in runes eye-high on the sacred oak of Cill Dara. My days are laid out for me like stones over a river.
> **FEARGHAL**: Ah, you're a Druid, then?
> **AOIFE**: As are many like me.
> **FEARGHAL** (producing a flute from the grass beside him, pipes out a short melody, then sings):
> *Oh the oak and the apple and the yew.*
> *Wave a wand and your wish will come true.*
> *Live forever and a day,*
> *In my arms you will stay,*
> *With a willy willy wally wally woo.*

The scene went on like that for some time, sometimes silly, sometimes philosophical, sometimes erotic, or at least semi-erotic. In a way, it reminded me of some of the fat fantasy books I indulged in, but somehow contorted into funhouse images. I flipped forward to the next act, in which Fearghal is now a retired accountant in Pirates Well in The Bahamas. He is married to a rum-running redhead and having a very explicit sexual relationship with a young Bahamian man named Clyde, who is a practicing nudist with a fondness for brie and a particularly mellow Chateau D'Esclans rosé.

I kept thinking to myself, it can't be this horrible. There must be a redeeming feature, but I just couldn't see one. The first act was a veiled (but still obvious) take off on a story I had investigated the year before involving a goat killed by a group of high school kids. The second scene must have been regurgitated out of Benny's past or his fantasies. In the third scene, Fearghal is not even mentioned. Instead, a New York gangster named Blitzy and his daughter Blythe are planning to kidnap the mayor's rare Bengal cat, remove its tail, and sell it on eBay as a one-of-a-kind collector's item. Symbolically, the cat's name is Eva (which is almost, but not quite, how Aoife is supposed to be pronounced).

Comedy?—Well, not intentionally. Tragedy?—On a literary level for sure. I looked closely at the publisher, but it was one I had never heard of. The plain cover bespoke an amateur or vanity publisher, but one with a website and mailing address. So either Benny had found a reader with sensibilities as twisted as his own, or—

Someone was rapping heavily on the glass door of *The Courier* offices. Must be Dilly because Mark had a key. I put down *The Gritty Goatherd* and went to let him in. It wasn't until I was reaching for the handle that I recognized Sgt. Joe Bickley in full uniform, arms crossed and legs slightly apart, on the other side of the glass. My body went stiff as cardboard, but I forced myself to open the door.

I doubt that I have managed to convey my uneasiness around Joey, which began the morning he came into my hospital room in what he considered fancy clothes. It was like I had millions of noxious organisms crawling inside me, coursing through my blood, and flooding my brain with poison. I can only liken it to my first month in Iraq when every minute of every day was permeated with the knowledge that there were people very close by who hated me, who were in fact aiming missiles at my hotel room or makeshift office. For once, I realized, I was glad that Gina was not around.

Joey entered and walked past me into the room. "You look like you were expecting someone else," he told me.

"Why should I be?" I bluffed.

"Just a little conversation I overheard back at the station," he said, walking around the room and looking in each cubicle, as if making sure that the two of us were alone in the office. "With Officer Dollar. I told him he didn't have to worry himself about coming by. I know more about Cletus Donnelly than he does."

I sat down at Mark's desk. "What did you find out?" I asked, then added, "Unless you want to wait for Mark to come back?"

"Who's Mark? Someone else you're 'seeing'?"

"I don't have time for this, Joey. Mark's the reporter who's writing the Donnelly story. He just went out for some breakfast. Now are you going to tell me what you know or not?"

"Do I get a finder's fee?" he laughed.

"I don't know what you mean."

"Oh fuck you, Sue-Ann. Everybody knows that you give Dollar a payoff if he tips you off to a story."

This was true, but I wasn't admitting it to Joey. Instead, I prevaricated. "Officer Dollar is a friend."

"What, and I'm not?" Joey raised his eyebrows in mock surprise.

"You don't make friends by threatening people and harassing them," I said calmly. "Why don't you tell me what you came to tell me."

Joey plopped himself down in the chair across the desk from me. "What I came to say was that I don't believe but about a tenth of what you tell me. Maybe not even that. I can't prove anything yet, but I will."

"Prove what?" I asked.

"Everything," he said pointedly. He took a can of Kodiak from his pocket and stuffed his lip. I hadn't noticed this habit before. As an ex-smoker, I knew that tobacco was a panacea for all kinds of things, but nervousness and uncertainty were both contenders for the top spot. He was treading on soft ground, then. His expression changed—the malice left his eyes like a ghost through a wall—and he looked at me the way he looked at me the night I was shot: professional and efficient. "You know Tequesta?" he asked.

I was so nonplused by this change in him that I stammered my answer. "Um, the night dispatcher. Sure. I mean, I've never met her but—"

"She woke me up at three a.m."

"Yeah?"

"Said she heard a car horn blaring and went outside to check it out. Know what she found? Clete Donnelly slumped against the horn of a stolen pickup—the same one they finally reported stolen from the hospital. There was a bloody arrow next to him on the passenger seat. Soon as she saw that he wasn't dead, Tequesta called Dollar and another patrolman to get him out of the car. While they were trying to lift him, he woke up and started yelling and punching. He managed to smack Tequesta so hard she fell backwards onto the street and almost got run over by an 18-wheeler. So Dollar tasered his ass and they carried him to a holding cell. That's when Tequesta called me and asked what they should do with the bastard."

Joey paused and I managed to ask, "Is Tequesta all right?"

But Joey ignored me completely and looked off into space. "Now here's the thing, Sue-Ann. When I was at your place I saw a couple of drops of blood that weren't in line with the way you said he ran. So just before I came here, I went by your place and checked out that dirt road you live on. Sure enough, I found a place where a vehicle had gone into the woods, then come out again. I'll bet if I made a tire impression they'd be an exact fit to the pickup Clete was in when Tequesta found him."

All this was total news to me, but I managed to come out with "That's what I told you yesterday—that I heard him drive away."

"Yep. It's what you told me. But once you start doubting a person, it's hard to believe anything they say." He cut his eyes directly down into mine. "And I don't believe *you*."

"That doesn't make any sense."

"I told Tequesta to call an ambulance to take Clete to the emergency room. By the time I got there, some doctor from India had slapped some salve on his taser burn and stuffed wood putty in that hole in his arm. They had drugged him, but he was conscious." He stopped and looked out the window at a couple of shoppers, winter coats on, carrying plastic bags of food from the Piggly Wiggly to their pickup.

"Let me guess," I said. "He told you another of his stories."

"That's right, Sue-Ann. Now how would you know that?"

I was saved from having to answer by Mark coming through the door, a bag in each hand and one gripped between his teeth. His eyes widened as he saw Joey Bickley sitting in front of his desk, but recovered nicely. When he had put his packages down, he stuck out his hand. "Mark Patterson," he said.

Joey took the hand reluctantly, but strongly. "Joe Bickley." I used the opportunity to get up from Mark's chair, grab the bags with my coffee and sandwich, and retreat a few feet to Annie's desk.

"Sgt. Bickley just captured Cletus Donnelly," I told him.

"Wow, that was quick." I haven't mentioned this before, but because Mark was a relative newcomer to Jasper County, he had a tendency to kiss ass. So I wasn't surprised to see him hurriedly dive into his desk for a notebook and a pencil. "Do you have anything I can write down? Can I get some quotes?"

So Joey—not without some sense of importance—recounted how Cletus had mysteriously shown up in front of the Sheriff's office, had cold-cocked poor Tequesta, been tasered by Dilly, and finally been transported to the emergency room. Mark wrote furiously. And here's what appeared the next day.

Escaped mental patient attacks locals

Drives himself to jail after being shot by champion archer

By Mark Patterson

COURIER STAFF WRITER

It was déjà vu all over again for *Courier* reporter Sue-Ann McKeown on Saturday evening. McKeown, who a decade ago won the U. S. National Championship in archery, was demonstrating a new bow to a friend when an intruder stepped from behind a tree on her property and threatened her with a sword.

McKeown recognized the man as Cletus Donnelly, who two weeks ago had been sent to the Regional Mental Health Facility in Waxahatchee for trying to kill Sgt. Joseph Bickley of the Jasper County Sheriff's Department. When McKeown's friend started to run to the house to call 911, Donnelly, who was dressed as a Japanese ninja, ran at her with the sword raised. That's when McKeown skewered his arm with a Wolverine 6070 carbon arrow, causing Donnelly to drop his sword and run back into the woods.

From there, Donnelly made his way back to a vehicle he had stolen from the hospital and drove away. He was later found passed out in the vehicle in front of the Sheriff's Office in Forester.

It all started the day before, when WRMHF employee Elijah Neel, a plumber, picked up a washer and dryer from the unit in which Donnelly was confined and transported it to an area designated for scrap metal. When he arrived at the location, Donnelly, who had hidden behind the appliances in the truck, jumped out, knocked Neel unconscious, and drove the truck from the hospital grounds.

It was not until several hours later that hospital security noticed the unlocked scrapyard gate and found Neel still unconscious.

Sgt. Bickley, who was formerly a neighbor of Donnelly's in Pine Oak, reconstructed the series of events which led Donnelly to McKeown's residence.

"The mental patients at WRMHF wear their own clothes," stated Sgt. Bickley, who has investigated both cases involving Cletus Donnelly. "Maybe if they had to wear some kind of uniform, somebody would have reported seeing Donnelly and we could have captured him earlier." As it was, Donnelly hid out until nightfall. Then he broke in the back door of the Jin Jin, Chinese Restaurant in Waxahatchee, stole the sword and an undisclosed amount of money, and drove to Pine Oak.

In fact, according to Sgt. Bickley, it appears that Donnelly actually drove back to his own house, where he donned the ninja robes and possibly even took a nap. "There are a number of hours we can't account for," he said. "All we know is that he showed up at Sue-Ann's house just before dusk on Saturday."

Sgt. Bickley went on to theorize that Donnelly was out for revenge.

"After all," he said, "Sue-Ann was the one who alerted us the first time he was arrested."

Donnelly was treated for his wound and transported back to Waxahatchee. Elijah Neel was taken to Jasper County Memorial where he remains in serious condition.

But there were several aspects of the story that never saw print. When Joey finished talking, Mark looked up from his notebook and asked, "But why did Donnelly drive to the sheriff when he could have made it into the next county—or even to Alabama?" Mark glanced at me but I could only shrug my shoulders, so he looked expectantly back at Joey.

"I asked him that," said Joey.

"Yeah? What did he say?" Mark was poised over the third or fourth page of his pad.

"He said he *didn't* drive there," Joey replied.

"What the hell did he mean by that?"

"He said he didn't get back in the pickup at all. Said he ran into the woods, bleedin like a stuck pig. He figures he must have run at least a mile before it got too dark to see much, so he sat down by a tree to rest. He says that he just closed his eyes for a second, but must have dozed off. When he opened them again it was pitch dark and there were noises in the forest. All of a sudden the moon came out of the clouds and he saw that he was surrounded by marines with automatic weapons all dressed in camouflage."

Mark wasn't sure what to say. "Um, do you think he managed to get some drugs somewhere, Sergeant? Sounds like he was hallucinating."

Joey smiled thinly. "He said that these marines had war paint on their faces. They appeared one by one, like out of the air, and just stood there until a half dozen of them surrounded him. They didn't say a word. Then something *really* weird happened."

Mark's eyebrows went up. He opened his mouth, then closed it again. As for me, I had no intention of getting involved in the conversation. I just sat back in Annie's chair and listened to Joey answer his own question.

"He said that a zombie rode up on a white stallion."

"A *zombie*?"

"Some creature with his face half rotted off and wild hair sticking out like porcupine needles. He whispered something to the marines and then whirled and galloped off. That's when the marines blindfolded him, tied his wrists together, and led him through the woods for what seemed like hours. Finally they pushed him in a car and started driving he didn't know where."

Joey stopped his story and looked squarely at me. "Know what happened then?"

"Not a clue," I told him.

"He heard a voice whispering in his ear. It said, 'Don't ever let us see you again,' then he felt someone grab his arm tight and yank on the arrow. That's when he passed out. He didn't wake up until Tequesta tried to get him out of the car."

"Boy," Mark breathed. "A great story, but Cal would kill me if I wrote bullshit like that."

I sat tight, without speaking. I had an idea that Joey wasn't finished.

And he wasn't. "Interesting thing, though," he mused, as if to himself. "When I saw him at the hospital he had some red marks on both wrists, as if he really *had* been tied up." I could see that Mark wanted to ask a question, but Joey went on before he could open his mouth. "Another thing," he said. "I would have expected to see blood on the driver's side of the truck, and

I did. But there was some on the passenger side too, although it looked like somebody had tried to wipe it up."

"Somebody . . . ?" Mark started to ask.

"And here's something really interesting, or maybe you won't think so. Just on a hunch, I dusted the truck for fingerprints. Know what I found?"

I shrugged and Mark just looked at him.

"Nothing."

"Nothing?"

"Not even a partial. Hmm." And with that, Joey got up and made toward the door. He reached out for the handle, then stopped and shook his head wonderingly. "Shot a man right through the arm. Yes sir, I may not believe a word of it, but I sure do like it."

Chapter 13

While Mark put the finishing touches on the story, I browsed the internet. It was a way to avoid thinking about Joey's suspicions for a while, but I also needed certain pieces of information if I wanted to move forward on the tasks I had set for myself: writing Cletus Donnelly's story, learning the fate of Ashley Torrington's first love, and finding Gina. So far, I had been doing a piss-poor job at all three. And although Joey's words still stuck to the roof of my mouth, a few minutes' browsing took away a bit of the bad taste.

Now you'd think that after he had tried to kill me twice, I'd just shuck off Cletus Donnelly like a torn and bloody shirt, but that's not what happened. In fact, I was even more interested in what made him tick now that he had—for the second time—gone to a great deal of trouble to locate me. Why me? If what he had told Joey was true, then he was just [illegible]elieved that there was more to it t[illegible]ld Joey that he suspected *himself* of [illegible]k so. Nothing really added up. I [illegible]r had much chance of visiting Cle[illegible]ed to know what my boundaries were. On line, I tried to find some information on the Waxahatchee Regional Mental Health Facility, but even on the internet, a veil of secrecy hid its history like a *niqub* shields an Iraqi woman's face. It looked like Myra was my only hope there. Not only might she finagle a meeting—or even just a phone call—but she might know some of the place's history that I could use as background.

I went on to search for Robin and Marian, and was surprised when I got a few hits. One—from an oldies dealer—offered a near-fine copy of their only LP for $30 plus shipping. Several others offered a remastered CD—the same one that Krista had burned me a copy of. The label's website printed the liner notes, which told me pretty much what I had already learned from The Creeper. But then I came on a very obscure music blog which asked the simple question: "Whatever happened to the folk duo Robin and Marian? They had a minor hit in the late sixties called "Pay the Moon." The song has haunted me for years and I always wondered what happened to them." The original question was dated March 30, 2007, and there were several responses. All but one simply mentioned the LP or CD; the last, though, was dated only a few months before, and was of a more personal nature.

> *I knew "Robin" back in the 70's. His real name was Michael Simmons. I called him Mickey or sometimes Mick. We both worked in the men's dept at J. C. Penny in Pensacola. He left after 4 or 5 mos. and I dont know what's happened to him after that. Hope this helps.*
> *Billy Carrothers, Pensacola, FL*

Following that was an email address. I wrote Billy a brief note, hit the send button, and then went back to Google and tried to find information on Meher Baba. The book I had purchased from Benny had some interesting facts, but was written by a disgruntled follower. I wanted something from another viewpoint and almost immediately I came upon a link to a 20-volume, 6742-page biography, every word of which was online for my reading enjoyment and spiritual enlightenment. I read for a while, copied down some information, and emailed my notes to my home computer.

By that time, Betty Dickson had come in and was set up at her desk in the darkest back corner of the office. Tomorrow's paper was going to press that afternoon and the lead story would have to be changed. I went back to Mark's desk and read what he had written so far. I suggested a few word changes and a brief cut-and-paste, then left it to him again. At noon, Cal came in, followed a few seconds later by Linsey Colley.

"I got your message," Cal said, as he strode briskly into his office. "How's the story coming?"

"Just finished," I answered. "Mark's printing out a copy now for you to look at."

"Can you bring it in?"

"Sure."

I sat in the familiar visitor's chair and waited for Cal to read through the piece. He wrote a few comments in the margins, then he looked up.

"Hell, Sue-Ann, you're a dangerous person to be around."

"So I'm told,"

"Maybe they'll keep Donnelly locked down this time."

"We can always hope," I responded.

"This is good, though. How much is yours and how much is Mark's?"

"Mostly his," I told him truthfully.

"He's going to make a good reporter." He gave me back the pages, then changed both the subject and his expression. "Listen," he began. "Have you made any progress finding Ginette?"

"You haven't heard from her?" I prevaricated.

"No. Of course I haven't." His words were clipped, terse, almost angry.

"Isn't Linsey working out?" I looked through the door and saw the new office manager back in Betty's area, seeing if any advertisements might need moving.

"Hmm? Linsey?" He made a dismissive gesture with his hand. "Linsey's fine, but she—"

"I didn't expect her in today," I said. "Betty could have dealt with the ads."

"She's conscientious," said Cal. "And that's good. She's learning her job. It's just that I need to talk to Ginette. I need to get on with my life one way or another. Don't you have any idea where she is?"

"I'll find her, Cal. I told you I'd find her and I will." Then I stopped. It was not like Cal to lose any part of his cool. "Has something happened?" I asked. "It's not your son, is it?"

"Hmm? No, no. He's fine. A growing boy's bones heal quickly."

I waited for the but, but I had to coax it. "But?" I said.

"Umm. Yeah, there is something. "My ex-wife is thinking of moving back to Shreveport."

"Is that where she's from?" I asked. Although I had been working for him two years now, I knew virtually nothing about his ex-wife.

"Born and raised."

"Where did the two of you meet?" I asked.

"Little Rock. At a Bill Clinton fundraiser. She was an organizer from Louisiana and I was covering Clinton for *The Arkansas Times*. She was seven years younger, but we hit it off."

"This may be out of line, but what happened between the two of you? Was it, you know . . . ?"

"No it wasn't Ginette," he said quickly. "Or maybe she was the dot on the last i. Carol never wanted to come down here to the backwoods of Florida. She's always been close to her family. Her parents still live in Shreveport and so do her brother and sister. Her *twin* brother and *twin* sister."

I had to think hard about that one. "You mean she's . . . she's a *triplet?*"

"Right. So we got married and lived in Little Rock. It's only about a three-hour drive to Shreveport, so she got to see her family as much as she wanted. And it was an exciting time for us—the Clinton presidency. I had a lot to do and so did she, so it worked for us."

"How long did you stay in Arkansas?" Now that I had started him talking, he seemed to want to go on and I was glad to be his audience.

"Almost fifteen years. We waited until we were fairly well off financially before we started a family, but the twins were born in '98. Problem is, it never seemed like I had time for them, especially after all that 911 stuff started happening. I literally busted my butt on that paper and I just got burned out."

"Tell me about it," I said.

He smiled. "But *you* got back on the horse," he said. "What *I* wanted was a desk job. Turned out that one of my old bosses had bought a few small-town newspapers. This one, *The Courier*, needed to be revitalized, so he asked me if I would take over as editor. Carol tried to put a good face on it, but after Jessica was born, she got more and more homesick and we grew farther apart."

"You still had a career and she didn't," I guessed.

"You nailed it, Sue-Ann. I'm surprised our marriage lasted as long as it did. Even more surprised that she's stuck around Pine Oak so long after the divorce."

"Is there any chance you two can make up?"

Cal shrugged. "People just grow apart, Sue-Ann; there's nothing anyone can do about it. Anyway, I think she's been emailing this guy she went to high school with in Shreveport. I hope it works out for her."

"But it's a long way from your kids," I told him.

"A long way," he agreed. "If she does go, we're going to have to work out some custody arrangements."

"A tough thing to do," I said. There was a silence, then I asked, "Do you miss being the man on the street?"

"Not really," he said. "I had a decent career as a reporter. Not stellar like yours or Jack Stafford's, but solid."

"I don't think I'd agree . . . about me, I mean."

"Come on, Sue-Ann. You were so close to the heart of the world that you could hear it beating. Your stuff got picked up by the wire services. When you came in here that day and told me you wanted a job, I about fell on the floor."

"I'm surprised you'd even heard of me."

"What, not heard of the local girl who made good? One way or another I probably knew about every story you wrote. And shit, that piece you wrote on Nonnie Gray knocked me out."

"Umm. Me too."

There was another silence as he expected me to talk about Nonnie. When it was obvious I wasn't going to, Cal straightened up in his chair and put on his business face again. "Anyway, sorry to heap my problems on you like this. Have you heard from Jack lately?"

"A few emails."

"Any more books in the works?"

"Can't speak for Jack, but that was a one-shot deal for me," I said, then came out with something I had only that instant decided. "I'm driving up to see him after Christmas."

"Oh yeah? Well, that's great. Tell him I said hello."

"I'll be sure to do that."

"Give those pages back to Mark and run with it. I'll break the news to Annie that her biomass story gets put under the fold. We'll postpone some of the other stuff until Thursday."

~ ~ ~

On the way home, I listened again to the Robin and Marian CD that Krista had given me. There was a song called "Pismo Beach," an orchestrated pastoral, sung sweetly and quietly. Another was about visiting a friend in Los Angeles. So Mickey Simmons had traveled to California at one time. Maybe he was there now. It wasn't much of a lead, but at least it was something.

In the twenty minutes it took me to get home, I listened to most of the songs on the CD, and by this time, I was at least semi-familiar with them. Most were sweet and flower-powery. Too much so. Only "Pay the Moon" seemed to have lasting substance. It dealt with sensitive emotions, while the others described only fleeting sensations. The public had liked "Pay the Moon," but none of the other songs had ever charted. Like so many other groups that made music in the '60s and '70s, Robin and Marian had been a one-hit wonder. And it had not been much of a hit at that. I admired the song, both for its lyrics and for Marian's—Maryanne's—haunting which was much more prominent in this song t the others. I might not be making much headway i ing her, but I was gathering information little by Sometime I hoped to be able to put it all together.

Inside the house, I spent a couple of hours on line and on the phone. I flicked the radio station on and wasn't surprised to hear these lyrics:

We sit in the sun between eleven and one
Staring at the clock, having fun
Watching Booker T get over his electric shock.

So The Creeper was still on his lunacy kick. Or, I guess, even deeper into it now that he had helped capture an escaped mental patient. I called Torrington and Krista answered. "Let's ride," I said.

Gina's horse Irene hadn't been worked since Gina left, so I brought her into the wash rack and gave her a good grooming and trimmed her bridle path. The temperature was in the low 40s and I would have had second thoughts about taking her out into the woods except there were some questions I had to ask Krista. It was not quite four o'clock when we met near the fifty-acre-long stand of pines that was the borderline between my property and the thick forest of oaks that shrouded Torrington like a garment of green and brown. Each row of trees was a dim tunnel with soft but luxurious footing for the horses, and Krista and I raced side by side down the leafy corridors until we were breathless and our horses blowing. Neither of us had to say a word; we were both thrilling in the enjoinment of woman and horse, something we both ached for after being cooped up most of the time. It was particularly bad for Krista, marooned as it were in a compound filled with the crazy and the wounded. She rode with such a breakneck abandon that I always feared for her safety, although I liked watching her. The horse she was riding, Trigger, was a 16-hand gray gelding that had been trained by The Creeper. In fact, it had been Trigger that The Creeper had been riding the night that Cletus Donnelly was picked up.

At the end of a row, we transitioned into a walk and veered out into the dense hardwoods. "So tell me," I said.

"You mean about that guy they found out here?"

"Yup."

"You won't believe it, but Creeper has a drill for that kind of stuff. It's like a fire drill, except instead of big coveralls, the guys get into camo, grab their rifles and walkie talkies, and fan out in the woods. Everybody knows exactly where to go and what to do. Jeremy was the one who discovered the guy thrashing around in the bushes. He called in the location and followed him until he sat down and seemed to go to sleep. Jeremy wanted to strip him down and nail him to a tree, but that was voted down when Grandpa rode up on Trigger."

"Were you there?"

"Are you kidding? I was right behind him on Goldie. He told Carl that Donnelly—is that his name?—Donnelly should be searched. The only thing they found was a truck key, but where there's a key, there has to be a vehicle and they needed to find it. Grandpa figured it must be within a couple blocks of your place, so he sent a couple of us to look for it. Smokey was the one who found it so he drove it the long way back to Torrington. By the time he got there, they had led Donnelly blindfolded into the compound. Then they threw him in the truck and drove him to Forester. Smokey followed in his own car. Outside the sheriff's office, they put him in the driver's seat, took off the blindfold and whatever they had tied his wrists with, and honked the horn. They even remembered to wipe their fingerprints off the car."

"Which is something that Cletus Donnelly wouldn't have done, by the way."

"What does that matter?"

"One of the sergeants—Joey Bickley—dusted for prints and got suspicious when he didn't find anything. You need to warn The Creeper about Joey. Cletus told him about you all finding him in the woods and Joey half believes it."

"What can he do?"

"Well, one thing he can do is come out in these woods and look around."

"But Donnelly was blindfolded the whole time."

"Just tell Creeper to be careful, okay?"

"Okay, I will."

The sun was going down as we approached the back gate of the compound. A couple of times I noticed Krista watching me, but when our eyes met she looked away. Then Trigger whinnied and we heard an answering whinny from the pasture. "Listen," I told her. "I need you to feed for me for a week or two."

"You going to find Gina?" she asked.

"How did you know?"

"I'm surprised you've waited this long."

"Been busy," I said.

Krista dismounted and took Trigger's reins in one hand, opening the padlock with the other. Then she stopped and turned around with a serious look. "What's it like to be with a woman?" she asked.

That took me aback. The question jibed neither with Krista's normal tone—which was mixed cowgirl and tomboy—nor with her on-air persona, which tended (or was it pretended, I wondered) to be silly or scatter-brained. "I've only been with one," I answered. "With Gina, it's marvelous."

"Umm." Then she looked at me again the way she had during our ride. This time she didn't look away. "But you've had a lot of boyfriends, right?"

"Way too many," I laughed.

"Do you still think about any of them?"

"Krista, some of them—at least the ones in Iraq—didn't even have names." Then I spoke in a teasing tone. "What's this all about? You're not coming on to me are you?"

Krista spoke quickly. "No, of course not."

"Anyway, your grandpa asked first."

"That old buzzard breath," she said. "When are you leaving?"

"As soon as I can. I'll give you a call before I go."

It was dark for most of my ride home, but the trails were well mowed and the moon was bright—a little world all its own, and I realized that it would soon be full again. The wolves howling and the crazies out shooting. Not Cletus Donnelly, though. He was strapped down in a world of his own making. I thought of Mickey and Maryanne Simmons; their own world of music had dragged them out to sea. Had they washed up on shore somewhere? The world was a big place. I had my own worlds: the newspaper world to venture out in and the world of horses where, sometimes, I could hide. Worlds within worlds. Like Torrington.

Back at the stables, I mixed the horses their feed, then began forking hay from a new roll into a large yellow wheelbarrow. With each forkful, motes of hay dust flew up into the glow of the barn lights, small galaxies traveling outward in space.

Chapter 14

My worst day in Baghdad began with a mortar shell rocking the foundations of my hotel, shattering my skull and sending fragments of shrapnel slicing through my brain. Or at least that's how it seemed. The noise and vibration jerked me out of sleep and I opened my eyes wide to a bed that looked like it had been detonated. But that was nothing new. Neither was my extraordinary headache. A glimmer of light through the faded curtains told me it was morning. The clock on my nightstand read 8:33 but it was already hot and my pillow was wet with sweat. The other side of the bed had damp stains too, and I didn't think they were mine. I was naked and when I touched between my legs, I discovered that I had been having unsafe sex again. The trouble was—and this was a first—I couldn't remember with who.

Beer bottles were strewn across the stained and threadbare carpet, but that was nothing new, either; nothing to account for my lack of memory and outright nausea. I ran both hands through my damp hair and tried to think.

The night had started off peacefully enough. There had been the report of a car bomb, but no word on the details. A number of us—reporters from the agencies of half a dozen countries—got together in what was left of the hotel bar, comparing notes and talking about what we were going to do when we went home. Around us stood a few soldiers—boys really, most of them at least ten years younger than I was—trying to drink themselves brave enough to talk to me or the two other women in my group. It didn't matter that the youngest and prettiest of us was out on assignment; the saying in Iraq was that *all* western women were beautiful. We took advantage of it, but never let things go too far. If we paired up, it was usually with other journalists or officers, but the handful of young men still crowded around us like chickens. There was Red, whose hair told the story of his entire life; Campy, who hoped someday to become a mess sergeant; Doof, a lanky, towheaded young man from the deep south; Crazy Del, who liked to read books on true crime when he could get them; Mucker, who always seemed to get the shit duty. There were others, most of them with silly but endearing nicknames that made them a part of the American extended family.

It was early evening when the news came in. Mahmood 3 was of one of our Iraqi interpreters. He was a small man with a thin mustache and a generally twitchy disposition. But when he rushed into the bar, it was like someone had plugged him into an electric fence. He was wild-eyed. His white shirt had thick bloodstains and his already-dark face and hair were filthy with smoke and dust.

"What's happened, Three?" asked Clive. Clive was covering the war for a conservative British review, and like most of us, he was conservative in how he covered it. We rarely—or in the case of Clive, never—left our safe compound, relying heavily on Iraqi stringers and interpreters like Three to ferret out and assemble our news for us. The one exception was Nonnie Gray, a young telejournalist for one of the cable news networks. Blonde, petite, and still in her mid-twenties, Nonnie insisted on traveling to the site of breaking news anywhere in Baghdad. She was semi-fluent in Arabic and knew how to use a video camera. On extra-dangerous assignments, she sometimes set her camera on a tripod and taped her own story. Nonnie had become my great friend in Iraq. Although she was a decade younger than me, she had her head firmly set on her shoulders and both her short- and long-term goals fixed in her mind like sticky notes on a wall. She kept me from binging too heavily and inspired me to be the kind of journalist I knew I was and always had been. In fact, it was Nonnie who first suggested that I might be suffering from some kind of illness. Three was her special assistant.

"Miss Nonnie," he gasped, tears streaming from his eyes. "Miss Nonnie, she is killed."

I listened to Three's story as if in a deep trance. Nonnie had set out with her convoy to cover the car bombing of an Iraqi official who had become too friendly with the coalition forces. It was certainly newsworthy enough to take a chance on; the official was an up-and-coming politician; a man who, in time, could make a difference. But, as often happened in these killings, insurgents stayed nearby, hoping to attack any relief effort—police, army, medical staff, etc. And that etc. included journalists like Nonnie. She and Three had filmed the scene of the bombing and she had almost finished taping her report when a sniper shot her in the back. The tape was still running, and it was possible to see—just above her left breast—a tiny tent billow out in her vest an instant before the bullet burst through, taking her life with it.

No one else in the convoy was injured. Soldiers gave chase, but not far. It was too dangerous even for them. The sniper got away.

I felt like I had been shot along with Nonnie. Nobody wanted to, but we all had to watch the tape, then go to our offices and write our stories. I wrote mine with the help of more than one glass of whisky. And around midnight, we all migrated back to the bar and sat around talking about Nonnie. There was more alcohol, some of it purchased by the shy, off-duty privates that still hung around hoping to get into the conversation. They had all known—and lusted after—Nonnie. I remembered that I cried a lot. Looking back, I realize my thyroid illness was affecting everything I did and felt. I would have been devastated by Nonnie's death anyway, but my condition made it unbearable.

Through a heavy haze, I vaguely remember my colleagues fading away into their rooms to sleep off the horrible night. But what happened after that remained a mystery. I woke up. That's it.

I took what passed for a shower and managed to wash away all evidence of debauchery, but no amount of scrubbing could erase Nonnie's death. I shampooed my hair and dressed in my cleanest fatigues. I had to go to the scene. I owed it to her. Not for the story; that was already filed, but to honor her bravery and her commitment; to prove that I was not the complete washout I often thought I was. There *was* a story there, though. The story of how, several years after the U. S. invasion, terrorists were still able to roam like wolves into almost every section of the great city, leaving their bloody footprints as they passed. I wanted to see the shops, the houses, the people who lived there—things that did not show up on Three's camera. But what I think I really wanted was a bullet through my own breast. I was by then so jaded and sick that I would gladly have traded Nonnie's life for my own. Failing that, I could at least die the kind of courageous death that she had. But it was way better than I deserved.

It took a little pull to get the military to issue me an escort. Luckily, I had some. Along with Gabir, who was my own interpreter, I arrived at the checkpoint just after noon. We were met there by a Lt. Franks, who I knew only slightly, and whose sour expression made me hope it stayed that way. Our convoy consisted of a line of three Humvees and a dozen soldiers from Camp Victory. Lt. Franks steered me and Gabir to the middle vehicle, which had a driver and passenger-side guard. I saw soldiers in full body armor, helmets, and space-age sunglasses assuming their places in the two other vehicles making up the convoy. Surprisingly, one of them waved to me as he climbed up to the roof behind a .50 caliber machine gun. It was Doof, one of the young hangers on at the hotel bar. I also made out Red's sunny features just before he closed the driver's side door of his own Humvee. No longer were they shy young privates who couldn't say boo to a goose. They were all soldier, and proud to let me see them at their best. I nodded at both, then got in with Lt. Franks.

Outside the razor wire and 12-foot-high blast walls, the convoy moved slowly. Doof and the other gunner were constantly swiveling around behind their guns, searching for enemies. It was slow going; the concrete walls made the streets narrower, and much of what was left was filled with potholes. Traffic was congested, although most of the local vehicles ran up on the curbs when they spotted the convoy. Franks spent the forty-five-minute drive lecturing me about the irresponsibility of the press. I had heard it all before. I knew how dangerous it was; I had been outside the bubble only a handful times in five months. I nodded mechanically to everything he said, which didn't make him any more pleased with me. But at least I held myself back from questioning the responsibility of shipping 50,000 boys and men into a strange land and a strange culture for the sake of . . . of what? Oil, power, prestige, penis size? So I nodded.

Our route took us past the French Embassy and I was treated to my first sight of the murals. Iraqi artists had seen the depressing gray concrete blast walls as vast canvases and had begun covering them with exotic scenes of swirling color: flying carpets, minarets reaching like spaceships into the sky, medieval castles, and doves—the universal signs of a peace that most Iraqis could only hope for. My favorite image was an array of brown and white horses, tails in the air and manes flying, looking out at our convoy as if some ancient Arabian magic had made the images come alive. Their eyes, their ears, their whole body language conveyed the certainty that they didn't like what they were peering out at. For the first time in a very long time, I thought of Pine Oak and my mother. In her fifties, Cindy had already shown Trifecta at Fourth Level and was immersing herself more and more in equine activities. My time in Iraq would come to an end in just over a month, and I was planning to take mucho R & R in Pine Oak and to spend a lot of that time on horseback. Cindy was still alive then; when I finally got home, she was not. Like Nonnie.

The scene of the bombing had been cleared, the body parts of the official, the bits of automobile, Nonnie. All that remained was a hastily repaired hole in the road surrounded by a black outline made by heat and smoke. Before Franks could stop me, I opened the door and got out. He quickly followed, catching up with me only when I was standing in the spot where Nonnie had made her last report. A slew of small shops surrounded the square where the bombing had taken place. The shop owners looked out their doors with eyes like those of the painted horses. I just stood there for a while, trying to imagine how it would feel to be ripped apart. Nothing probably. As a teenager I had been bucked off a spooked horse and landed hard, my head conking against a fallen branch. For an instant, I was unconscious. Total blackness without sensation. When I opened my eyes, I braced myself for pain, but felt nothing. As Mrya had said the day before, adrenalin will do that. After a second or two, I began trying to breathe, but it took minutes before my bleeding head started throbbing. On my mother's last ride, she, too, had come off and landed on her head. Cindy had not gotten up, but it was consolation to think that her death had been painless.

I stepped into the doorway of several of the shops and Gabir asked questions for me—questions I have long forgotten. I remember only the eyes and the mustaches of the men he interviewed. I scribbled stuff in my notebook, but what I wrote were mostly personal memories of Nonnie. I was ready to leave. I picked up a spent round that had been overlooked by the cleanup crew and tucked it in my jacket pocket.

It wasn't until we got out of the immediate neighborhood that the firefight started. We had entered a section of town relatively undamaged, with gardens of gardenias, leafy ficus trees, and date palms with their lilting fronds. It was just a pop at first, as if someone in one of the palms had set off a firecracker. This was followed by a dither of machine gun fire as the two gunners from our convoy returned fire. Franks spoke into his portable radio and the three vehicles accelerated, weaving and bumping in the uneven street. I looked from window to window, trying to see our attacker, but saw only the waving fronds.

The firing stopped, but we didn't slow down. I looked behind us for signs of pursuit, but all I saw was the third Humvee, close on our heels. In the gunner turret I saw Doof. His helmet had been shot off and he was slumped redly over his weapon.

Chapter 15

Xmas came and went without me. With Gina in parts unknown, I felt like the season was weighing me down rather than cheering me up. I bought myself a bottle of brandy and a few trinkets for the staff at *The Courier* and let it go at that. Cal had gone back to Louisiana to be with his kids for a couple of days and had left me in charge of the paper, which I enjoyed, despite the fact that it was probably the least newsworthy week in the history of Pine Oak. Then he called, very apologetic, and said he'd be delayed for a couple days more. Was that all right? No problem. Tit for tat, though; I told him that when he got back, I would take my own little trip. What I didn't tell him was that I was afraid of what I might find.

And suddenly I was reminded of Trifecta, my mother's beautiful black Oldenburg mare. Sometimes, for reasons only she knew, Trifecta would balk at entering my mother's trailer come show time. She would walk up as far as the ramp, then stop and back away. If Cindy insisted, Trifecta would rear up—not to hurt Cindy, but just to show her displeasure—and back away further. Cindy never got mad at the mare, but would continue to gently insist that Trifecta load. "Come on, we're going," she would say patiently. It might take forty-five minutes, but Cindy knew that if she let the mare win once, she would always win. So she persisted until they were both exhausted, but loaded and ready to go. "Come on, we're going," she would repeat.

Now, I had to tell myself the same thing. "Come on, we're going."

But to take a trip, I needed another vehicle. No way did I want to ask the old Toyota, which already had over 180,000 miles on the odometer, to trot up and down the east coast. It was great for what I used it for—driving to work and hauling feed and supplies—but it wasn't a touring car. I wish I could tell you that I went out and traded it in for something snazzy like a new Acura or Mitsubishi, or a hybrid that would help ease the glut on the world's irreplaceable fossil fuel supply. But my next vehicle needed to be one that would pull a horse trailer. That is, if I ever had enough money to buy a horse trailer. A Ford F-250 like Joey Bickley's, maybe. Rugged and diesel.

Instead, I rented a car. A compact car. One with a CD player.

So on the Wednesday after Xmas I got up early, fed the three horses and rode Alikki in the ring for an hour. I showered, called Krista and asked her to look after the barn for a few days, and set out towards Pensacola. It was a drive of several hours, so I had time to think about all the reasons I didn't really need a new truck.

When my mother died, she willed me the house, the stables, and the hundred acres associated with them. Luckily for me, they were paid for. All I had to worry about were taxes—which in a small town were pretty low,—utilities, and the upkeep of the horses—which was considerable. My salary from *The Pine Oak Courier* was only about a third of what I'd made in Richmond, but it was enough to survive on and even rent a car for special trips. I didn't think, though, that I could afford to tackle a four- or five-hundred dollar a month vehicle payment. In the recession the country was just trying to recover from, I was lucky to be working at all.

I was never any good with money; always spent it as fast as I got it. In Richmond, Jack and I had expensive tastes. Despite his cooking skills, and he had some, we often dined out—especially toward the end of our relationship when I began to feel the need of a little freedom. We went to movies, attended art exhibitions, donated freely to worthwhile causes. I drove a leased car, only giving it up after I returned from Iraq. I had retired from archery competition by then, so I wasn't buying much in the way of tackle, but I had no qualms about surprising Jack with the latest high-tech photography gadgetry. It was silly, really; he didn't have any use for half the stuff I bought, but it gave him a sense of what was available and what he *did* use, he used uniquely. In Iraq, I . . . well, who knows what I did with my money in Iraq.

The county roads leading to I-10 were picturesque in a North Florida kind of way. Acres and acres of hay fields had gone brown and stubbly for the winter. Property lines were dotted with hay rolls from the last several years, and a good eye could tell from the color which were baled this year, which the year before. I passed a field of paint horses browsing among the stipple of weeds in their field. In an adjacent pasture, two donkeys and a mule glanced up from their own browsing as I raced past. The donkeys looked upscale in matching herringbone blankets.

The fields and pastures turned into patches of scrub pine and oak, and everywhere I looked, I saw puddles from December's frequent rains. The sky, too, was filled with darkish clouds, and showers had been forecast. Cold and wet. Here and there I saw small cedar sprigs nudging their way upwards and I felt a pang of regret. A month earlier, Gina and I had begun planning our first Xmas together. We had decided to cut our own little cedar tree from the woods surrounding the pasture and decorate it with whatever baubles we fancied. I had been looking forward to mulled wine, comfortable slippers, light music, and a warm closeness between us. It hadn't happened.

To ease my depression, I found a National Public Radio station and listened until it, too, started to get me down. Wars, wars everywhere. But I had gotten out of Iraq alive, sort of. And Jack, too, was safe. I had not seen him since he got back from Iraq, although we exchanged frequent emails discussing our joint book of photographs. But I would think about Jack later. I flipped in the Robin and Marian CD and prepared for my interview with Billy Carothers.

Billy had returned my email within a few hours, saying that he'd welcome a chat about his "old friend Mick". I combined the directions he gave me with a more precise printout from Google Maps. I got off I-10 on exit 22, crossed over 90, and traveled north until the streets got smaller and the trees larger. The house, when I finally spotted the address in gold metallic numbers over the front door, turned out to be one of those old white clapboard boxes constructed around 1950 or so. It had a screened-in front porch and a slate roof that needed patching. The whitewash was faded from the woodwork and the bushes around the house were scraggly and unhealthy. A cracked cement driveway contained a green VW bug from the seventies. I parked in front of the house and opened the car door just as a burst of rain began pouring down, making me think of cartoons featuring various sad sacks with their own personal rain clouds following them about.

I didn't have an umbrella, so I dashed from the curb to the screen door, which was opened almost immediately by a round little man with a fringe of white hair surrounding a bald, red head.

"Miss McKeown?"

"Call me Sue-Ann," I told him, as he led me through the cold porch and into a very warm interior.

"Billy," he told me. "Billy Carothers."

Billy had the type of light complexion that, combined with a little sun, stays pink, and from the veins that reddened his nose I assumed he was a drinking man. This was turned into fact when he motioned me to a small table set with two glasses and a frosty pitcher brimming with something cold.

"Here, have a seat," he told me. "I enjoy a mint julep from time to time. Would you care for one?"

"No, not for me," I answered. He was one of those people who spoke much better than he wrote. His thin voice had just a touch of the feminine and a vestigial southern drawl.

"Are you sure? I use Woodford Reserve, just like at the Kentucky Derby."

I took my minicassette recorder from my purse and set it on the table. "That's a nice bourbon," I replied, "but I have to drive. Do you mind if I record this conversation?"

Billy Carothers waved my question away like it was one of no importance whatever. "You told me on the phone that you're writing an article on Mick Simmons."

"That's right, Mr. Carothers."

He smiled and sat down. I took the seat across from him and looked around the room. The word stuffy comes to mind because there was a lot of stuff. There were two plush couches and several thick armchairs all covered in faded chintz. Corner bookshelves were crowded with knickknacks, although I spotted a few western paperbacks on an end table. The walls, papered with a flowery design, were disfigured with half a dozen grayish photographs of old people. There was a fireplace with a mantle, but it was cold. The room was kept warm by vents on the floor, which was mostly covered by a dark grey patterned carpet, giving the room an illusion of shade. There was even an antique-looking étagère containing a selection of alcoholic beverages. I caught a brief glimpse into a bedroom with airy curtains and a carefully made-up bed. A single bed. A childless room in a childless house.

An aberration was the small round table at which we sat in the center of the living room. It was almost certainly a piece of lawn furniture with the umbrella removed from the center. The two chairs—dark metal with green naugahyde cushions—were part of the same set. Billy Carothers sat with an ease that assured me that he spent a good deal of time in his chair. I assumed, because he was contemporaneous with Mickey Simmons, that he must be somewhere in his late fifties or early sixties. The same age as The Creeper, more or less. On the whole, he gave the appearance of a man that would rather have been sitting on a verandah somewhere near Atlanta in the 1860s. I pushed the record button on the cassette machine and settled back in my own seat, facing him obliquely. But before I could ask my first question, I heard a door open and close somewhere behind me. I must have looked startled because Billy said, "Don't worry. It's only Charles."

From the kitchen, a lanky man about Billy's age with dark shaggy hair and a five o'clock shadow entered the room shucking off layer after layer of clothing—hat, overcoat, sweater, scarf—all of which he threw on an armchair. He looked first at Billy, then at the chair I was sitting in. "You the reporter?" he asked, but he might as well have said "interloper." For a big man, his voice was freaky-shreiky.

"Sue-Ann McKeown," I answered, and put out my hand. He put out his own, but not to shake hands. Instead he reached past me and poured himself a julep in my untouched glass. "I guess I have your chair," I said.

"I'll sit over here," he said, "while you two talk." Before he sat, he pulled out a length of toilet paper from his pants pocket and started snuffling into it. "You need to turn down your thermostat," he said.

"You'll live," Billy Carothers said with equanimity. He turned to me and said, "Charles owns the house just in back of me. We're both retired, and most days he and I just sit here, drinking our drinks, and looking out over the street at the people going by. In the spring, we take the table and chairs out to the porch."

I could see them sitting together like that, but I couldn't imagine either of them actually saying anything. Which, really, was kind of touching.

"Did Charles know Mick Simmons, too?"

But it was Charles who answered. "Never heard of the bastard until Billy told me you were coming over to talk about him," he screeched.

I decided to begin the interview. "Tell me how you met Mick," I asked Billy.

Billy leaned back in his lounge chair, took a tiny sip of his drink, and closed his eyes. "It was way back in about 1974. I had been working in the men's department of J. C. Penny for about a year when one day I notice this new guy. He was a year or two younger than me, smaller than me too. He still looked like a boy, really. He had all this hair pouffed up on his head like he was prissy, but we got to be kind of friends."

"Sounds like an effing faggot," squawked Charles, who was now sprawled out on the sofa, his heavy shoes threatening to sink through the threadbare fabric. I supposed that I was an effing faggot, too, but I knew that if I flared up, I might not learn what Billy had to tell me. Billy, who was obviously used to his friend's outbursts, ignored him. "Back then, we all listened to the radio. I wasn't a hippie or anything, but I liked to hear all the latest music—Dylan, The Doors, Pink Floyd. I talked about it all the time, so one day, old Mick told me that he had made a record."

"The lying son of a bitch!" Charles burst out.

"I thought he was just making something up," Billy said with a laugh. "I didn't mind because he seemed like such a lonely kid and everybody's got their fantasies, right?"

"Just like you're fantasizing about ripping off that reporter's blouse and slobbering all over her tittays, haw haw."

Charles reminded me of a gelding my mother had once owned, before she'd shelled out a king's ransom for Facilitator. He was a horse who would try anything as long as he could get away with it, and until Cindy learned that she had to be the one that controlled the ride, he had effectively ridden her to distraction. I wondered if this worked on humans, too, so I pushed my chair back viciously and loomed over Charles' slouching figure. "How would you like me to rip your throat out?" I snarled. The man spilled what was left of his drink on his shirt and cowered, an old man, frailer than he looked. "I, um, I just . . ."

I turned my back on him, picked up my chair, which had tipped over with its cushions askew, and sat back down. Meanwhile, Billy had taken the pitcher over to his neighbor and refilled his glass. I suddenly realized that Billy and Charles were like two personalities in the same individual—Billy was the calm and refined persona while the Charles persona suffered from that disease that makes people scream out obscenities for no reason.

"Charles is sometimes inconsiderate," Billy explained. "But it's not really his fault. You see, he earned his living as a vacuum cleaner salesman for thirty years. That would make anybody crazy. I was luckier; while I worked at the department store, I was also taking classes in accounting at the junior college. And, oh, boy, that really ticked off poor Mick. He said that school was for fools, but I didn't want to sell men's clothes for the rest of my life. Or, ha ha, to sell vacuum cleaners. But by the time I finally got my certification, Mick was long gone."

"The effing knob-gobbler," Charles muttered, then cringed back into the upholstery when I gave him a dirty look.

I turned back to Billy. "Did Mick ever talk about his music?"

"Umm," Billy sipped. "Did he ever talk about anything else? He told me that he wrote a dozen songs a week and that he was going to make a comeback and be bigger than Judy Collins. He even showed me the lyrics of some of his songs. I don't know anything about poetry, but I told him they were good anyway. He seemed to want me to, you see, because a lot of people had told him they were dreadful. Maybe that was why he was always so angry and unpleasant. Kind of like Charles, ha ha." Billy raised his glass and saluted his friend on the couch. I heard a grumble in reply. "No," Billy continued, "Mick wasn't much fun to be around, but I didn't have any other friends and neither did he. Sometimes we would go to Duff's for the all-you-can-eat buffet, or maybe out for a drink somewhere—although even one beer would usually make him fly off the handle."

"Did you ever invite him here?" I asked.

"Oh, I wasn't living here, then. I inherited this house when my mother died back in 1990. But sometimes we went to his apartment, which was pretty close to where we worked. The first time I was there, he showed me the Robin and Marian LP. It had a picture of him and his sister, so I knew it was Mick even if he didn't use the same name. He put it on this cheap turntable and played a couple of songs from it. They were okay. Soft and sweet, kind of."

"Not as sweet as the inside of his ass, I'll bet!" croaked Charles. He quickly covered up his mouth and pretended to cough into his piece of toilet paper.

"He even showed me his guitar," Billy continued, unperturbed. "He played me a couple of new songs, but I didn't think they were as good. They lacked something."

"His sister's voice?" I asked.

"That was it. Mick couldn't carry much of a tune by himself."

"Did you ever meet his sister?" I asked.

"No, never. Saw a picture of her, though, on the record jacket. Taller than Mick. Prettier, too, ha ha. But no, she had moved away by then, I think."

"Do you know where she went?"

"Naw. To tell the truth, Mick didn't like to talk about her. Said something like she had ruined his career."

This perked me up. "Did he say how?"

"If he did, I don't remember."

I seemed to be coming to a quick dead end. "Do you remember anything about the songs he played for you—the ones not on the LP?"

"Ah. Well, it's been a long time now, but I remember he said he was going in a different direction. Tougher. One song might have had something to do with working in a coal mine, or maybe an ice plant. Something like that."

"Where would he have seen a coal mine?" I asked, half to myself.

"Oh, he didn't have to see one. As long as he could imagine it, he was going to write about it."

"Did he ever mention the time he was in California?"

Billy Carothers almost snorted into his glass, and I heard Charles echoing this from behind me. "California my rosy rear," Billy laughed. "He'd been to New York all right, but could never get up the money to travel to the west coast."

"But some of the songs on the LP are about places in California."

"Um. But they're not the best songs, are they?"

No, they weren't. And when I realized this I had the first inkling of what might have happened in Mickey Simmons' life. Or rather, in the lives of Robin and Marian. We talked for another half hour or so as the rain pounded down outside, but the image he gave of Mickey Simmons was generally the same as the one I had gotten from The Creeper. Small, angry, unpleasant, and maybe not so talented.

A break in the rain gave me the opportunity to pack up my recorder and make my goodbyes. "I'll email you if I need any more details, and you do the same if you remember anything else," I told Billy. "And happy New Year to the both of you."

"It was a pleasure, Miz McKeown," he said. I heard Charles skronk with muted laughter on the couch.

I saw myself out, pausing at the door to take a final look at its inhabitants. Charles had already wafted himself into my vacated seat and filled his glass, smiling at Billy. "I'll send you a copy of the article," I told him.

Billy waved it away, as if were of no importance.

The meeting gave me a lot to think about. I had learned little about Mickey Simmons and virtually nothing about Maryanne. But I had learned a lot about human nature, love, repression, and ingrained bigotry. Charles' anti-homosexual comments were delivered with exactly the same unthinking disregard that Joey Bickley would have used. Yet if I had ever seen a perfect couple, Billy and Charles were it. They were completely at home with each other, had the same interests, enjoyed the same pastimes, and suffered the same jealousies as any two people in love. Yet both would have rejected that word, would have been flabbergasted by it, in fact, and I suspected both had been chaste for the entire length of their friendship—if not always. It made me wonder about Mickey's own sexuality, and if it had affected his songwriting. Another carrot in the stew.

I cranked the car, turned on the heater, and was away. Next stop: Jack.

Chapter 16

I need to tell you the story of a photograph.

It's a picture of me topless in the heat of a summery July. Or maybe it would be more accurate to say that I was topless and in heat. That photograph is important to this story and to the next chapter, so here goes.

I started working for *The Richmond Times-Dispatch* at the very beginning of the new century. It was a good time symbolically—time for me to move on to a better job but also move away from a bad relationship. *The Times-Dispatch* office was a bustling, gray, two-story building with people rushing back and forth waving papers and the click of keyboards like night sounds on a pond. It was a hectic time for me because in addition to learning my duties, getting to know a lawyer I had just met named Matt, and trying to meet other people at the office, I was training hard for the Olympics. It took six months before one of the sports editors found out about my archery and decided to do a story about me.

"I'm not sure I'm comfortable with that," I told him. "I'm supposed to write the news, not be the news."

"Don't worry about it. I'll talk to the boss."

"But—"

But he was gone.

An hour later, I looked up from the computer in my tiny cubicle to find the handsomest man I had ever seen standing beside me. He stood six feet tall with wavy, jet-black hair. His square chin reminded me not so much of Batman, but Bruce Wayne. He had a smooth, light complexion with no hint of facial hair. He was smiling, so I was able to see perfect teeth.

"Hi," he said. "I'm Jack Stafford."

"I know who you are," I said without thinking. "but how did you get there?"

"Teleported," he deadpanned. "The technology is kind of new, but most of the major newspapers are converting to it." He walked around me and sat down on the only other chair in my cubicle. "What are you working on?" he asked.

"I, um. I'm writing a piece on aging inmates."

"Criminals?"

"Yeah. Some of them are over 70 when they get out and everyone in their family has either died or disappeared. I mean, what do you do with a guy who has diabetes, is confined to a wheelchair, and has nowhere to go? And why are you in my cubicle?"

As you can see from my weird conversational turns, I was flustered. Someone had pointed out Jack to me while I was still in my first week at *The Times-Dispatch*. Although he hadn't won any national awards yet, he was widely admired for his almost indescribably eloquent photographs of everything from cherry trees to tenements. And for his looks. I guessed him to be about my age—early thirties—or a little older, and it took no guesswork to know that every woman in the office had the hots for him. Unrequited hots, from what I understood. I had, however, once seen him in a restaurant acting cozy with a very well-dressed woman in her forties, bling dangling like tinsel from her wrists and ears.

"I'm supposed to take pictures of the famous Sue-Ann McKeown," he said, smile still fresh and dazzling.

"Why?" I asked.

"Something about you being on the Olympic archery team. Is that true?"

"Yeah."

"Well, listen. The sports editor wants you to dress in a skimpy green skirt and a Robin Hood hat. Green felt pixie boots. Then he wants us to go out in the woods and have me take a roll of photos." Jack looked at me evenly.

"The sports editor can fuck an ice cream cone," I said with asperity. "Did he really say that?"

"Yes, but I lied."

"That doesn't make sense."

"Right. He said it but he didn't say it to me. He said it to one of the sports photographers. I just happened to be in the room."

"So what are *you* doing here?"

"I said I wanted to do the shoot."

"You do? I mean, you did?"

"Umm."

"And so, what? We're going out in the woods?"

"Not likely."

I was almost disappointed.

"I'm not going to tell you that I haven't done fakey stuff before," he said. "You have to, really, if you're going to make a living. But to me, the business of photography is to record a real event, not create the event for a photograph."

"I usually shoot after work," I told him.

"It's a date," he told me.

Date? I thought. Not likely.

~ ~ ~

One of the first things I did after I was hired on at *RTD* was locate a place to shoot my arrows. And it wasn't easy, because I needed a place almost as long as a football field all to myself. What made it even harder was the fact that I had to have a place to store my tackle, my telescope, my targets, and target stands—which weren't light. A golf driving range would have filled the bill, but there would be no way to retrieve my arrows with all the golf balls flying about. The pistol ranges I found were all too small and my apartment didn't even have a back yard, much less space to shoot. In the end, I settled on a place I should have checked out in the beginning.

Chuck's 3-D Archery Playground was located on an out of-the-way 20 acres in the Upper Shockoe Valley, just east of town. Chuck, a redheaded, potbellied ex-Marine in his forties, had probably assumed that I was there to buy something for my husband—something in camo, perhaps, which was the motif of choice in most archery stores; I mean in *all* archery stores.

"You Chuck?" I asked.

The man looked up at me over a row of fletching jigs, with which he was attaching feathers to half a dozen shafts at once. "Chuck Zabala," he answered. "Kin I help ye?"

"I'd like to see your layout," I told him politely.

"Yeah?"

"I'm looking for a place to practice," I explained.

"What, you hunt?" he asked.

"Olympic archery team."

"Right."

I shrugged. "You have a target range?"

He just moved his head toward a side door. "Out there."

He didn't offer to accompany me, so I walked out the door to a surprisingly large, complete, and well-kept facility. On my left was a hundred-yard field set up with half a dozen full-sized targets, although they had pictures of game animals instead of the traditional bull's-eye circles. On the right was a patch of forest with a gated entrance. I peered inside and could see paths leading to what would turn out to be life-size replicas of turkey, deer, even bear positioned at strategic areas on the course.

Although I was wearing my work clothes, I decided to shoot for a while before it got dark. I walked back into the office with my aluminum carrying case and asked the redheaded dude what he charged to use the target range.

"Four bucks an hour." He looked curiously at my case. "Whatcha got in there?"

I set the case carefully on the counter and flipped the catches. I took out the riser and began to attach the limbs. Then out came the stabilizers, which I screwed in to their respective holes. As I was stringing it, I heard, "Where are the pulleys?"

"It's not a compound," I told him. "It's a recurve."

"Never seen a recurve that looks like that," he said.

"It's an Olympic recurve."

"Bullshit," he said.

I told Jack Stafford about my first encounter with Chuck as we drove east after work. Jack had insisted on driving because of the cases of camera equipment he had stashed away in the trunk and back of his Lexus SUV. It was still roomy enough for my archery case, my telescope case, and the bag holding my sports clothes. In fact, it was probably the most comfortable car I had ever sat in.

"So let me guess," he smiled over the steering wheel. "He decided to outshoot you with his souped-up compound and you kicked his ass all over the valley."

"Um, yeah. We've gotten to be pretty good friends, though. After a while him and some of the other guys started coming out to watch. They call me Ms. O. Some of them have asked me to come out and hunt deer with them."

"Have you taken them up on it?" he asked, turning off the highway and into the parking lot of Chuck's 3-D Playground.

"I don't hunt," I told him. "I mean, I don't believe in hunting. It's giving in too much to macho instincts.

My mother used to say that some people don't feel alive unless they're out killing something."

"Yeah, well. I've never hunted, either." There were only two other cars in the lot, so Jack was able to park close to the office. As we were taking out our gear, I asked. "Is this your car?" I was really wondering how he could afford it.

"I lease it," he told me. "But my mileage expenses for the paper almost cover the cost. Leasing's the best way to go."

A path from the parking lot led to the office, but veered off to the left through a hedge to the shooting range.

When we walked into the office, Chuck was talking to one of the regulars about taxidermy. A TV on the wall was showing a video touting a new arrowhead called "the guillotine," the purpose of which I don't want to discuss. When Chuck saw Jack and I enter with our cases of equipment, he looked in my direction and asked, "Another Olympic Team member?"

"His name is Jack Stafford and he's a photographer from *The Times-Dispatch.* They're going to do a story about me."

"That's great. Do you shoot football games, too?"

I left Jack with Chuck and his friend—I'm pretty sure he went by the name Bubba—while I went into the rest room and changed into my shooting outfit: dark blue running pants, white, knitted shirt with a collar and with the Olympic emblem above the pocket, and Nike running shoes. I tied my hair—which I was wearing down below my shoulders at that time—into a ponytail with a red scrunchie.

The range was deserted, as it usually was, although I could hear brush rustling inside the 3-D compound where someone was getting off on penetrating a 10-point buck molded from solid, self-healing polyfoam with a 100-grain, easy-to-pull-out target point.

Jack and I set our cases on the ground and began removing our equipment. First, I went about the mechanics of putting together my bow and placing my arrows in a ground quiver. At the same time, Jack was screwing a long lens on his Nikon. A thought passed through my head that we were like a young couple unpacking suitcases in a motel room. I banished the thought, but when he took out a tripod from his case, I did the same, attaching a telescope and focusing it at one of the targets.

"Holy wow, Sue-Ann," Jack burst out. "What's the telescope for?"

"When we're shooting at anything more than 30 meters or so, we can't see exactly where our arrows hit so we can't make adjustments. I saw you with a woman in Harold's Grill the other night. Are you dating?"

He didn't look at me as he attached one of his cameras to the tripod. "Yeah, I guess."

"Yeah, me too."

"She's a lawyer," Jack said. "Libel."

"It that right? I'm dating a lawyer, too. Estate, I think."

"Umm."

I was doing a series of stretching exercises when Chuck and his pal came out to watch. After a minute or two, Chuck came out with, "Listen, um, Jack. Would you take a picture of me and Sue-Ann?"

"Me, too," said Bubba.

Jack took the request with good grace and shot a few pix—the guys with their arms around my shoulder and smiling mightily. "Might be good for business," Jack told Chuck. "I'll make some prints and have them delivered."

"Thanks, man. We'll pay you."

"No charge," Jack said.

I began shooting—just 30 meters at first, but within a half hour had moved out to 50. Chuck watched for a while, but soon he and Bubba went back into the office to watch guillotine videos. Just after that the gate to the 3-D Playground opened and a man and his young son exited. They were both dressed in camouflage and carrying different-sized, but matching, blue compound bows. They both looked hot, but satisfied.

Chuck came out to tell us he was closing up for the night. "You all can stay; just go out the hedge path."

I nodded.

It was hot hot hot and as I shot—and as Jack shot—sweat was creeping down our crevasses and making dark patches on our clothes. Jack loosened a button on his shirt and kept shooting. I tugged my shirt away from my sweaty body and kept shooting. We both continued what we were doing with rapt absorption. After retrieving my arrows for about the 20th time, I moved back to 70 meters and began shooting in earnest. The sun began to go down but it was still hot.

I kept tugging my shirt away from my body. Jack snapped and snapped. I hit four tens in a row and tugged my hair loose from its scrunchie and whipped it around my face. I stripped off my shirt and sports bra and threw them on the ground. My wet, target-pointed nipples were aimed directly at the camera. Click click.

"Holy wow, Sue-Ann," Jack said breathlessly.

"I've never been so turned on in my life," I replied softly as I shot my last arrow, which completely missed the target because Jack had left his tripod and had his hands on my breasts. Then we were kissing like I had never kissed before.

It was the first and last time I ever made love on an archery range. And we didn't do it just once, either.

"Tell me about your girlfriend," I panted.

"She's . . . she's . . . uhhhhhhhh . . . she's an arrow shooter." When he calmed down, he said, "Tell me about your boyfriend."

"What boyfriend?"

The truth is, I never saw Matt again. He called, but I put him off until he stopped. After Jack and I moved in together, I sold the old Chevy I'd been driving for the last few years and leased a new Toyota Camry.

One of the pictures Jack had taken—the one of me topless and all a-sweat—hung in the bedroom of our apartment. It was far and away the best photo ever taken of me. I looked flush, healthy, athletic, and way more naked than I actually was. My skin was sepia-tinged and running with sweat; my hair like Medusa snakes plastered across my face and neck. My eyes were filled with everything. For the several years I lived with Jack, whenever I felt bad or sad or overweight or tired, I would stare at the photo, wondering how I could possibly have been such an extraordinary being. As far as I knew, the portrait was still on the bedroom wall in Jack's apartment.

And I wanted it.

Chapter 17

It was already dark when I passed through Atlanta so I stopped in Lawrenceville at one of the new motels that had sprung up around the Braves' triple-A farm team in Gwinnett County. The room was clean and the prices were down because of the off-season. It even had a wireless hookup for my laptop, which I didn't even bother to take out of the car. I turned on the TV and began mindlessly browsing through the channels. I stopped when I recognized a scene from *The Princess Diaries*, in which a young Anne Hathaway shoots a flaming arrow through a hoop using a beautiful Martin Dreamcatcher. It was the same model that Gina had selected as her first bow, and which still hung on the wall of the archery room in my barn. The movie was kind of stupid, but I liked it anyway. And the girl had good form. I fell asleep thinking of Gina.

It was still dark when I pulled out from the motel parking lot just after 6:00 the next morning. It had gotten colder, but my little rented car had a warm, silent heater and I drove in comfort, munching on a blueberry muffin and sipping on the several cups of coffee I had scarfed from the free motel breakfast. On the CD player, Robin and Marian, like most of us, attempted greatness and fell short. As I drove along, I thought of my own failures, and there were many. My track record with men was abysmal and my competitive archery career had ended on a sour note. But it was my journalism that really fell short of my expectations.

I haven't had a lot of jobs. My mother wouldn't let me work in high school; wanted me to concentrate on my grades. That was okay; I liked school and didn't want to get a job anyway. I had my small circle of friends, but no one really close and I spent most of my time at home. And the grades thing paid off—I got a free ride to the University of North Carolina, one of the top journalism schools in the country. Some of the guest lecturers included Marcia Ladendorff, who I envied because she was the CNN anchor that broke the AIDS story nationally; Dan Rather, whose bones I wanted to jump despite his already-graying temples; and Christiane Amanpour, who I quickly wanted to become because . . . well, because she was Christiane Amanpour.

But despite a few semesters of broadcast journalism, I was a print reporter my entire career. As a senior I was appointed Editor-in-Chief of *The Daily Tar Heel*, which gave me a lot of cred in my employment applications. After a few jobs as a stringer and a couple of years on the political beat for *The Chapel Hill News*, I was offered a job at *The Richmond Times-Dispatch*. Not only was it a good job, but the timing was right. An innocent friendship with a lobbyist for Greenpeace turned into a dilemma when I realized that I was becoming attracted to this happily married father of three. Time for me to move on.

My new job gave me a much higher profile and concomitant responsibility. No regrets; the years I spent at *The Richmond Times-Dispatch* were increasingly good ones. I soon graduated from local news to writing about the state legislature, and from there to national news. My byline was well-known and I received a couple of local and statewide awards for journalism. When I was posted to Iraq, I thought that I would get my chance to rival Christiane. It didn't happen. I saw friends killed, I fucked total strangers, and I drank what was available. I wrote what I could, and maybe some of it was good, but I only lasted six months. By the time I left, I was a nervous and physical wreck.

And now, driving back to Richmond, where my journalistic talent had begun to bud with promise, as it were, it was like stepping into a pool filled with cold pudding.

~ ~ ~

My first few months with Jack Stafford were hardly what you would call a whirlwind romance, if you use those kinds of clichés. Although he knew a lot of people, he was not the least bit social and rarely went out. This was okay because we enjoyed staying in our apartment, watching TV, and discussing our workdays. He had surprising newspaper savvy and helped me—sometimes just by my watching him—improve my own knowledge of the business in general and of *The Times-Dispatch* in particular. His way with people was almost mesmerizing; he could have charmed the beard off Colonel Sanders.

We were a pretty attractive couple and we were both good at what we did. When Jack won his first NPPA award in Conceptual Photographic Illustration a couple of years later, our circle of activities widened. We started socializing on a small scale, we spent money, we had fun. At least it seemed like fun at the time. And the relationship helped us both.

It took years before I realized that Jack was not the person I wanted to spend my entire life with. Even then, it was more of a subconscious whisper than a full realization; a pulling away synapse by synapse. That he was gorgeous and talented I knew before we met. But during the half dozen years we lived together, I also found that he was naïve, overly fastidious, and curiously unsexed, despite our first furious entanglement at Chuck's 3-D Archery Playground. He enjoyed cooking and delighted in preparing elaborate three-course meals. Trouble was, I'm a fast food junkie who enjoys a Big Mac as much as a plate of spaghetti alfredo with mushroom and shrimp.

Nor could we bond using music; In college I had developed a passion for alternative rock while Jack actually had Mantovani records in his scanty collection. And don't even get me started about cleanliness. Jack once joked that he was going to buy his own bed so that he could make it every morning and wash his sheets every few days while my own languished for months in slovenly disarray. It isn't that he wasn't affectionate; it's just that . . . shit, I don't know. I have no idea why I finally broke up with him. As far as I can remember, we never spoke a harsh word to each other. I've written a lot about our relationship and I've described it honestly, so I'll leave it to you psychologists to figure out.

When I first moved to Richmond, I was renting a little hole in the wall near the university. When Jack and I decided to live together, it made sense for me to move into his much larger and newer apartment. Located near the Forest Hills area, the Enclave was a magnificent stretch of white, three-story buildings with steep roofs, dormer windows, and balconies with trellises. Jack's two-bedroom had a large and shiny kitchen with its own breakfast nook and separate dining area. The parlor was roomy and comfortable, and the den was fluffy and cozy. Central heat and air kept the place at about the same temperature year-round. No wood stoves for Jack. No lawn mowers either—the plush lawns surrounding The Enclave were manicured by staff professionals. He used the smaller bedroom to sleep and the larger to store his camera equipment, mainly because he had set up a sophisticated darkroom in the spacious walk-in closet. It was in that bedroom that I built a wall rack for my bows.

Although the price was kind of staggering for a small-town girl, I insisted on paying my share of the rent. It was silly, really, because Jack was well off and economy was one of the many things that simply never entered his head. If something struck his fancy—from a new three-seater leather couch to a newly marketed piece of photographic wizardry—he simply ordered it and had it delivered. Although he didn't play competitive sports, he was a decent swimmer and he tried to work out in the Enclave's Olympic-sized pool two or three times a week.

By the time I pulled into the parking area early that afternoon, the rented Hyundai was awash with Styrofoam coffee cups and fast food containers. I turned off the engine and just sat there for a few minutes, feeling a real trepidation. The truth is, I really didn't want to see Jack. I visualized him healthy and trim from swimming, smiling at me in front of an aluminum Xmas tree set up in the corner of the den. Smiling because that was part of his charm, part of the essence of Jack that allowed him to obtain whatever he needed. Like me, for instance. But I had been explicit in my email; it was just a short visit to pick up a few of the things I had left in the apartment—my picture, a few books, letters from my mother.

I got out of the car and was hit with a gust of frigid air. The sky was dark with clouds and I had lived in Richmond long enough to recognize approaching snow. The lawns surrounding the long apartment building were strangely devoid of the accoutrements of the season; no manger scenes, reindeer shaped from metal rods, balloon snowmen. I did spot an electric candle on one second-story window and a holly wreath on the door of Jack's neighbor, but for the most part it was as if the residents had moved to the Enclave to get away from not just ostentation, but celebration.

It was odd to be knocking on the door of an apartment I had lived in for six years, but I did it. I still had my old key, but didn't want to use it. It wasn't my place anymore. As I waited for an answer I stuffed my hands in the pockets of my too-thin fleece pullover and hunched up my neck into the collar. When Jack opened the door, he smiled and immediately gave me a big hug.

"Hey, girl," he said heartily. "It's about time you got here." I smiled and tried to return his hug. Well, no I didn't, but at least I didn't pull away. Jack was dressed in Khaki trousers and what looked and felt like a cashmere sweater. He was barefoot on the thick rug and I noticed that his toenails were too long. That's when I knew that something was wrong.

I stepped back and handed him a beribboned bottle of a mid-priced Chianti Classico wine that he enjoyed. "Happy New Year," I told him.

"You, too," he said. "Come and sit down."

I took a seat on the end of the brown leather couch and took a look around the place I hadn't seen for over a year. It looked the same, almost. But there was something that was subtly but disturbingly different. For one thing, the pictures on the walls were different. As usual, they were all photographs Jack had taken, but the stylishly aesthetic pictures I was used to seeing had been replaced by starker ones. Each was in black and white except for a single color somewhere in the photo—a yellow sun over an abandoned tank that lay half overturned in the desert sand, a blue glint from the pistol of a U. S. Sergeant at an ID check, a red hole in the thick cotton shirt of a dying insurgent.

"Shit, Jack," I burst out. "When did you start experimenting with color like that?"

Jack sat down facing me in a leather armchair he had purchased together with the couch. He put his feet up on the footrest and blinked at the photos as if he had never seen them before. "Awhile ago," he finally said. "I was looking through some rolls I took in Iraq and I just saw those colors there, like some kind of weird auras. Pretty crazy, huh?"

"They're good, Jack. A little freaky, but good."

"So tell me about *The Courier*," he said.

And so for a while we just chatted about Cal, Becky, and small town life in general. I mentioned some of the stories I had been working on and my new interest in horseback archery. He made all the appropriate replies and with just the right amount of interest in his voice, but I could tell that it was false—he was really listening to a voice within his own head. When I tried to change the subject and ask what stories *he* had been working on for *The Times-Dispatch* lately, he just shrugged. "I'm between assignments right now," he said. "Hey, let's call out for a pizza. I've got some beer in the fridge."

"Pizza?" I asked, astonished. "You hate pizza."

"I've acquired a taste for it lately," he said, smiling. "No muss, no fuss."

"There's something off kilter here," I told him.

His eyebrows went up slightly. "You think?" he said.

"Fuck it, Jack," I said louder than I had intended. "When's the last time you went more than three days without worrying your toenails with those damn hedge-clippers of yours? And what's with the military magazines on the coffee table? And as long as I've known you, preparing food was always more important than eating." Jack held up his hand to ward off anything else I intended to bring up.

"I have PTSD, Sue-Ann," he said bluntly.

"Huh?" I said. Talk about naïve—especially from a reporter who had been in a war zone—but I really had no idea what he was talking about.

"Post-Traumatic Stress Disorder." He pronounced the words carefully.

I felt like someone had stuffed me into a small box. "I don't understand," I managed. "I mean, I do understand, but why didn't you say something?"

He shrugged again. "It comes in spurts," he said. "Since I got back from Iraq I found that there are just some things that I don't care about anymore."

"Like?" I asked.

"Most things, really. I mean, most of what we do is really a waste of time, don't you think?"

"Doing something you enjoy is never a waste of time," I told him.

"Yeah," he said. "I'll need to think about that."

"Jack—"

"Listen," he interrupted, brightening. "Speaking of Post-Traumatic Stress Disorder, I just heard about this guy who came home from a tour of duty in Afghanistan. He hadn't seen his wife in a few months so he was looking forward to a night of passionate sex. Unfortunately, she came out of the shower with a towel around her head, so he shot her." Jack chuckled. It was the first time I had ever heard him chuckle, and I hoped it would be the last.

I shook my head.

"Not very funny, huh?"

"Not for a lot of reasons, Jack."

Jack took a cell phone from his shirt pocket, found a stored number, and called for a pizza. Then we chatted for a while about our book. It was supposed to be a collaborative effort, something Jack had cooked up to bring us back together. He took the pictures, I wrote the copy. But it had evolved into more than that.

Jack had gone to Iraq as a freelancer. He had a deal with *The Times-Dispatch* that they had first refusal on any photos he sent in, but whatever they didn't use Jack could market elsewhere. As soon as he reached his hotel in the Green Zone he made contact with several reporters who agreed to write stories for their own media outlets around some of the pictures he took. In return, he sometimes went along on their assignments. In that way he quickly was brought up to speed on what was going on in the country—the safe zones, the hot spots, the decent places to eat. And, of course, being Jack, he made many friends.

So it was only right that some of these reporters were represented in our book, although I edited their copy into the proper size and format. I hadn't really minded; after all, it was Jack's idea—his book. And the contributions from the other journalists would give it an international flavor—and audience.

It wasn't until we had eaten most of the pizza and drank several bottles of Heineken that Jack was oiled enough to talk. The uncorked bottle of Chianti sat like a lonely woman at the bar. But oddly, it was me that started talking first. Talking about the book had put me back into Iraq and brought back some of the old, bad feelings. Before I knew it, I had told him about my friend Nonnie, who had been killed right on the brink of greatness and at the height of beauty and confidence. I remembered bodies I had seen at the sites of car bombings and in hospitals. And then there was the convoy, a dead young private slumped in his turret . . . but that's something I couldn't think about yet.

"Nonnie shouldn't have been there, Jack. None of us should have been!" I cried. The tears I felt running down my face were like pesky gnats and I kept brushing them away. "She got shot for absolutely *nothing*."

"For Corporate Journalism," Jack said. "For the Nightly News, the Mighty Dollar, Big Oil."

He sat back and pushed away his plate. He rinsed out his mouth with the last of the Heineken, then stood up. As he was clearing away the things, putting our plates in the dishwasher and packaging the remnants of the pizza, he started talking.

"I was in a bazaar in Al Kut," he began. "You've probably been in something like it: lots of tents with banners flapping, incense burning, and chattering shop owners. I was looking for something for you, actually.

I'm not sure what, maybe something like a bracelet or a ring. A souvenir, maybe to prove I'd been there and that I was thinking about you."

Although his cleaner-than-thou housekeeping used to make me want to jump through the window, I was glad to see him wiping the crumbs off the table into his hand and drying the water rings with a thick wad of paper towels. Maybe it was just some kind of muscle memory, but his earlier strangeness had worried me.

"It was a shopping trip," he went on. "Not even an assignment, although I had a camera slung around my neck. I had gone out with this radio journalist from Australia and a guy named Phil who worked for Blackwater." Anyway, we were spread out in this pretty big tent and I was bending over some baubles when someone grabbed my camera and started to strangle me with the strap."

"My god, Jack. Were you hurt?"

"It was a good strap. I mean, you buy good accessories so you won't lose your good equipment, so all he did was pull me over backwards. It was so sudden that I didn't even cry out—even when the guy started pulling harder on the camera and choking me. I tried to fight him off, but I was in an awkward position and I was gagging. And I was scared; I couldn't even get my fingers between the strap and my throat. As far as I knew, the man was somebody who hated Westerners and had seen an easy opportunity of getting rid of one. It was strange, though, because instead of keeping an even pressure on my neck, he kept tugging at the camera harder and harder. Then he just let go and started to run. I looked after him just in time to see the Blackwater guy pull out his pistol and shoot."

Jack paused for a moment as he surveyed his work in the kitchen, then he walked back into the living room and sat down in the brown leather armchair. I followed him and sat across on the couch. "It was a stupid thing to do, really," he said. "I mean, we were surrounded by about a hundred nationals. What if Phil would have hit one of the shoppers? Or what if they took exception to some bionic Western Robocop shooting one of their own? But most of them were too scared to care about any of that and had run out of the tent. Not ten feet away from me, the guy who'd tried to kill me was screaming in pain and his blood was soaking into the sandy floor of the bazaar. The bullet was a hollowpoint, and it had hit him in the ball of the shoulder. When I stood up, Phil was standing over me and talking into a radio, asking for back up."

"So there was no more trouble?" I asked.

"No, no trouble, but I was numb. I don't even remember driving back to the hotel. All I could think about was that someone had tried to kill me."

"Jack, he was just trying to steal your camera."

"Yeah?"

"That man would probably have had to work for a year to buy that camera—if there was any work for him to do. He must have been desperate."

"Wait a minute, Sue-Ann. Are you siding with a murderer?"

"Of course not, Jack. If he would have killed you I would never have forgiven myself."

"Forgiven yourself for what?"

"If I hadn't gone to Iraq, do you really think *you* would have?"

"I was just going to say that," he said. "In the hotel bar that night, I was thinking that if you had married me instead of going off to Baghdad, things would have been different."

"Yes."

"I don't think I'll ever forget that man's scream."

"I'm sorry that happened to you, Jack. But going to Iraq was your choice. Maybe it wasn't the right thing to do—for either of us. But getting married wouldn't have been right, either."

"But I need you here, Sue-Ann. Don't you see that?"

"You need a mother."

"I have a mother."

"You need to call her."

And I could see in his eyes that it was a solution he had never thought about. Jack's mother lived in Portland, Maine, knocking about in a house much too large for her. She doted on Jack, who called her far less than he should have.

"What are you doing for your PTSD?" he asked.

"What am *I* doing?"

"Why do you think you were acting so crazy when you got back from Baghdad?" he asked. "You were stressed to the max. I didn't realize it then, but it's clear as a bell now."

"I had just lost my mother," I burst out. "And I had a thyroid disorder that almost killed me." I continued more gently, "And add to that the fact that I had realized months before that spending my life with you was not what I wanted to do. That's pretty stressful."

"But . . ."

"Jack, I don't have *time* for PTSD! I have my own life now. I've moved on." And having said that, I got up, went into the bedroom and started gathering up the few things I had left that had any value to me. Jack tried to convince me to stay, but I could see that the fight was gone from his words. Suddenly he perked up a little and said. "Golly wow, I almost forgot. I have something for you." While Jack went into the other bedroom, I removed from the wall the photo—all sweaty and hair-streaked—he had taken of me at Chuck's 3-D Archery Playground. I placed it on the bed and was looking around for something to put it in, when Jack came back holding a small, wrapped gift. "Here," he said.

"You shouldn't have," I told him, meaning it. But seeing the expectant look on his face, I stripped off the simple snowflake wrapping and extracted a set of new Ray-Ban Aviator sunglasses in a leather case. Black lenses, gold frames. Top of the line—none of your Malaysia knockoffs. There was even an authenticity card. "They're great, Jack. But this is kind of why I left. *You* wear sunglasses, I don't."

"They'll make you look cool," he said.

"You were the cool one in our relationship, dude," I said, putting the glasses back in their case and laying them on the bed. In the closet, I found a thick plastic shopping bag from a major department store. I placed the photo inside.

"I'll always treasure this photo, Jack," I told him. But I knew that looking at it would sometimes hurt.

"You're not leaving now, are you?" he asked, following me around the room.

"Places to go, people to see."

"It's late, how far can you get?"

"Far enough, I hope."

"I guess you're probably dating someone in Smallville, now," he said.

"Pine Oak," I corrected him. "And I'm not ready to talk to you about my personal life." At the front door, I dropped my shopping bag on a table and fished in my pocket for my key ring. From it, I clumsily extracted the key to the apartment and handed it to him.

"No, you keep it," he said.

"Jack—"

"I don't want it," he said evenly.

I shrugged and put it back, loose, in my pocket. Then I gathered my things and left the apartment. It was freezing so I started the car and immediately turned the heater up to high. As I was shifting the bag with the pictures and books on the front seat, I noticed that Jack had somehow managed to slip the Ray-Bans inside. Shit. Then I remembered that I still had a key to our mailbox, located on the side of the building along with the mailboxes of each of the other apartment dwellers. I drove there, unlocked the box, placed the Ray-Bans inside, relocked it, then slipped the key through the slot. I followed this with the key to the apartment.

Goodbye, Jack.

Chapter 18

That's two things out of the way: I had interviewed Billy Carothers and let Jack down once and for all. But there was a third reason for my trip, one that made the other two seem like minor distractions. I had to find Gina; and not because Cal wanted her back. *I* wanted her back. Even now, I longed to tell Gina about my adventures with Cletus Donnelly, what I had found out about Mickey Simmons, about Olympic horseback archery. I even wanted to fill her in on what had been happening at work. And in burning my bridges with Jack I was deliberately confirming myself in a much different kind of relationship. I didn't want anything to fall back on; I didn't need it. Gina was always popping into my head; she was always there, really, strolling, sitting, drawling in her marvelous voice, and listening with interest to every word I said. I had changed a lot in the few months since we had become close, and I liked the change, even though it was still pretty scary.

And something else was pretty scary: I knew where she was. I did. Pretty sure, anyway. I had lied to Cal when I said I had called her mother and sister, but I had to tell him something. Anything but where she was.

Although Gina had been born and raised in Pine Oak, her parents were originally from Tyler, Texas. Her father worked cattle on a farm that supplied beef to McDonald's and her mother was a traveling representative for the Texas Cattle Feeder's Association. When Gina's sister Laurel was born, they decided to change their lifestyle and sold some stock, pooled their earnings, and bought a Western-style tack store to which Gina's dad had the prescience to add a section of fishing equipment. Cartwright's Tack and Tackle was located in Jasper County, Florida, just off I-10. Jasper County was hardly a vacation paradise, but it was a decent enough place to raise a family. Gina was born several years later and virtually grew up in Cartwright's. It was a pretty good living, and gave Gina access to horse people and a comfortable life. But when Gina graduated from high school, the Ruby Tuesdays Corporation bought the property that Cartwright's was on and put in a restaurant. Gina's mom and dad took the money and ran back to Texas, where they retired to a small ranch near Abilene with a few cows and lots of goats. Laurel had already married and moved to Toronto, but Gina had just won a scholarship to the local vocational college and gotten a job in the cosmetics department at Wal-Mart, so she decided to stay in Pine Oak.

I only knew a little of this at the time. You already know that Gina and I were intensely jealous of each other in high school and rarely spoke. I even insisted that my mother use a tack store in Forester so I wouldn't have to see her outside school. Since Gina and I had finally become friends, though, I had learned a lot about her family. I knew that her parents' ranch was larger and more organized than mine, but I also knew that her freedom was important to her. She had spent her first 18 years in almost constant company with both her parents and she didn't want to spend much more. So I was pretty sure that Gina wasn't in Texas.

I had never met Laurel Cartwright. Ten years older than Gina, she ran in far different circles than I did. Like Gina, she worked in Cartwright's and rode horses. Like Gina, she had been pretty and very popular in high school, but unlike her, she had hated Pine Oak with a passion, and had shocked everyone she knew when she joined the Marines the day after graduating from high school. From what Gina told me, Laurel had been stationed in Japan when she met a young Canadian who was there studying microtechnology. They fell in love, married, and moved to Toronto when Laurel's enlistment ended. They settled down, had a couple of kids, end of story. She and Gina corresponded only occasionally and the chances of Gina driving to Canada for a visit were remote.

That left, what? everywhere else in the world? Not quite. While Gina was still in her mid-twenties, she ran away from Pine Oak. Her popularity and beauty had gotten her nowhere after high school, at least nowhere she wanted to be. Her small-town relationships were doomed by her attempt to better herself—in music, in finding the right career, in anything that made her feel more whole. Her boyfriends preferred docility, so after a brief and unsuccessful marriage to a used-car salesman, Gina, sick unto death of life, had gone a-traveling, with only a few changes of clothes and a heavy old Eko acoustic guitar.

She drove around the country for almost a year, stopping in places like Delta, Colorado, where she got a job working horses. She waited tables at Perlie's Pancake Factory just outside Nashville, where she spent as much time as she could in lounges and bars just to study the way music should be played. But Nashville brought home the fact that she was still a nothing and a nobody who had little talent—she was too self conscious to even bring her own guitar out in public. And so it was off to someplace else. Her peregrinations brought her, finally, still tired and disgusted with just about everything, to Myrtle Beach, South Carolina and to the Meher Baba Center.

She had never heard of Baba before she arrived, but not many people have nowadays. He was a mid-Twentieth-Century spiritual leader who had given up speaking for the last 40-plus years of his life. This might seem to be a drawback for the self-professed Avatar of his age, but I suspect that it kept him from putting his foot in his mouth from time to time. From what Gina had told me (and from my own readings) I learned that his "religion" was more like a recipe for life rather than a strict dogma. His "Don't worry, be happy" motto has become clichéd, but still gives off the essence of his beliefs. Baba himself was a strange-looking man, with scraggly hair, a wildly hooked nose, and a thick mustache. How persuasive his doctrines were is attested to by the millions of his followers who actually believe that he was a deity. As Gina once told me, "If that funny-lookin little man could convince people he was God, then maybe the rest of us have a chance to make somethin of our own lahves." She was intrigued by this idea and by the idea of becoming better than she was. She spent many happy weeks in Myrtle Beach on that first visit, studying, meeting like-minded individuals, and playing music whenever she got the chance—music was something that Baba had always encouraged his followers to enjoy. She had brought home not only a new resolve, but a new-looking Gretsch G400 hollowbody acoustic guitar that she had picked up for a song from a musician who had decided to divest himself of all his worldly possessions. "It was set up for lefties," she said. And it was in Myrtle Beach that she had learned some guitar chops and become more confident in her playing.

So I was convinced that, unless Gina was making a pilgrimage to Baba's shrine in Islamabad, she would be in Myrtle Beach. I had even made a reservation the week before at a motel within a few blocks of the Center.

Ergo, when I left Jack's comfy condo, I headed straight to Myrtle Beach, right? Wrong. I decided to get my hair done, instead. I mean *really* done, and who better than the hairdresser I had used when I worked in Richmond?

I'm not very stylish, and the number of times I actually used her for more than cutting off split ends was probably close to the number of Robin Hoods I had scored in archery. That's, you know, when you split one arrow with the next. It's pretty hard to use archery for similes because most people just don't get the references and the ambiguity. But there you go. Suffice it to say: only a few.

My hairdresser's name was Pepper. She was in her late twenties, but talked with the experience of somebody who had been molding and shaping hair for twice that long. Whatever you were going through, Pepper understood because she had been through—or was presently going through—the same thing. She listened like a bartender and gave advice like a therapist and, although we weren't exactly friends, we knew each other pretty well.

Pepper's own hairstyle often reflected her moods. Today, she looked kind of punk-pixyish, with short but wild—almost wiry—dark hair highlighted by red streaks on the left side and in the middle. She always dressed neatly, but kind of outré—today she wore green slacks, a heavy-metal t-shirt washed just often enough to look stylish, and her usual low-topped black sneakers. Her look was not quite emo, but she *did* seem to be always depressed about whatever man she was seeing at the time. What I liked most about her were her hands: long, slim, and gentle with unpolished nails manicured short. She was surprised to see me, but was just able to fit me in for her last client of the day. I had to wait decades for her to finish with all the debs and divas preparing for New Year's parties, but I didn't mind. I looked around the familiar room with its yellow walls and its row of occupied chairs. In one corner stood an Xmas tree festooned with brightly colored lights and ornaments. It was homey and I was comfortable waiting there. I also got a chance to look through the fashion mags and determine what I wanted to look like. But when I finally got into the chair, leaned my head back and let Pepper wash a couple days worth of driving from my scalp, I still hadn't a clue.

"I haven't seen you for a long time," Pepper said casually.

"I moved away. To Florida."

"Isn't it hot there?"

"North Florida. But, yeah, it gets hot there."

"Your boyfriend go with you?"

"No. We broke up."

"You sound like me," she said, giving me a last rinse. "What are you doing back, then?"

"Came to see you," I joked.

"Ha ha. That would be a first."

"No, I came back to get some of my stuff from my old apartment, but I wanted to come in here, too. I feel like I'm a different person now and I want to look different."

"I feel that way every day."

"Bullshit, Pepper. You just like to make people think they're better off than you so you'll get a bigger tip. You're good at your job and you're a walking advertisement."

"Yeah, well, I spend a lot of time experimenting on myself."

"Experiment on me," I told her without thinking.

"Say what?"

"I want my hair to look just like yours." Then I added, "But maybe a little more mature. I've got ten years on you and I don't want people to think I'm trying to look younger than I am."

"You sure?"

"Um, yeah. I'm sure."

'It probably won't help you in the man department," she told me.

"Still having trouble with boyfriends?" I asked.

"Is there any other kind of trouble?" she asked.

I flashed back to the instant when I saw Cletus Donnelly running toward Myra with an upraised samurai sword, to interviewing people like Dick Smerk for *Courier* Office Manager, to my mother's death, to . . .

"Except for flat tires, maybe," Pepper mused. "Or trying to make rice pudding. That's bad trouble, there. But men are usually at the top of the list."

"I'm, um, I'm into women now," I told her. I don't know if I shocked her, but I sure surprised myself.

"You mean like a lesbian?" she asked in a voice loud enough for the two women in adjoining chairs to glance over at me. She began combing out my hair—like a groom putting her hands through a silky mane.

"Kind of like that, yeah," I replied. "I have a girlfriend."

"How about that?" she said in a lower voice. "Big reporter like you."

"I'm probably not the only one," I told her. "Besides, I don't work for a big paper any more."

"What do you do?"

"Mostly ride horses."

"Yeah?"

She went silent for a few minutes and I felt her hands becoming even gentler than before. Her fingertips massaged my scalp while her fingers sifted through my hair like a breeze. She was a woman who knew how to use her hands, all right. Then I heard and felt a snip here, another there, and I saw inches of dark strands falling to the floor.

"How is that?" she asked after a while.

"Turn me to the mirror and I'll tell you," I said.

She laughed. "No, not the hair. How is it being with a woman?"

"It's great; like being with a man, but different."

"Smart aleck," she said

"Seriously, it's wonderful," I said. "It's got to be the right person, though."

"I suppose," she answered. "I don't know if I could do it."

"Let me tell you something," I said. "If you ever decide to go that way, your hands are a natural."

"You think?"

"I know."

And when I walked out, just after sundown, I was sporting a look that I never had before—maybe one that nobody ever had before. The hair at the top of my head was short—almost spiky—but soft. Pepper had copied her own pixie look around my ears and neck, but had made it longer on the left side than the right, so that the bang on that side covered my left eye. As the *pièce de résistance*, she had put a white stripe an inch and a half wide starting from the middle of my head down over my left ear. If I had been twenty pounds fatter, or half a dozen years older, it wouldn't have worked. As it was, well, I hoped it would do. I had wanted to look different; now I looked different. Felt different, too.

In the car, I kept looking in the mirror.

I spent that night in a cheap motel at the edge of town, mostly trying to finish the biography of Meher Baba I had purchased from Benny's bookstore. It put me to sleep.

It was plenty cold when I got up the next morning. I turned the heater of the rented car up high and drove toward Interstate 95. It was a route I had traveled dozens of times before on my way to and from Pine Oak to visit my parents during holidays and vacations. But this time there were no parents to go back to; my mother was dead and my father was enjoying a second childhood in Italy. And I wasn't going home. At least not yet.

I drove for a couple of hours before snow started to fall, light at first, but increasing to a semi-flurry—confetti from a hundred marriages at once—but I kept driving, wanting to make Myrtle Beach by noon or so. After that, I didn't know. I wondered how cold it was back in Pine Oak, and hoped that Krista remembered to put blankets on the horses and a little warm water in their feed. I missed them, kind of like I think I would miss my shadow on a sunny day or maybe the way my soul—if people have souls—seemed missing without Gina. One without the other didn't seem right.

The snow and the holiday traffic slowed me up and I didn't arrive at Myrtle Beach until after 2 p.m. Without much fuss, I found and checked in to the fairly expensive Starlight Motel on Highway 17—The King's Highway—in the northern part of the city. The snow was still coming down as I hurried inside the small room, in which the heater was already going full blast. No wonder the rate was so high, but it was considerate. The first thing I did after I brought my things in from the car was to take a long and very refreshing shower, being careful not to ruin my new do. In the steamy mirror I watched myself primp my hair and tease it to where it belonged. The whole thing still looked a little weird, but I was getting used to it.

Three o'clock. I was naked and restless. I picked up the TV remote and put it back down. I opened my suitcase and started taking out clothes. I put most of them back, slipping on a pair of jeans, a blouse, and my fleece barn jacket. Time to go out and find Gina? Evidently not. Instead, I got back in my car and went to the nearest mall. A couple of hours and several hundred credit-card dollars later, I was back in the motel room trying on my new clothes—a heavy cotton skirt with a lot of purple, brown stockings, leather boots reaching almost to my knees, and an ankle-length brown coat. I had to do a double take when I looked in the mirror.

But still I waited. I watched the Weather Channel for a while, browsed the motel literature on the writing table, took a thyroid pill, made myself a cup of coffee; well, more than one. Then I took out my archery case and assembled an old Bear Kodiak takedown. That's another thing I feel naked without—my archery equipment. I always carried at least one bow and half a dozen arrows with me on trips. There were archery ranges everywhere and always opportunities to practice, even in a motel room. I strung the bow and took the points off all the arrows. For a target, I slipped the mattress off the bed and stood it on its edge, leaning against the wall. Then I got an alarm clock from my suitcase—one with a second hand—and put it on a table to my right.

I backed up a few steps and loaded six arrows in the same hand that held the bow. Then I practiced transferring arrows from that hand to my right, positioning and nocking the arrow, then letting it fly—very gently—at the mattress. Over and over: pick the arrow from the bunch, push it between the string and the riser, nock, pull and release. Pick, push, nock, pull, and release. Over and over until my fingers were sore and tired. And, in my new, flashy clothes, what an image I made in the mirror.

When I could release six arrows in fifteen seconds, I was ready to go out hunting.

Chapter 19

Outside, the sky was full of the crazy moon, and it was watching me. I tried to hide by getting in the car and driving to the Baba Center, but when I went through the gate and parked in front of the office, it was still up there. I got out of the car, shivering in the moonlight, and looked around. The Center, what I could l see of it in the early darkness, was clean and well-landscaped, but if you want to know more, you'll have to visit the place yourself. Dickens would probably have described it—and Hardy would still be describing it—but all you really need to know is that I was there.

My education—topped off by my experiences in Iraq— had caused me to distrust spiritual leaders, even one as seemingly beneficent as Meher Baba. But if Gina felt the need to commune with his spirit from time to time, that was fine with me.

I made my way through the few snowflakes still lingering on the blacktop, and knocked on the door of the office. The young man who opened it looked at me and my outfit as if I were ten years younger than I was. But that would still not have been nearly young enough for him. Fresh-faced and shorter than the average, his sandy hair was short and neatly combed. He said apologetically, "I'm afraid we're closed for the day, but if—"

"That's okay," I broke in. "I'm not here for a tour or to sign up for anything. Just looking for someone."

"Someone here at The Center?"

"A woman about my age. but blonde and a little taller. Ginette—Gina—Cartwright."

The boy's face broke into a smile as if I had said something about cookies. "Gina, sure."

"Oh, good," I said. "I was afraid I might have come to the wrong place."

"Are you a friend of hers?" he asked.

"Yeah," I said. "We went to school together in Florida. Do you know where I can find her?"

"Sure. She's at Baba O'Reilly's. I was just on my way over there. I'm Jeff, by the way. I volunteer in the office a couple days a week."

"Sorry," I replied. "My name is Sue-Ann." We shook hands. "What's Baba O'Reilly's?"

"A little bar and restaurant about half a mile west of here. If you'll give me a ride, I'll show you."

"Sounds like a bargain."

Jeff turned out the lights in the office and locked up while I went back to the car and tossed all the empty coffee containers and fast-food packaging into the back. Jeff hopped in and closed the door. "Go out of the parking lot and take a right," he told me, and we were off. On the way, I learned that Gina volunteered at the Center almost every day. She typed donation letters, did filing, made up beds in the rental cabins, raked leaves, whatever had to be done. "Once a week she gives music lessons for kids," Jeff finished. "She's really good with them."

"Guitar lessons?" I asked.

"Right."

"Are you from Myrtle Beach?" I asked.

"Born and raised. At The Center, though, I can pretend I'm somewhere else."

I glanced sidewise and looked at his face. I doubt he had even started to shave yet. "Are you in school?" I asked.

"Yeah. Community college. Basic stuff. My parents went me to go into business, but I don't know, you know?"

"I do know," I laughed.

"This is the place coming up."

I turned in the parking lot that Jeff indicated and found a spot around the side. We got out and walked toward the entrance. A lilt of music came from inside—live music from the sound of it. Country or some kind of country-pop hybrid: an amplified guitar backed by electric bass and drums. Female lead singer. Just the kind of thing that would attract Gina.

Jeff and I walked through the dark, thick, wooden door into another world. The walls were all made of logs and the tables and chairs were rough-cut timber. A fire blazed in a fireplace on one side of the room and glasses clinked over the music. I felt like a traveler in a Walter Scott novel who has ridden all day through the Scottish Highlands and finds, in the thick of a raw storm, an inn with a crackling blaze and the smell of meat and strong ale. As the song ended, I turned to Jeff and asked, "Do you see Gina?"

He looked at me like I was an idiot and pointed toward the stage. I looked. I blinked. Maybe I *was* an idiot. Gina was standing on the stage wearing jeans, short black boots, and a long, ruffly beige sweater. She was also holding that huge, left-handed Gretsch sunburst and looking right at me. I was so surprised that I couldn't even move. What was Gina doing on stage? As far as I knew, Gina had never performed for an audience. For that matter, she had only played for *me* a handful of times. I dropped like a snowball into the nearest chair. Jeff sat down beside me.

"Hey, are you okay?" he asked.

"Oh. Oh, yeah, sure, thanks." I didn't look at him because Gina was speaking into the microphone.

"Listen up everybody," she told the audience. "Ah was plannin ta play that Taylor Swift song everybody was so wahld about a few months back, but somebody special jist came in so ah wanna play her a special tune." Gina was looking straight into my eyes as she spoke. "It was written by a young woman almost 40 years ago. It played on the radio for a few months, but she never got no credit for it. Her name was Maryanne Simmons, and ah'm givin her the credit now." Gina spoke in a whisper to her band, counted out a silent beat, then began picking out a melody with her fingers. The bass and drums joined in a few seconds later, but in a quiet way. Then Gina began to sing in a voice huskier than you would have guessed, and though there was a country tinge to it, she pronounced each word without what I call "the Pine Oak twist."

Pay the moon to stay bright.
Monsters travel at night.
I've got my chains but you've got my light.
I'm not so sure where I am.

Was I born just for breeding?
Was I brought here because I'm bleeding?
Pay the moon to make me smile,
The distance widens every mile
That I'm receding.

So The Creeper had given a copy of the Robin and Marian CD to Gina before he had given one to me. But I knew the song well enough by now to be able to sing along.

When I feel the dying pain?
Will I ever laugh again?
Or spend odd moments walking in the rain?
I'm not so sure I ever will.

I don't know why I'm being tested.
I've been examined and dissected.

Before I reach the danger zone
Take my lead and walk me home
Until I'm rested.

Gina's voice was enough like Maryanne Simmons' that I could actually visualize the tall young, horsey-faced woman on stage, but no way could I visualize her little wimp of a brother. Instead of the orchestration on the record, Gina and her band were spare and raw, and on the choruses, Gina's guitar playing became more active and forceful. More full, strummed chords and an occasional searing lead note that she accentuated by hugging the guitar closer to her and bringing the neck almost vertical and up against the microphone. I was totally amazed. Not only was Gina a really, really good artist, but she had solved part of the mystery that The Creeper was so anxious to solve.

Pay the grass not to grow.
Pay the farmers not to hoe.
I'm trying hard, but I feel so slow.
I'm not sure I'll ever change.

I thought I knew just what I wanted,
So tell me why I feel so haunted.
Pay a shrink to tell me why
I have to live before I die
So disappointed.

The song ended with a lot of bar-chord changes and a soft fadeout. But Gina's eyes did not leave mine throughout the entire song. The audience—and Baba O'Reilly's was pretty packed—broke into applause that put a smile on Gina's face and caused her to look away—finally.

"Thanks," Gina told them. "Y'all are nahce. Maryanne'd think you were nahce, too and if ah ever see her, ah'll tell her. We're takin a break now, but stick around. Ah'm a playin fool an ah still have a few songs ah'd lahk to get your opinions on." Then she set her guitar on a stand and walked down the three steps from the stage to the floor. Then she was walking toward me with no expression at all on her face. I stood up, not knowing what to expect. We were the only ones in the place not sitting, which was weird, and everybody else was looking at us, which was way weirder.

Gina stopped dead in front of me, her arms held akimbo. I held my breath, I mean, I *would* have held it if people really did that. Gina stood there looking at me and I saw her expression soften into a smile. Then she stepped forward, placed a gentle hand behind my head, and kissed me. It was a really good kiss, soft and deep and as full of emotion as the song she had just finished playing. I closed my eyes and heard clapping. Then hooting. "Get a room," someone called out playfully. Gina knew exactly when to break the kiss, although I wouldn't have minded if it had gone on all night.

"Hold that thought, Sue-Ann," she told me, then turned to the crowd of people ogling us. "Y'all go back to your business," she told them loudly, then she turned back to me.

"Umm, nahce duds," she said. "You gotcha a new do, too, huh?"

"Do, um," I managed. "Do you like it?"

""I lahk it a lot, darlin." Then she noticed Jeff for the first time. "Jeffrey," she said. "Kin you git for a little wahle? Ah need to talk to Sue-Ann for a minute before ah finish mah set. Go buy you a Pepsi or somethin."

Jeff scurried away. "Let's sit down, okay?" she said.

"Okay."

"Nahce place, huh?" she said.

"Gina, we just made out in front of a hundred people!"

"Yeah, I guess. It was fun, though, wasn't it?"

"But you've always said . . ."

"We're not in Pine Oak now, Sue-Ann. We can do what we want." She reached across the table and took my hands in hers. "Ya know, ah've been waitin for you to show up," she said.

"How did you know I'd find you?" I asked.

"You're a resourceful gal," she said. "And you know me."

"A lot of people know you and I'm not the only resourceful person in the world."

"Yeah, but you love me."

"You knew that already!" I cried.

Gina looked down at the table and ran her fingers across its rough surface. "Ah wanted to make sure," she said softly.

Before I could reply, Jeff came back to the table with a pitcher of beer. He set it carefully on the table along with two glasses and the words "Compliments of the house." And before either of us could thank him, he had merged back into the dark crowd. A gust of wind blew across the chimney outside causing a puff of smoke to billow out of the fireplace and flit harmlessly up into the rafters.

I pulled my hands away, filled up one of the glasses, and drank half of it down. "So what, this is all a test?" I asked.

Gina looked at her empty glass on the table, then at me. "No, Sue-Ann. It's more than that. Ah caint explain it all raht now, but . . ."

"But what, Gina? Damn it, what am I supposed to—"

But Gina jumped up from the table. "Gotta play," she said.

As if to make me even crazier than I was already, Gina started off the set with a rollicking version of Katy

Perry's "I Kissed a Girl." And, as they say, the crowd went wild. She followed that up with a combination of different kinds of songs, from Patsy Cline's "I Go to Pieces" to Augie Rios' "Donde Esta Santa Claus" to Tracey Chapman's "For My Lover" to Elvis Presley's "Blue Christmas." I finished the pitcher by the time Gina finished playing. I needed it, because despite the cold outside, I was sizzling inside. She had quit her job, left two lovers, and traveled hundreds of miles just as a test? Without a word of explanation, without taking with her any means of communication, without . . .

"That's it for now, folks," Gina told the crowd. "But come back around midnahht when we'll celebrate the New Year with a few new songs. "Don't drink and drahve and you'll get home alahve." I watched her put her guitar in its case and flip the catches to the lock position while she said a few words to the bass player and drummer. Then, carrying the case, she threaded the other tables until she came to mine.

I stood up to meet her. "You have a lot of fucking nerve—" I began, but Gina took me firmly by the arm and led me out the door. It wasn't until we reached her PT Cruiser that I managed to shake her off. "Let go of me," I shouted. "You're a monster."

Gina shoved the guitar into the back and opened the passenger door. "Git in, Sue-Ann," she said.

"Forget it," I said, getting in. "I'm not going anywhere with you." She shut the door in my face and got in the driver's side and started the car. While it was idling, she looked at me and asked, "Where you stayin?"

"Starlight," I said grudgingly. "It's—"

"Ah know where it is," she said, looking straight ahead. I turned and looked out the window, although I have no idea what I saw out there. Neither of us spoke a word until I had slid the plastic key to open the motel door and Gina stashed her guitar case against the wall.

Then she stood in the middle of the room and faced me, her hands on her hips again.

"Okay, Sue-Ann. Give it to me. Ah probly deserve it. Come on, bring it on."

But all I could do was sink into the room's only chair and start crying. I cried and cried without saying anything and only when I looked up a few minutes later did I notice that Gina was sitting at my feet, her own feet curled up under her.

"What's that all about?" she asked gently.

I said the first thing that came into my head. "I found you," I said. "I didn't know . . . I mean, I wasn't sure . . ." Then I gave myself a mental shake. "But you left me!" I said. "And I'm drunk. And you're this big singing star now and you won't want to know me anymore. And this cretin shot me in the side with a crossbow and I almost died and you weren't there. And I've had to feed and put the blankets on the horses all by myself. And I have Post-Traumatic Stress Disorder."

"Wah don't we take them one at a tahme," Gina said. She hadn't moved from her position on the rug. The heater was still blowing big time so I stood up shakily and took off my new coat. Then I sat back down and closed my eyes. I felt Gina gently taking off my boots. "Look, Sue-Ann. Ah wanted to go to Iowa with you, ah did. Ah wanted it more'n anything, but ah had a duty to Cal to trah an run things whahle he was gone."

"I understood that . . . "

"But ah told you once that ah couldn't choose between the two a you, an ah had."

"You didn't have a choice, Gina. I don't understand what you're trying to say."

'Ah'm trahin to say that when ah decided to stay in Pine Oak, ah did it even though ah didn't want to—because Cal was mah boss, not because he was mah friend. Ah resented it every minute. Ah had made a decision, see? Ah had chosen *you*, and it scared the pants offa me."

"Me?"

"Raht. From the second ah said ah'd run his damn paper for a week, ah knew that ah was never gonna be in his bed again. It was suddenly as clear as sittin on a tack that it was you I wanted to be with. But Sue-Ann, that was a hellava realization. Ah was this beauty queen who useta be proud of the fact that ah had every man in Jasper County sniffin after me like tomcats and suddenly ah'm a lesbian. What was ah gonna tell Cal? Ah brooded about it for days, but in the end ah just wimped out an disappeared. Ah needed tahm to think."

"You didn't even leave me a message," I said softly. "You left Cal a message, but you didn't leave me one."

"Ah did, though." She was massaging my feet through my stockings.

I thought. "What, you mean that little throbbing heart thingy? That could have meant anything."

"No it couldn't, darlin. And ah didn't send one to Cal."

"Um," I began. "I had the same realization you did."

"Hmm?"

"I just came from Richmond. I broke it off with Jack for good and all."

"For me?"

"For you, but now you've become this singing sensation who's never going to want to come back to a bullshit little town like Pine Oak, even though you hardly ever played for me despite my begging you to scads of times and—"

"But that's another thing ah wanted to tell you. Seems lahk every minute ah wasn't either with you or Cal or The Creeper, ah was home playin music. And singin music and listenin to music and learning about music. At first ah thought it was just somethin to take mah mind off things, but then it hit me that ah loved it. An one day ah realized that ah could play and sing good—ah mean really good. So ah decided to go after it. But ah had to be bah mahself for awahle. Ah didn't wanna play in front of you unless ah was pretty sure ah wouldn't embarrass mahself."

"What, you'll embarrass yourself in front of an audience, but not in front of me?"

"That's raht, Sue-Ann. Ah would. And ah did lotsa tahms. But ah didn't tonaht. Least ah don't think ah did."

"You were wonderful," I told her. "And you even played that Robin and Marian song."

She smiled. "Ah wasn't sure ah had that one under mah fingers yet, but it came out okay." She let go of one foot and took up the other.

"And you figured out that it was Maryanne who wrote it and not her brother."

"Yeah. It's a girl's song. It's about goin crazy, ya know. And that lahn about "take my lead and walk me home;" that's a horse reference. Mickey wouldn't a come up with that lahn in a million years. Did The Creeper tell you that he met Maryanne and gave her rahding lessons?"

"Yeah. He told me to find her. Almost the same day that Cal told me to find you."

Gina dropped my foot and stood up. "Is that whah you came lookin?"

"I . . ." I began. Then stopped. "What if it was?"

Gina smiled. "Fuck you, Sue-Ann. You came for me because you love me and that's that. If you didn't, you'd a stayed put and jumped in Cal's bed lahk a rabbit."

"It never occurred to me," I answered.

"An did you fahnd Maryanne?"

"Not yet. First things first."

Gina walked the few steps to where I was standing and began to unbutton my blouse.

“What are you doing?” I squirmed.

“We gotta git you outta these new clothes,” she said.

“You’re funny,” I said, but stood there on my not-too-steady legs.

“An you’re cute.”

“I think I’m too drunk to make love,” I told her.

But I was wrong.

And when we found ourselves standing outside Baba O’Reilly’s for Gina’s midnight performance, she was dressed in a heavy cotton skirt with a lot of purple, brown stockings, leather boots reaching almost to her knees, and an ankle-length brown coat. I had on Gina’s jeans, black boots, and roomy gray sweater. And the full moon cast its light down and around us and I felt warm and cozy amid the drifting snowflakes. I looked at the moon, then at Gina’s face.

“I’m crazy about you,” I said.

Chapter 20

I stayed in Myrtle Beach for two more days, spending most of my time with Gina. It wasn't all pleasant. For one thing, she refused to come back to Pine Oak with me. After her midnight set at Baba O'Reilly's, which I enjoyed more than I can possibly describe—and did it on diet Pepsis instead of beer this time—we were camped snugly back in my motel room, heat on halfway and nestled under sheets and comforters.

"Caint, baby. Ah don't have it in me to say no to Cal if he asks me to do this or that. Ah've always had trouble sayin no to anybody."

"You don't seem to be hav[illegible]ing any trouble saying it to me," I remarked.

"And [illegible]cause ah can be honest with you. Besahdes, [illegible] ah'm raht. Ah'm doin okay with mah music now and I need to pursue it, at least for a little wahle. If ah came back now everythin would be the same, cept ah wouldn't have a job. Ah'd have to wait tables with Linda C or somethin. The two of us'd be havin to sneak around to see each other again and be freakin out if anybody ever saw us together."

I had a retort on the tip of my tongue, but then a thought hit me. Cletus Donnelly. "Oh, shit, Gina. I haven't told you yet. Someone *did* see us. Cletus. He saw us that night we were at Cypress Lake Lodge together."

I had already told her the story of some of my adventures with Cletus Donnelly (when someone is tonguing their way down your naked body, it is kind of hard to miss a not-quite-completely healed, star-shaped wound on your side), but I had not gotten around to telling her that he had seen us.

"That was our first naht together."

"And probably the best night of my life," I told her. "Although this one is pretty good, too. But evidently Cletus was working at the Lodge doing some flunky work and saw us go in together or go out in that canoe or something. Maybe he was even peeping in the window at us, I don't know. I just know that he told Joey Bickley that we were, you know, intimate."

"Joey Bickley's not gonna believe somethin a crazy man says. An he was there both times Cletus attacked you."

"He was at Cletus' house, but not at mine."

"No, ah mean both times that first night."

"Well, yeah. He did shoot at me, but when he ran out of the house he came at Joey, not me."

"The way you described it, Sue-Ann. You and Dilly were standin raht behahnd Joey when Cletus ran out."

"Yeah, but we ducked behind the police car."

"Didn't it ever occur to you, Sue-Ann, that he was [illegible] oey just got in the way?"

[illegible] y would he single me out?"

[illegible] out when he called you on the [illegible] e shot with that crossbow. And it [illegible] came to after he broke out of Wakoville. Of course he was comin at you."

"Fuck," I breathed. "I think you're right. But why? What does he have against me?"

"Maht be just one of those obsessions, Sue-Ann. Like the guy that shot John Lennon or the one that was [illegible] You're about the most famous per- [illegible] Olympic archery team, world-class [illegible] -Ann, everybody in Pine Oak has [illegible] man's just not raht. Ah wouldn't [illegible] ll he has is the wild story of a crazy man, and if ah'm your girlfriend, whah did ah leave town?"

"I'm still having trouble with that one, myself, Gina, but I guess you're right about Joey. But he also thinks that there's something suspicious about how Cletus drove himself to the police station without leaving his prints on the vehicle. And the blood trail that led toward Torrington instead of out to the street." I paused and took a breath. "And there's something else . . ."

"Um?"

"Joey's been coming on to me. At first it was a bunch of flowers when I was in the hospital, but then he followed me across town. As much as accused me of being a lesbian because I wouldn't have dinner with him. If it hadn't been for Clarence pretending he was my boyfriend, things could have gotten really ugly. Shit, Gina, it was ugly already and it could get worse."

Gina stared across the room for a few seconds with a pensive look on her face. In the mirror, I saw her eyes harden. Then she took my hand and squeezed it. "Some day ah'm gonna haveta have a talk with that man," she said. "Does Ashley know about Joey?"

"I told Krista to warn him."

"Good, but better talk to him yourself when you get back. Now let's go to sleep."

Gina had gigs on both of the next nights, which were Friday and Saturday, but we spent a lot of those two days dressed warmly, walking through Myrtle Beach—both in the downtown area and actually on the beach, although it was windier there. Strolling in the sand, sometimes holding hands, sometimes picking up whatever shells might have been washed up on the tide, I thought of Mickey Simmons.

"The beach," I said.

"The beach?"

"That's when I first suspected that there was something strange about that Robin and Marian album. Some of the songs were about California, like that one he called "Pismo Beach." But Billy Carothers told me that Mickey had never been to California. He was just making up fantasies. But "Pay the Moon" is very emotional. Maryanne wrote that song; we both know she did."

"An she let her brother put his name on it."

"She must have loved him a lot," I said. "But all he had to say about her later is that she ruined his career."

"Ah expect that the record company wanted more songs lahk "Pay the Moon," but there weren't any. Mickey couldn't admit to anybody that he hadn't written it or they would've dumped him and wanted Maryanne to go solo. That sound about raht?"

"Right as a razor and just as sharp," I smiled. "That's why he wouldn't talk about his sister to Billy. She had ruined his career by being the only really good thing about his music."

"Ah hope you can fahnd her."

"I *will* find her," I said firmly, but I was not as confident as I tried to sound.

~ ~ ~

I arrived back in Pine Oak to find Krista sleeping in my bed again, which was kind of a surprise since I had called her the night before and told her I would be home that morning to feed. The covers were pulled up to her neck and she didn't stir when I walked into the bedroom and put down my suitcase. It was about 7 a.m. and I had driven all night to get home and was about to fall out. I noticed that my answering machine light was flashing so, tired or not, I instinctively pushed the playback button and plopped myself on the edge of the bed to listen. There were three messages. The first was from Myra, telling me that she needed to see me as soon as I got in.

The second was Cal, asking if I had any news for him. "Oh, right, I almost forgot," his message continued. "That weird guy from the bookstore came in this morning looking for you. No idea what he wanted. He just hemmed and hawed for a while and left. So I guess you should call him. Call me, too." The third message was from Smokey asking if I had seen Krista.

In fact, I was seeing more of Krista than I had ever expected to see, because as I was listening to Smokey's voice she got up out of the bed and stood between me and the doorway, starkers. "Hey," she said. "You just get back?" She yawned and stretched her arms over her head, showing me short tufts of blonde hair spriging her armpits. "I've been waiting for you," she smiled. Her breasts were large for a smallish young woman, and her nipples were erect in the chilly room. She kept her arms stretched upwards, fluffing out her unruly hair. My first impulse was to . . . but I'm not going to tell you what I was thinking right then. I'll just tell you what I said.

"You need to put some clothes on, Krista."

"Really?" she said. I saw her eyes, her mouth, her whole body language relaxing into disappointment.

"Now." I said.

I busied myself in the kitchen making coffee and breakfast for both of us—scrambled eggs, sausage, toast and butter. When Krista came into the kitchen—fully dressed this time, she had a hangdog look. She sat down at the kitchen table and said, "I guess you must think I'm disgusting."

"You're a beautiful young woman, Krista. I can't imagine anyone not wanting to jump your bones. Man or woman."

"Then why . . .?"

"I'm not into women, Krista. I'm into Gina. You're not Gina, ergo . . ."

"I guess. But if you didn't have Gina?"

"I do have her. And damn it, Krista. I'm almost forty years old. Twice your age. I've made a lot of mistakes in my life. I'll probably make a lot more, but one that I'm not going to make is to jeopardize my relationship with Gina to let you have a little experiment. Sex is not the same thing as love, although sex is good. Real good sometimes, I'll admit." I filled a plate and set it in front of her. "Here, eat all this stuff while it's still warm."

Krista took a bite of toast. Her hair was still flyaway, but for some reason that always looked good on her.

I glanced at her, then looked away when I saw how she was looking at me. I could have buttered my toast with the sexual tension in that room. Suddenly I started giggling—something that's almost impossible to believe—I mean, giggling was Krista's thing, not mine—but it couldn't be described as anything else.

"You're laughing at me, now?" Krista asked. "I'll just go." She didn't make any attempt to get up, though.

"No, no. I just had a silly thought."

"What?"

"I have a hairdresser—well, I used to have a hairdresser when I lived in Richmond. I saw her about a week ago when I was picking up some stuff from my old apartment." I remembered my new hairdo, seaweedy now with two days of heavy driving, and ran my hands over my head. "She did this for me, but it looked better then."

"I think it's gorgeous. I think *you're* gorgeous."

"And I think *you're* just horny," I told her. "But I want to tell you about my hairdresser."

"Kind of like making me take a cold shower, right?"

"No, Krista. Pepper is—that's my hairdresser's name –Pepper is hot."

"Ha ha."

"Sorry about that. Pepper is thin and looks like a cute but depressed pixie. Late twenties, maybe. Mod hair and clothes but she never seems to be able to meet any really nice guys."

"Tell me about it." Krista, after a slow start, was wolfing down her breakfast like, well, like a wolf. Gradually, we were relaxing back into a semblance of our normal relationship and I could start breathing easier.

"When I was in her chair the other day, I told her about my relationship with Gina. She's the first person I ever talked to about that—which let me know a lot about my own feelings. And you know what; she reacted just about the way you're reacting."

"She took off her clothes?" Krista sipped coffee with cream and sugar.

I laughed. "No, it wasn't anything overt. She just got really curious."

"You mean you could have picked her up or something?"

"Or something. Maybe, who knows?"

"Do you, like, have her business card?"

"Business card? What are you going to do, drive over 600 miles to Richmond and ask out someone you've never even seen because I'm vain enough to think Pepper might have . . ." I waved the idea away with my hand and turned my attention to my own breakfast.

"Maybe," she said eagerly. "Do you have a picture of her?"

"Now why would I—" But I stopped, realizing that Pepper's picture was actually part of her business card, which I had carried in my wallet for years. I got up, went through my purse and finally extracted it from the mess. I slid it near Krista's empty plate. "Fuck it, Krista," I said. "Do what you want."

Krista picked up the card and stared at it for almost a minute. "She is kinda cute, isn't she?" she said. "I'm keeping the card."

"I hope the two of you live happily ever after," I joked.

"Well, you know, Sue-Ann," Krista said in an entirely new tone of voice, "I'm not sure I'm ready to marry her quite yet."

We both laughed. And it was that easy. As soon as I had given her Pepper's card, it was like it was before between Krista and me. Together we went outside and fed the horses, broke the ice on their water trough, and did general barn duty. When Krista trotted off back toward Torrington, I took a short nap (I was convinced I could still feel the heat from Krista's skin on the sheets and blanket), took a long shower (but not a cold one), and called Myra. In her message, she had given me her work number in case I called on a workday, so I assumed that something was up.

A secretary picked up and transferred me to Myra's office. "Block 12, Myra Van Hesse speaking."

"Hey Myra. It's Sue-Anne."

"Sue-Ann. My land, girl, where you been? I been callin you for days."

"Taking care of some business out of town, Myra," I replied. "What's up? Have you got some more information on Cletus Donnelly?"

"Some. I found out something else, too. But I just got out of a staff meeting and it'll take me a few minutes to get my notes together. Can I call you back?"

I looked at the clock on my nightstand; it was already after noon. "Would it be all right if I drove out there?"

"To the hospital? You're forty-five minutes away."

"I need to clear my head. And I've always wanted to see where you work." I didn't tell her that I hoped I could wrangle a way to see Cletus as well.

"I'll be happy to see you, Sue-Ann."

She gave me the directions and I got back in the rental car and drove east. My encounter with Krista, weird as it was, made me feel a lot younger and prettier than I actually was. It made me feel, in some redounding way, that my relationship with Gina was actually getting stronger, even though I hadn't been able to convince her to leave Myrtle Beach. Not yet, anyway.

By driving to Waxahatchee, I was also putting off Cal and Benny for the moment. I knew I had to see Cal eventually—soon even—but I had news for him that he wouldn't like. And I assumed that poor Benny wanted to see if I had written the review of his play. The longer I could avoid that, the happier I'd be.

The Waxahatchee Regional Mental Health Facility was spread out on a hill just across the eastern fork of the Okachokeme River. The entrance was well landscaped and colorful—even in the dead of winter—and as I drove through I could see a dozen separate red-brick buildings looking a lot like Monopoly hotels, arranged on invisible radians, each pointing toward a larger white building that I assumed housed the hospital administration. The streets were winding and narrow and I soon got lost, despite Myra's fairly explicit directions. I spotted a white van parked at the side of the road with several men in blue work uniforms getting into it. I rolled down my window and drove up next to the driver's side of the van, where a man in street clothes was speaking into a walkie talkie.

"Thirty Seven to Dubya Arr Dispatch," he said. The squawked reply that issued back from his unit sounded like barn fowl to me, but he must have understood it because he pressed the his talk button and replied, "Dispatch, ah have six ten-fifteens ten fifty-one to Block 22" The man, who was in his early thirties and wore a John Deere cap, looked at me as he clipped his radio to his belt. "What can I help you with, ma'am?" he asked. "You lost?"

"Yeah, I guess I am," I smiled. "I'm looking for, um, Block 12. Myra Van Hesse."

"Ten-four. Miz Van Hesse is on the ground floor in that building raht over there." He pointed east, beyond what looked like a water treatment plant. "You see that building yonder with the two big pines in front? Raht past the hortitherapy greenhouse? Well, that's it. They'll be a big sign out front that says Block 12."

"Thanks, I really appreciate that," I said. From the inside of the van, several pairs of eyes stared out at me.

The road to Myra's building led me in kind of a curlicue past a fire station, a water tower, and several buildings similar to the one the man had pointed out. Despite a temperature in the 40s, it was sunny and there were a handful of people walking along the sidewalks or lounging in the entranceways. I saw a black man with a long beard stepping along and swinging his arms like two broken windmills that couldn't quite make a full circle. Another man was wearing only cut-off shorts, a t-shirt, and leather sandals. His hair was long and spiky. Another—man or woman I wasn't sure—slouched along bent over, head covered by a thick, dark hood. I found a parking lot next to Myra's building and walked toward Block 12. There was no security, but that didn't mean I could just walk in without any scrutiny. As I made my way through the automatic door, a dozen eyes turned my way. I was in a foyer with a nicely patterned carpet and sturdy and attractively upholstered chairs. In some of these chairs sat half a dozen patients and a large black woman with a hospital badge on the shirt of her scrubs. I tried not to stare, but couldn't help seeing that one of the patients, who was wearing pajamas, was sitting in a chair with his head cocked almost straight down, as if he were a dodo trying to burrow into his own chest. Another patient wore a crash helmet; a third wore thick dirty-white mittens. As I passed, their heads followed my progress like plants bending toward the sun.

Myra's office was located at the end of the foyer and to the left of an elevator. A patient was speaking into a wall telephone nearby and, as I knocked at Myra's door, I heard him croaking nonstop in a hoarse but hyper voice. I could make out: " . . . and all the walls should be made out of Styrofoam. Right. Don't tell me my business, man, I've got forty thousand dollars riding on this—don't fucking interrupt when I'm . . ." But Myra opened the door and that was the last word I heard. I walked in and Myra welcomed me with a smile. "Sit down, Sue-Ann," she said while she closed the door again and made sure it was secure. It was a small office that gave the appearance of being larger by its particular feng shui. In addition to the smallish desk, there were two visitor chairs; two beige, four-drawer filing cabinets; a computer desk; and a knickknack cabinet filled with equine figures. A couple of photos were hung on the walls—one of Myra's husband Phil and another of Myra in her younger days competing in a saddlebred show. "You have to lock your doors?" I asked.

"Some of the other Ward Block Supervisors had some trouble with residents walking in their offices and either breaking their computers or their heads, so we had new locks installed that keep everyone out that doesn't have a key. And I'm the only one with a key to this door. Myra seated herself behind her desk. I noticed that her chair had a heating pad for her back attached with Velcro straps, and she settled into it with a sigh.

"Thanks for coming out, I would have had to mail—Gosh sakes, Sue-Ann, ah *love* your new hairstyle—did you get it done around here or did you have to go to Tallahassee?"

"I had it done in Virginia last week when I went back to pick up the rest of my things."

"So that's where you were?"

I nodded, but I couldn't keep back my curiosity. "Myra," I began. "Do the patients do work around the hospital? I saw some men in blue uniforms outside when I was coming in and I was wondering if you had some kind of a halfway program for patients that have, you know, been cured."

"I won't say that we don't cure people here, Sue-Ann, I won't. But most of our residents are crazy as rats in a can. I spect that those workers you saw were convicts from the prison down the river—inmates. The hospital contracts a couple of hundred to come in and do most of the landscaping, painting, and whatnot. But they're all in for nonviolent offences. We have a lot more trouble with the residents than with the inmates."

"Is that guy I saw at the telephone a . . . a resident? He was talking to his broker or somebody."

"He was talking to the inside of his own skull, Sue-Ann. I've seen him talking on that phone a hundred times and to a hundred different people, but I've never seen him dial it even once. Those other residents in the foyer there aren't as hyper, but I doubt they'll be going anywhere soon either."

"What's with the crash helmets and the mittens?" I asked.

"The crash helmet is for people that tend to have seizures—sometimes their medication will cure that and sometimes it will cause it. The mittens are for biters."

"Biters?"

"That's people that want to eat themselves. They'll start with their fingernails, then the ends of their fingers, and then onward. Some of em have to wear those mittens on their feet, too. There are a million stories at this hospital, Sue-Ann, and every one of em's different. But I've got some news about the ones you're interested in."

"Cletus Donnelly?" I asked.

"Cletus is still in the forensics block, but he's in isolation because he keeps trying to kickbox with other residents or give them karate chops. There are some big bruisers in that block, Sue-Ann, that will tear him to pieces if he tries that stuff on them. But he's medicated now and the wound in his arm is getting better every day."

"Can you access his files?"

"You mean the sessions with his psychos and so forth?"

I nodded. "Anything like that, yes."

"Ah've been here over thirty years now, Sue-Ann, and I've learned how to do just about everything. Trouble is, those files are confidential and if anyone tries to view them—not just me, but even the person who wrote them—a red light shows up in the administration office. Same happens if you try to see how much money the Chief Psychologist or the Head Dentist makes. I can do it if you want, but I'm not sure what you're looking for and even more important, I'm not even sure that his doctor has written up all his notes and put them on a computer file yet. So I'd be investigated for nothing."

"Let's not worry about it then," I told her. "The last thing I want is to get you in trouble." Then I added hopefully, "Maybe I can get in to see him."

"When he gets out of isolation and goes through a boatload of therapy, I can help you with that. But it will take awhile." As Myra spoke, she extracted a file from a locked desk drawer and placed it in front of her on the desk.

I let out my breath slowly. I would either have to wait or figure out another angle.

"In the meantime, Sue-Ann," said Myra, sliding the file folder across the desk, "you might be interested in this."

I opened the folder and saw a few pages of computer printout. I glanced at them as Myra explained.

"I started searching through the records for the woman you told me about—Maryanne Simmons, but I didn't come up with anything under that name. I tried looking through all people named Simmons from 1970 or so and on up and I had more luck. Back in the early eighties—only a few years after I came to the hospital—there *was* a Simmons admitted. In fact, there were three, but one was a black man and the other was a woman in her seventies who only stayed a month or two. But I found a Michael Simmons who would have been about the right age and I made a copy of his file. That's what I just gave you and you can take it with you if you want."

"It's Mickey!" I said excitedly. "That's Maryanne's brother."

"Now in the wards, Sue-Ann, only a few people know our residents' last names. We would have known him as Michael S. And you know what, Sue-Ann? I remember Michael because he was in this building."

"Really?"

"I was only a Senior Clerk in Transportation when he was admitted, but when I finally made WBS and came to Block 12, Michael was still here. I think it was 1995. Michael was probably only in his late forties, but he looked a lot older. He was small and scrawny and had real thin hair that he let grow down past his shoulders. He was one of our most popular residents, Sue-Ann. He didn't say much, but a lot of the time, if there weren't too many people around, he would start singing. He didn't have a great voice, I guess, but the songs he sang were as sweet as could be. He told me—well, he told everybody—that he was a big singing star once, but when one of the music therapists tried to get him to go to the music room where they have guitars and keyboards and drums and such, he about had a hissy fit. Wouldn't go. Wouldn't sit in the dayroom when she came in with her guitar and had singalongs with the residents. No, not Michael." Myra smiled at her recollections.

"So I guess he's gone by now, huh?" I asked.

"He died in 1997, Sue-Ann. Heart failure. He's buried right here on campus in the hospital cemetery."

"So no one claimed his body?" I asked.

"Someone did," Myra recalled. "A tall woman. I had seen her a couple of times before when she came to visit. And here's a weird thing: she told us that he should be buried here—it was where he had lived a lot of his life and where all of his friends were. She told me that it's what *he* wanted, too. They had talked about it."

"Do you know the woman's name?" I asked.

"It's there on the last page of the file."

I turned to the back of the folder. On the line after Next of Kin was written the name Maryanne Marshall. And there was a Tallahassee address.

Chapter 21

Myra had done her work well; now I had to do mine. I knew I had to go in to *The Courier* office, but I didn't want to. And Waxahatchee was halfway between Pine Oak and Tallahassee. I chose Tallahassee. Cal and Benny would have to wait a bit longer.

Myra had Googled the address on her computer before I left, so it was an easy trip along I-10 to Exit 203, then right onto Thomasville Road. My watch read 4:30 as I approached the residential section where Maryanne lived. A little too early; if she was a working woman, she probably wouldn't be home yet. At the same time I didn't want to arrive unannounced after dark, so I spent a half hour in a nearby McDonald's eating a fish sandwich, quaffing cup after cup of coffee, and going over the file that Myra h [illegible] lot of it was technical, but essentially it b[illegible] [illegible]aryanne had told Ashley Torrington bac[illegible] [illegible]ckey had a type of hereditary schizophre[illegible] [illegible]y that was more common in days gone [illegible] [illegible]ugs, like Zoloft and its ilk, could give 21st Century sufferers a normal life; I mean, except for having to take a pill every day. But you didn't have to be schizophrenic to have to rely on your daily little pellet; you could have your thyroid irradiated, for instance. There was no mystery about Mickey's death. Halfway through smoking a cigarette (Myra told me he had been a heavy smoker all his life) in the garden behind Block 12, he had had a seizure and dropped dead on the spot. It took no real thinking to realize that his sister had gotten married and taken the name Marshall.

Like most of its neighbors on the block, the Marshall house was constructed of red brick with shingle roofing. These small houses were crammed onto small lots. They were solidly constructed, but without any attempt at artistry. Small-family houses—two or three bedrooms and a single bath was what I guessed. Maryanne's house, with a tiny lawn, a boxwood hedge across the front, and a pine tree between it and its neighbor, looked cozy. There was a car in the driveway, so I parked on the street, walked up the sidewalk and rang the doorbell. Expecting for some odd reason that the door would be opened by a tall, horsey-faced, white-haired lady in her sixties, I was taken aback when a thin, gray-haired man peered at me across the threshold. He had a mild face under his thin hair, but looked at me warily, like I was some kind of living spam.

"I'm not selling anything," I hastened to reassure him. "In fact, I'm not even sure I'm at the right house. I'm a writer and I'm looking for a woman named Maryanne Simmons."

"Maryanne?" His eyes softened. "Why, that's my wife. But I'm sorry to say she died more than two years ago. I'm alone here now."

"I'm so sorry," I said. And I was; not only because I was too late, but because this man so obviously missed her. "You're Mr. Marshall, then?" I asked.

"Jim Marshall, yes."

"Mr. Marshall, I'm sorry I didn't call ahead, but I was in the area and I thought I would just drop by in the hope that . . . do you mind if I asked you a few questions about her?"

"About Mary? I would like nothing better, but. . . . But forgive me, come in and sit down. Can I get you something to drink, some coffee maybe?"

"No thank you, I just had something." I never thought I would refuse an offer of coffee, but there you are. And I'm lucky I had used the bathroom at McDonald's before I left. I sat down on one of two matching recliners set in the middle of the room facing a TV set. The chair had obviously been Maryanne's and I felt very strange sitting in it, feeling the contours her body had made in it over the years. The room was small and spare—the room of a couple who spent most of their time alone with each other. A third person in the room would have been one too many. There was a couch against the wall, but it looked unused. Two coffee tables—one to the side of each chair—had probably been used for just that, coffee. There were no books or magazines anywhere. Two photographs, in plain but neat frames, adorned the otherwise bare walls. One was a picture of Maryanne and her brother in their younger days. It was a casual shot of the two of them laughing at something off camera, none of the sternness I had glimpsed in other pictures of Maryanne, and none of Mickey's snobbish pique. The other picture showed Maryanne and her husband together. Jim looked only a bit younger in the picture than he did in person. Maryanne herself looked the picture of a loving wife. Her hair was still light, her face still long. What beauty she had when she was twenty had all but faded, but what had taken its place was a look of contentment.

"Mr. Marshall," I began.

"Call me Jim if you'd like to," he said, turning his chair slightly so that we were face to face.

"All right, thank you. I guess you're wondering why I'm here."

"To tell the truth Ms . . ."

"Sue-Ann," I said.

"To tell the truth I can't imagine what would interest you about Mary. We lived such a quiet life here."

"I'm interested in her music," I said.

"Her music? She didn't . . . but that was so many years ago! She made a record with her brother, you know."

"I've listened to that record dozens of times," I told him, smiling.

"But that was long before she met me."

"When *did* you meet, if you don't mind my asking?" I asked.

"Well, it must have been about 1977 or so. We were both working in the same real estate office. We got to know each other pretty well after a while, and we decided to get married the next year. It wasn't long after that when we decided to start our own business and it worked out pretty well."

"My mother was a real estate agent," I told him. "In Pine Oak."

"Is that in Florida?" he asked.

"Just this side of Forester," I told him.

"Aha."

I did a quick mental calculation. "So when you met her, Maryanne was close to thirty years old."

"That's right."

"What had she been doing before that, do you know?"

"Oh yes. She liked to talk about it sometimes. Especially after her brother died. But do you mind if I get myself a glass of beer while I talk?"

"Please."

"And can I get you one?"

"I'd love to join you," I told him.

He came back with two foaming glasses and handed me one. Sitting down, he took several large swallows and when he put his glass on his coffee table, it was half empty. "Mary always told me that I guzzled beer," he said. "She drank slower, but we always ended up at the same place in the end."

I smiled and saluted him with my glass.

"Mary's brother was two years younger than she was. His name was Michael, but everyone called him Mickey. When they were teenagers in Pensacola, Mickey started listening to all the folksingers that were popular back then—Joan Baez and Bob Dylan and all the rest. He got himself a guitar somewhere and started writing songs. He asked Mary to sing harmony."

"And she was really good at it," I said.

"Yes, she was, but, you know, Mary had years of piano lessons when she was a girl and wanted to play on the songs, but Mickey wouldn't have it. He said no folksingers used the piano. So she used to practice in secret, and she even learned a few guitar chords."

"She wrote one of the songs on that album didn't she? And she let Mickey take credit for it."

"So you've figured that out, have you. Ha. You're a bright young woman. But it was Mickey that had the drive and the ambition to be famous. He found them some jobs playing in bars and coffeehouses around North Florida. Then they went to New York and actually got a record deal. Mickey stayed in a hotel room all day writing songs while Mary waited tables to pay the bills. For someone like me, who's never done anything exciting or gone anywhere very interesting, this would have been fascinating, but to Mary, it was just, you know, another day at the office. She wasn't obsessed with music or fame or anything like that. What she wanted was to be with her brother and help him achieve his dreams. She believed in him. She always believed in him."

Jim Marshall took a small gulp of his beer and collected his thoughts. "Well, they managed to get a record deal, but it was mostly because of that song of Mary's—and because her voice was so much more pronounced in that one. It got some airplay—even *I* heard it on the radio one day. But the album went nowhere and their label dropped them. Mickey got depressed then, started to get a little crazy, but Mary wouldn't let him give up. She wrote a couple more songs and told him he could have them; you know, to take to the studio and try to get another record deal."

I perked up in my chair. "She wrote other songs?" I asked.

"Yes she did. I have them on tape along with a couple of practice sessions she did. Would you like to hear them?"

"Are you kidding? I would love to hear them!"

"Mary kept the tapes for all these years in a small box up in our closet. I don't think she ever listened to them, but when she died, I took down that little box and I've listened to the tapes many times. I never actually heard her play or sing in person. She gave all that up, as I said, before she met me."

"But what happened in New York?" I asked. "Did they ever make any more records?"

"No, I don't think so. What happened is that Mary met a man somewhere—another musician—and went to California with him. Mickey went back to Pensacola and lived on any little jobs he could find. I guess he was still writing songs and hoping to make a comeback, but his health was poor."

"He had a hereditary mental illness," I said.

"You know more than you let on," Jim Marshall said, surprised. "But you're right. He managed to function longer than you would think—more than ten years—but he was finally committed."

"I found that out earlier today," I told him. That's how I located you, in fact. Maryanne's name was listed as next of kin." I hesitated, then threw out the words, "I have a friend who knew Maryanne and Mickey just before they went to New York. Even then, Maryanne was afraid that she had a hereditary mental illness."

"It ran in her family, yes. She told me that her grandfather died in a mental hospital and that her dad was crazy, too. Maryanne always thought she would get some form of it, but she never did. Instead, it was her brother that . . . but that's the reason she left from California. The guy she was with turned out to be heavily into Scientology. She hung out with those kinds of people for several years, but I don't think she never really believed in any of it. She was playing music again, though, and that was a good thing. Then the man she was with wanted to have children, but because of her family history, she said no and I don't think he reacted well. I gathered that she was pretty unhappy for the last year or so she was in California, so when Mickey was committed, she ran off and came back to Florida. Put herself through real estate school and got that job where we met."

"So the two of you never had children either?"

"No. I never really wanted to be a father. Sometimes I wish I had a son or daughter to talk to, but not often. I do wish that I had Maryanne back again, though."

"Did you ever meet Mickey?" I asked.

"Once. I went with her to see him in Waxahatchee, but I could tell he didn't want anything to do with me. To tell the truth, I had already formed a bad opinion about him from the stories Mary used to tell. But to her, he could do no wrong. According to her, you see, he didn't actually steal her song, she gave it to him gladly. He was moody because he was a genius and aren't all geniuses moody sometimes? He was antisocial because his mind was fixed on higher things."

"I get the picture."

"He didn't talk to her much. Never called on the phone and even when she visited him in the hospital, which was every month or two, he mostly just sat there and stared out at the trees or bushes or whatever was in front of him. She seemed to think that her presence there was comforting to him, though, so she kept going."

Jim Marshall finished his beer and sat back in his chair. "Would you like to hear one of the tapes now?" he asked. "I mean, if you're not in a hurry . . ."

"I'm not going anywhere," I said firmly.

It was another couple of hours before I left Jim Marshall's cottage. While I listened to the tape, he cooked us both a hamburger and served it with some potato salad he had made the day before. And another beer, of course.

It's not hard to describe what was on the tape. There were fourteen songs, made on a cassette recorder but made well—Maryanne had learned in the studio how to set her mic levels, how to modulate her voice and pronounce her words for the best effect. Most consisted of just her voice accompanied by her strumming a guitar. Four had her playing the piano, and a couple had a lead guitar player in the background, adding notes that brought the song up a level. Hearing these made me realize that, with a good band behind her, Maryanne could have made some incredible music. If she had wanted to, that is.

I thought back to Billy Carothers and his friend Charles in Pensacola. Two different parts of a single personality. It was the same with Maryanne and Mickey—Robin and Marian. Mickey had a desire, not necessarily for stardom, but for recognition of his abilities. But his talents simply didn't measure up to his dreams. Maryanne had natural talent, but none of her brother's obsession with proving himself.

The most interesting thing on the tape, for me, was a song entitled "Ashley and Me." This was the chorus.

The wars raged on around us,

The world tried to surround us,
Before they came and found us,
We rode on.

It was late by the time I got back to Pine Oak. I still had to feed up, but luckily it was warm enough so that I wouldn't have to fool with the blankets. I had extracted an invitation from Jim Marshall to come back and make a copy of the tape. Not only that, he said I could make copies of the few diaries Maryanne had kept throughout her life on the road.

I had a lot to tell The Creeper. More by far than he had hoped. If things worked out, I had hopes of writing Maryanne's biography. Woo hoo!

Chapter 22

The Courier office was full of busy reporters. Mark Patterson, Randy Rivas, and Annie Gillespie were in their cubicles, hammering away on their keyboards, Betty Dickson was hunched over her paste-up table, and Linsey Colley was closeted with Cal in his office. I wanted to slip into my own office unseen, but when I walked in it seemed that every eye stopped what it was looking at and swiveled around to me—just as the residents' eyes had followed me across the foyer of Block 12. Mark's eyes were friendly, Ricky's and Annie's expressionless, and Betty's a little sour, as if chiding me on being away for a week when everyone else was busy working. I guess that's the thanks I get for suggesting to Cal that she get a raise. I gave a small wave and a smile, and went into my office. I had barely put my coat and purse on my extra chair when an unfamiliar phone rang on my desk. One with a lot of lighted buttons. I pushed the one that was flashing and heard Cal's voice.

"Sue-Ann, welcome back."

"Thanks, Cal. When did we get new phones?"

"Last week. Linsey thought it was a good idea if we got some with intercom capabilities."

"So we have intercom, now?"

"There's a list on your desk with everyone's intercom number."

"Cool."

"Can you come in here when you get settled?"

"Sure. Okay." But I took my time getting settled. There were a stack of phone messages in Linsey's smallish but neat handwriting. I glanced through them and set them aside. I booted up my computer and checked my email. There was nothing really pressing. There was one message, though, that made me smile. Gina had sent me another small throbbing heart—maybe in thanks for me bringing her cell phone and laptop to Myrtle Beach, or maybe because she loved me. It bucked me up, and I went to Cal's office with a lighter heart than I had walked in with.

Linsey was just leaving and as she passed, I imagined she gave me a look that one dog sometimes gives another. Linsey was still an enigma to me. Although I had been the most enthusiastic about hiring her (much to her daughter Becky's disgust), I had never really sat down and talked to her. She dressed impeccably—better than Gina, really, because she dressed in the business fashion of larger cities, where Gina would have felt out of place. And although she had the same people skills as Gina, Linsey was logical while Gina had been folksy. Both could have learned from the other, but both did their jobs well. As Cal motioned me to close the door, I resolved to ask Linsey to lunch some time, get to know her.

I sat down without being asked, looked Cal square in the eye, and delivered the news he didn't want to hear. "I'm sorry, Cal. I couldn't find Ginette. I tried."

Surprisingly, he shrugged it off. "I know you did, Sue-Ann. I got an email from her this morning."

As it happened, I had helped Gina write the substance of that email before I left Myrtle Beach, so I knew it almost by heart. Here's what it said.

> *Calvin,*
>
> *I know that you sent Sue-Ann McKeown out to find me, and I appreciate your concern for me. I do. You and I have been through a lot together and we had some great times. But I really*

don't want to be found. It's hard when one person knows something and the other doesn't, but that's the way it is, and I've known that our time has come and gone. I've known it for a while now. I'm sorry I didn't tell you in person before I left and I'm sorry I can't do it now, but you need to believe what I say. I'm in a new city now and I have a new life. I have a job in the daytime, just like I did there, but some nights I'm playing music—sometimes with a small band, sometimes all by myself. It's something I have to experience before I'm too old, just to say I tried. I think you can respect that.

I've made some new friends here already, and, yes, I'm seeing someone. It's a serious relationship and I'm very happy. I will not be coming back to Pine Oak, Cal.

I wish nothing but the best for you. I'd like to know that you will move on and settle yourself the way you wanted to be settled with me. Be good in everything you do.

Ginette

"So?" I asked Cal, pretending to be concerned. It was a hard situation. Gina and I both felt tenderness toward Cal, but we had our own lives to think about. This email was the best we could come up with. I knew that Gina already had a new email address and would cancel the one she had used to write Cal. She had also asked to have her cell phone number changed. If I had brought Cal the letter in person, saying that I had found her, he would have asked me where she was. I would have pleaded confidentiality and he may not have taken it well. After all, I was supposed to have been doing this for him, not for her. I didn't like to lie to him, but this way I was off the hook, this way he would feel no resentment toward me. "What did she say? When is she coming back?"

"She's not coming back, Sue-Ann." He seemed not just resigned, but very professional. Like someone who had come to a resolution. He sat tall in his chair like a dressage rider, impeccable in his gray coat and baby-blue shirt. He fingered his tie absently. "She said she's seeing someone else. She's got a job and she's playing music in a band." At once, his demeanor softened and he looked at me almost at a loss. "Sue-Ann, I didn't even know she *liked* music. What does she do, sing? Does she play an instrument?" He looked as lost as a man might look if his wife suddenly told him that his son was really the result of her union with his best friend.

"Those are things you needed to know." I said softly.

"Did *you* know?"

"I'm not her boyfriend, Cal. But if I was, yes, I would. I should." And at that moment I think both of us came to the same realization: that Gina's affair with Cal could never have succeeded. Cal had not known it until this moment, had not had a clue. I had wanted to believe it, and now I did. Completely. Gina had known it all along or else she would have shared her life with him more fully. I remembered that Cal had not even known that Gina had a sister.

"Are you okay?" I asked.

"Yeah. Sure. I can get on with things now, you know?"

"I do."

"Hey, how's Jack?" he asked in a more jovial voice. "Are the two of you still, you know, getting along?"

"He's doing okay, I guess. Working hard. It's tough, but . . . yeah, everything's fine." Halfway through my last sentence I had realized that with Gina in Myrtle Beach, I was the most eligible woman in Pine Oak. I had been interested in Cal when I first came to work at *The Courier*, and he knew it, but as Gina had said in her email, times had changed. The last thing I needed was him rebounding onto me. I hated the prevarication and wanted it to end. Hopefully in a week or a month, three months maybe, Cal would be back to normal.

And for the rest of our meeting, he *was* normal. He brought me up to speed on the stories the paper was working on, the budget, the new phones; in fact, his briefing was even more expansive than usual. I got an assignment to interview the new City Manager, who turned out to be none other than Panhandle Slim, a man I had met the year before at a Cowboy Mounted Shooting event. I decided not to tell Cal about the research I had been doing on Maryanne Simmons. It wasn't local enough and both Maryanne and Mickey were dead. I knew, though, that I would write up the story and submit it to a few music magazines.

I got up to leave, but had a thought. "Wait," I said. "One more thing. You know Benny from the bookstore?"

"Sure. I told you that he—"

"Right, in your phone message. Well, he wrote a play and somebody published it. Now he's asked me to do a review."

Cal leaned forward with both elbows on the desk, looking at me over clasped hands. "Is it any good?" he asked.

"I haven't finished it yet. But from what I've read so far, it's worse than bad."

Cal chuckled and shook his head. "Poor guy. Well, just tell him, you know, that we don't run reviews."

"I already mentioned that, but Benny is kind of a pal. You wouldn't think to look at him, but he's really a bright guy and knows something about just about everything. He's done me a lot of favors—favors I'd like to repay somehow, but there's really no way I can write anything good about the play."

Cal sat back and thought for a few seconds. "Okay, how about this? Tell him that we don't review books, but we'll run an announcement that the book was published and give him a free ad for a week."

"Thanks, Cal. I think he'll like that."

"Just give Betty the book and have her scan the cover. Write up a few words for the announcement. And hey, tell him that if he ever gets his play produced, we'll be in the first row."

"Thanks Cal."

I spent the rest of the morning answering my phone messages and emails and setting up the interview with Panhandle Slim. After a quick lunch, I stopped in at The Best Little Bookstore in Pine Oak and for once, Benny was not sitting at his desk going through piles of books. I noticed that the Xmas decorations were gone and that one of those new little computer notepads sat on his desk. And, as was true most of the time, the store was devoid of customers. "Benny?" I called out. "Are you here?"

I heard the noise of a toilet flushing in the back room and a few seconds later, Benny waddled out, drying his hands on a brown paper towel. "Emptying me bladder, heh heh," he said. "Aha. Brenda Starr. Haven't seen you in donkey's years."

"I've been out of town," I told him. "But Cal told me that you wanted to see me."

"Um. Uh huh. Ah."

"I know I told you I'd try to get in a review of your play, Benny, but Cal says we just can't do reviews right now." He tried to speak, but I cut him off. "But we're going to run a small column announcing the book and give you free ads for a week. I just need to ask you about—"

"Arghh. That's not what I wanted to see you about. Good, though. Hmm, like the idea of an ad, harrumph. I can show it to the wife."

"What, then, did you get in another book on Meher Baba?"

"Naw. Nothin like that. But I did pick up something that you might want to see."

"Tell me." I sat down in a chair located at the end of the Occult section. But Benny, instead of sitting down at his desk to talk, hurried into the back room again. When he came out, he was holding a thin sheaf of papers. A couple of them looked like letters of some kind. He took them to his desk and sat down.

"Hmmm," he started off. "Need your good advice."

"I'll help if I can," I said.

"Thinking of changing the name of the bookstore."

"Again?" I asked. He had made noises (literally) about changing it several times already—always to a name even worse than the one it had. Names like Books-a-Dozen or Books 'R Us. I had always managed to talk him out of it.

Benny got up from his desk and handed me one of the sheets of paper he had brought from the back room. It contained a sketch of his building, but with the outside decor completely redone. The façade in the sketch was red and above the door were three Chinese characters in gold, below which was, presumably, the English translation, also in gold. Wong Fuk Hing Book Store. I stared at it for a few seconds before the meaning hit me. I handed it back and simply said, "No, Benny. No."

"Yeah, well. Thought you might say that. But, erm, that's what most people must think—that this place is the wrong place. Need more customers."

"If you want to change the name, just call it Benny's," I told him. He had a point, though. I had often wondered where he got the money to pay the rent when his sales probably didn't average more than a couple hundred dollars a week. I assumed his wife worked, but at what, I didn't know. And didn't want to ask. "Are you short of money, Benny?" I asked.

"Naw," he said. "Makin it. Just sold one of my inventions. Dough re mi fa so."

"That's great, Benny. What is it?"

"Whiskey flasks shaped like binoculars. To sneak the booze into football games. Gurgle, heh heh."

I was—and not for the first time—completely impressed. "That's a super idea, Benny," I told him honestly. "Do you know how many of those you could sell for father's day?"

"Got another."

"Another what?"

"Another invention, harrumph. Black coffee creamer. You know, creamer, but black instead of milk colored."

"Black—but that doesn't make sense."

"For macho people who like cream but want to make their friends think they're tough enough to drink it black. Ha ha. Got a name, too: Old Black Joe. Haven't quite got the ingredients figured out yet, though. Bummer."

"That's a little wackier, Benny," I said. But I had a feeling that it could be a hit nonetheless. "But keep at it."

"Yowser."

"So, what are those other papers you have there?" I had work to do and needed to get back to the office.

"Hmm. Yes yes. The guy next door," he cocked his thumb toward the lawyer's office in the next unit, "came n last week and, ah, gave me a scoop. Said he had a client that needed some quick cash for legal expenses."

"I didn't know Joe came in here," I said. Joe Rooney was one of Cal's golfing buddies, but I had never known that he was a reader.

"Every few weeks," he said. "Likes true crime, bang, kapow, he he. But guess who his client is?"

"No idea," I said. "I didn't know he had clients."

"Yeah, well. Hargh. It's your old nemesis Cletus Donnelly."

"Clete? Really?"

"Right-oh-rooney," he said. "Wanted to know if I could come and make an offer on Cletus' books. And I told him 'That's the name of the game.' So I drove out to Sawdust Street and he let me inside. The police had taken all his weapons out already, but there was a pretty big box of books. All martial arts stuff—Japanese, Chinese, some of them hard to get. I made an offer—tried not to go too low, he he, but you know. Ka-ching! And I got the box. Brought it here. Went through it more carefully; use to dabble in that kind of thing meself long ago, Hoo." Benny made karate-chopping motions with both hands. "Kung fu, Gatka, Hapkido, ai yi!"

I had long since given up on expecting Benny to come to the point quickly—or ever—so I prodded him a little. "Any archery books?" I asked.

"Hmm? Ah, ooh, don't think so. Maybe."

"Then what . . .?" I left the question open ended.

"Letters." He held up the papers. "Found em between the pages of some of the books."

"Cletus's letters? You mean suicide letters or plans to kill somebody? You have to give them to the police, Benny."

"Nuh uh. Letters *to* him. For your eyes only."

I almost snatched the letters out of his hand. Maybe they would give me a piece of the puzzle I needed to write Clete's story.

"Found your name in em," he said. "Um. You know, just a glance."

"My name. But what about? Who wrote them? What do you mean, for my eyes only?"

Benny tried to put on an inscrutable gaze. Then he made a zipping motion across his mouth. "Just call me Baba," he said.

Chapter 23

I sloughed off my catch-up work to read the letters. I wish I never had. I wish Benny had never given them to me. There were six of them, written over a half-year period. The writer was Rufus Donnelly, Clete's younger brother, who had been stationed in The Middle East. I arranged them on my desk in the order in which they were written. Writing came hard to Rufus, as attested to not only by his grammar and spelling, but to the brevity of the letters. Six sheets for six letters, sometimes both sides, sometimes just one. Rufus's handwriting was the scrawl of a preadolescent, but I was able to make it out well enough. And although my first impulse after reading them was to tear them into little pieces and burn them, I owe it not only to Clete and Rufus, but maybe to history as well, to include them here.

> 16/02/08 (that's military style)
>
> Dear Clete:
>
> Just got here into bagdad. You should see it. If Bagdad was a car, it would be like that Chrysler old man Johnson had up on blocks in his field that we shot up with buckshot. Holes everywhere. Even our Forward Operating Base has a lot of bombed out bildings, but its better than being deployed in Tikrit or Falllujah or one of those places.
>
> Some of the guys got computers that they can send letters to their friends

with. If you had a computer I could maybe send you one instead of havin to write it out this way. And we have TV whenever theres power. The gear I have to wear is hot and heavy, its like bein rapped in a electric blanket made outa steel. Because Im a gunner I have a place I stand on the top of a humvee with a turret gun. I aint shot nobody yet. I aint even been on a convoy—the Lt. says that we don't go out less we haveta. The foods all right and next week we're gonna get to go and check out the beer in some of the hotels where the newspaper writers live. That will be great.

Rufus

13/03/08

Hey, Clete—

I went out on three convoys this week. It was scary at first, but all the guys in my platoon stick together and protect each other. Theres 3 humvees in a convoy most times and everbodys got a weapon even the driver and we all got on flak gear. The sidewalks are shot up pretty bad with mortar and the streets are to so we go real slow which isnt real good because it gives the enemy time to set up for a good shot. So far we havent been fired on but a lot of these towel heads look at us like they wish they could. Theres no front line in this kind of war. Or maybe the front line is everywhere.

Hey guess what. Remember that girl you used to go to school with? Sue Anne. Sue Anne Makowen. Shes here. Shes working in bagdad as a reporter for some paper. I might try to say hi to her some time. After all, were both from Pine Oak. Theres more girls here, too, but most of them are reporters like Sue Anne. Theres this one girl named Nonnie and shes a real knockout. If she was a car, she'd be a yellow sports car like a Corvette-with only a little mileage. Real pretty and smart too, but she hangs out with the other reporters or the officers and dont pay much attention to us enlisted men.

Wish you could be here with me.

Rufus

P. S. Im putting this letter out to be posted as soon as I seal it up. You never know if you ul come back from a mission.

22/04/08

Big Brother Cletus—

Everythings the same here every day. We go out on convoys sometimes but most times we stay in our barracks. We can watch TV and read or just sit around. And its scary all the time knowin that we might get shelled any time but were here for a reason. Were protecting the American people, wether there in Pine Oak or in NY. I'm kinda proud to be doin what Im doin. In fact, if I was a car, Id probly be a new Chevy Silverado pickup. Dark military green. Extended cab. Yeah.

Ive got some buddys that I hang out with. There's this one guy we call Cracker because, you know, his moms always sending him Cracker Jack. There's a guy with red hair so we call him Red. And then there's Mucker and Crazy Del and this black guy we call Mr Soup but dont ask me why. I got a nickname too. The guys call me Doof, maybe short for Rufus but maybe because they think Im a doofus ha ha. We get drunk a lot but were all friends and we ud die for each other if it came to that which I hope it dont.

We all go into the Palestine Hotel compound every weekend now and drink at the bar. Thats the hotel where all the reporters bunk. Sometimes I see Sue Anne Makowen there. I waved to her once, and she waved back and smiled. I guess the reporters are no different from us. They seem to be drunk all the time, too.

Gotto go out on patrol now bye.

"Doof" (Rufus)

07/05/08

Hey big brother—

Cracker got killed today. The humvee he was drivin ran over a IED and turned over. His buddies got shaken up some but they were all right. Crackers neck got broke like a stick. I was in the back of the convoy so I saw the whole thing—I could even see the tarmac in the street roll up like a wave just before the humvee went over. We were passing by one of the big concrete walls that line all the streets here and there were some houses on the other side. Some shots got fired from the window of one of the houses but none of us didnt get hit, only the vehicles and theyre really tough. By the time we finished firin off rounds at that house, the whole wall fell in. If that building woulda been a car, well, all cars look alike when there in the crusher. We put Cracker in one of the other vehicles and the other guys from that humvee too and we got out of there plenty fast. By the time we came back with more power, that humvee was nothin but a black shell smellin like burnt tires and smokin like all the cigars ever smoked. Cracker was my buddy and Im gonna miss him a lot. Id hate to have to be the one to tell his mama. Things here seem to be gettin worse instead a better.

Next week were goin back out so that Nonnie can get a story. Shes the prettiest of the girls at the Palestine Hotel and she goes out into the streets more, too. I'm on speakin terms with Nonnie—all the fellas are now. And with Sue Anne, too. I even bought her a beer once and she smiled and said thanks. Ill mostly be glad to get back home so I can get my own girl. Its lonely here that way.

I hope your doin good in your job and keeping all those hoodlums from breaking out ha ha.

"Doof"

12/05/08

Whats up big bro—

When I first got here I never thought Id get used to the sound all these helicopters make. Seems like theres one in the air all the time, comin and goin. And if there not in the air, there crashing down somewhere, killin folks. Im glad Im not assigned to one, because if they was cars, theyd be like those jalopys in demolition derbys you used to take me to when I was a kid.

Today I had to watch a helicopter fly Nonnie out of the city because she's dead. Some bigwig Iraqi politician got himself bombed into a lot of steak and we took her and her camera man to the scene in our convoy so she could do a story about it. But while she was talking into her microphone she got hit by a lone sniper. One bullet right through the heart. We didn't catch the sniper and the mood of everbody here is black as smoke. In a few minutes we're all goin down to the Palestine to get drunk as skunks.

Doof

13/05/08

Hey Bro—

You'll never guess.

We went down to the bar at the Palestine last night all feelin pretty bad about Nonnie bein killed and us not able to protect her like we should have. But we werent the only ones. The other reporters that live there were already drunkin hard when we got there. They saw how down we were so they bought us some drinks, and we bought them some. I started talkin to Sue Anne, the girl from Pine Oak. She remembered my nickname and was real friendly, but sad as could be. A couple of hours passed and most of the other reporters went to their quarters, but Sue Anne stayed. It was hot and she was sweating bad. I guess we all were. She was not really lookin very good and I asked if she was sick. After a while, I had to help her up to her room, which I did like any gentleman, but when we got there, we kind of fell into her bed together and things happened. I was real excited and not so careful, if you know what I mean and I hope that nothing happens. But I was thinkin that if she gets pregnant, maybe she'd want to get married. That ud be great, huh, Clete?

> Tomorrow she's goin in to the city to see where Nonnie died. Maybe Ill be part of her convoy. I hope so.
>
> I think Im in love. If Sue Anne was a car, she'd be a Cadillac, but maybe one thats out of gas. Theres a lot of that here, though. It ul be better for us all when we come home.
>
> Im getting a collection of artillery shells to bring back with me when I come. For you, so you can have something that was really in war.
>
> Your brother, Rufus Donnelly

Joey had suggested that Clete's brother was in Afghanistan. Not so. He was with me in Iraq. And he was evidently in my bed. The tall, quiet, shy boy with the accent. Why didn't I realize that he was from Pine Oak? My last memory of him was slumped over the turret, blood covering his head and dripping down onto the bombed-out street.

No wonder Cletus Donnelly hated me. He knew that I had gotten his little brother killed. For nothing.

But he didn't hate me as much as I hated myself.

Chapter 24

I couldn't work. I couldn't even think about working. I just sat at my desk, rereading those simple, touching, heartbreaking letters and wondering how I was ever going to live through what I had just found out. If I hadn't insisted on going into the city—into one of the most dangerous places in Baghdad—there would have been no convoy and no sniper fire and Doof would still be alive. In fact, he might even be home now, talking about his collection of artillery shells with his brother, discussing all the different cars and trucks that they would like to drive.

Somehow, time passed. Mark Patterson and Randy Rivas went out somewhere, doing something for the paper no doubt. Linsey Colley went out to forage for advertisements and Cal left a few minutes later. Becky came in looking flustered, saw that her mother was not at her desk, and turned back around. Through my window I saw her get into her rusty yellow Honda and leave rubber as she left the parking lot. Thinking I was alone in the office at last, I buried my head in my hands and gave myself up to the stupid relief of sobbing. I was still crying ten minutes later, but it was a soft crying, just a tear here and there and a shudder every minute or so. My head was on the desk and my new hair was damp with tears. I remember thinking that if I concentrated hard enough I could make Doof's letters disappear, or that I could just repress the whole thing. Yet, even if I could, the fact would remain that I had caused an innocent man to die. I tried to tell myself that I had not been in my right mind. That I had been too drunk, too devastated by the news of Nonnie's death, to have been able to think rationally. That my thyroid gland had already started its drop-by-drop destruction. If I had been halfway sane I could never have made the ridiculous decision to venture into a part of town where several people had been killed only hours before. What the hell had I been thinking? There was no answer to that question, no way to go back and negate what I had done and turn Doof's letters into ones of happy memories and missions successfully accomplished. I found myself wishing with all my being that it had been me that had been killed instead of Nonnie. That way both she and Rufus would still be alive and I would be a lot better off than I was now.

"Sue-Ann?"

I was so startled that I jerked my head off the desk and sent a tensor lamp bumping to the carpet. The light in the doorway was bright and Betty Dickson was standing there like a shadow with her hands on her hips. "Shit, Betty. I thought everybody was gone." I scrambled to pick up the lamp.

"I was back in the back," she said. "Can I come in?"

"I guess. If you want," I said reluctantly. I took my purse and coat from the chair and offered it to her. "But I'm not good company."

"We're even, then. I'm almost never good company." She sat down and looked at me over the desk. "I'm not going to ask you if you're all right, Sue-Ann, cause you're obviously not. But if it's any of my business, tell me what's wrong."

"It's *not* your business, Betty," I said evenly. I had always thought of Betty as kind of an old biddy, even though she was only in her mid-fifties. Other descriptions might have included the words spinster or dowdy or even butch. She preferred her hair short, her clothes dark, and her contact with the rest of the office limited. So I was shaken a little out of my morbid tree when she seemed interested in my pain. And, of course, any port in a storm. "But I'll tell you anyway," I said. "I have PTSD. Post-trau—"

"I know what it means. Sue-Ann. I was in the marines."

I wiped my face as best I could and swept my hair behind my ears. "I didn't . . . I mean, I knew that. It was on your application. Listen, Betty, I'm sorry you didn't get that job. I think we made the best choice, but I'm sorry if you were disappointed."

"I can handle a little disappointment," she said, giving me the tiniest of smiles. "In these times, we're all lucky to still have any jobs at all," she said.

"I know that's right," I said.

"But I want to hear about your PTSD. I know you were in Iraq; you must have seen some horrible things. I was only in the service for the minimum and I schlepped around Camp Lejeune the whole time. Never even left stateside." She stopped and pointed to the letters that I had positioned just out of tear range. "I guess it has something to do with those," she said.

"Yeah," I replied. "Sad, sad letters."

"Friend of yours?"

"I guess you could say that. He was a private in Iraq. Turret gunner for a Humvee. Killed in the line of duty. Him and his buddies used to hang out in the bar of the hotel I was staying in."

"I've heard that sometimes fresh memories can trigger your old stress."

"Yeah, well."

"Tell me about your friend," she said gently.

And so I told her a little about Doof and his buddies and his death. I left out the part about the sex and even that he was from Pine Oak. It was a cogent, but heartfelt memorial. But to my surprise, I kept on talking. I spent most of the next hour talking about Nonnie. I told Betty about her brilliance on camera and in person, the courage that had gotten her killed, and my silly, stupid attempt to emulate her. And by the time I had finished, with more tears flowing at odd intervals, I still felt like I wanted to be dead. But maybe not quite as dead as before.

"Do you bowl?"

"Hmm? You mean, like bowling alley bowl?"

"Yeah."

"I . . . I was on the bowling team in high school," I answered. "But I haven't bowled in donkey's years."

"I have a league tonight," she said. "Come with me—one team or another always needs a sub."

"I . . . I really don't want to go home, but I'm not sure I want to bowl either."

"All right then. You can just watch if you want. Drink some beer."

Beer sounded good. "All right, I will. What time does it start?"

"About seven. Warmups ten minutes earlier."

"I'll see you there." I didn't have to ask which lanes she bowled at because Hi-Score was the only bowling alley within 50 miles in any direction. Counter to what I told Betty, I *did* go home, but only to feed up and change into something more casual. I toyed with the idea of calling Gina and telling her about the letters, but Gina had her own problems. That is, Gina didn't really have any problems at the moment and I didn't want to burden her with mine. If she knew how depressed I was, she would probably fly back immediately and lose all her gigs—at least I hoped she would. And I wanted that, yes I did, but it was a hard time to be selfish. I needed to get through this without her.

Hi-Score Lanes was located just before you hit the downtown area of Forester—only a couple of blocks from the Eat Now restaurant, but on the opposite side of the road. It was a deep, drab-looking building that had been there since I was in grade school. The façade was painted with rollicking tenpins, and the parking lot was just large enough for a full league of bowlers without anyone having to park at the Taco Bell next door. But it was a tight squeeze. My little rented Hyundai was dwarfed by the preponderance of mostly American-made pickups of all sizes and colors. I was a few minutes late and everyone else was already inside. Sitting in my car, savoring the warmth from the heater, I wondered what the hell I was doing there. Then I remembered the letters and I hurried inside.

If any of you have never been in a bowling alley, you have missed out on a truly unique experience. And if you have been an avid bowler even once in your life, you simply miss it. As soon as I set foot inside the door, I was assailed with so many sensory impressions that everything I carried in with me was crowded out like a coyote in a field full of donkeys.

The clunk of balls dropping onto the oiled wooden lanes; the click or clatter or crash when the pins were struck; the high murmur of voices on every lane; the smell of resin, talcum powder, and onion rings; the mustiness of Bowling Alleys Past: each called up the same sensations I had experienced in every bowling alley I had ever been in. Although Jack and I never went bowling together, I often searched out lanes in towns I had to spend a day or two in on assignment (if I couldn't find an archery range). And every time I entered one, I wondered why it had taken me so long to return. The answer was less in the bad scores I usually managed to rack up than in my too-deadline-oriented schedule. But it was also more than that. Bowling was usually—at least in college and in the more sophisticated or artsy surroundings I traveled in in Richmond—looked down upon, like a cousin in jail, or like MD 20-20. You could visit once;

even go bowling once on a date, but not more than that. But once it got into your blood, you had to love it—despite your friends and your circumstances and your bad scores—even if you didn't admit it. And books can—and will—be written about the characters you'll find in these sometimes seedy, always exotic establishments.

Just inside the door was a long, oval-shaped desk, within which two people were employed to rent shoes and run the cash register. Two pool tables stood on each side of this desk and, against the wall, there were pinball machines and a snack bar. Beyond the oval desk were twelve lanes of clunking, clicking, clattering, and crashing noise. I looked around for Betty Dickson, but before I could spot her, I heard a familiar voice on my right.

"Sue-Ann. What are you doing here?" It was Randy Rivas, *The Courier's* sportswriter, dressed in dark pants, shiny black Dexter bowling shoes, and a collared bowling shirt with Randy stitched in cursive over the pocket.

"Hey, Randy. I forgot you were a bowler, too. I'm looking for Betty Dickson."

"All the way over to your right. Lanes eleven and twelve. We're on the same team." He turned his back so that I could read the words "Krissy's Moving and Storage" embroidered on the back along with a bowling ball that had green eyes and a long, red, tongue. He turned back around and said, "Come on."

I followed him over, where I saw Betty on Lane 12 waiting for the bowler on Lane 11 to finish her approach before throwing her practice ball. I gave her a quick wave and sat down at a round table behind the bowling area. I had no purse to stash—I carried some cash in my jeans. Betty threw a ball and the lanes went dark for a few seconds, signifying the end of practice. Betty sat down beside me. "I thought you might have changed your mind," she said. I just smiled and shook my head. We were soon joined by Randy and a couple I had never seen before. The man was in his late forties, with brown thinning hair and a mustache, also brown and thin. His name was Barney and his accent was all Jasper County. The woman was about Barney's age, but had long, dark hair tied into a ponytail that reached halfway down her back. A formidable looking woman, she stood about 5-10 and was thickly set.

"And this is Krissy," said Betty. We all shook hands. Barney's hand was kind of dead-fishy, but Krissy's was firm and confident. "Glad to meet you, Sue-Ann," Krissy said in the relative silence of the short break before the games began. "I've read a lot of your stories. And of course Betty has told me a lot about you."

I doubted if any of it was good, but made the proper response.

"Are you here to bowl?" she asked. "I'm not sure if any of the teams are short tonight. There are a couple of ringers that always hang around because subs don't have to pay. I can check at the desk though."

"No. I just want to watch tonight. Maybe another time. What I really want is something to drink."

"Me, too," Krissy piped up. "How about we all split a pitcher?"

"Sounds good," I said. The others nodded, just as the lane lights came on again and the pins were reset. "Here, I'll get it."

A young black woman was behind the counter cooking up something on the grill and I realized I hadn't eaten since before noon. When my turn came at the counter, I said, "Let me have a pitcher of, um, Honey Brown, a cheeseburger, and an order of onion rings." She wrote it down, rung it up, and drew my pitcher.

It wasn't the only pitcher we had that night.

And, although my thoughts sometimes drifted back to the Palestine Hotel, the night went along quickly.

Betty was not quite an average bowler. Her approach was slow and her delivery precise—bending low to place, rather than launch—her ball onto the surface with no spin at all. Although Betty was characteristically quiet, I found Randy Rivas to be a lot funnier than he seemed at the office. Nothing specific; just a quip here and there and goofy body antics at the line. When everybody except him got a strike in the same frame, he would grab his neck in an exaggerated manner and stagger back to the table. When he managed to score two strikes in a row, he turned and struck a gorilla pose—stomach in, arms out to his sides, and fists clenched. For an ex-athlete, his bowling was reserved, almost prissy, with heavy spin that rarely achieved a tight line. Barney, like Betty, was soft spoken, but he was the best bowler of the four, with a graceful approach and delivery and a smooth curve into the headpin. Krissy was kind of outrageous in everything. Garrulous at the table, her bowling was all arms and legs. If she hit the headpin, she was likely to get a strike because of the odd backspin she put on her ball, but she rarely hit it, and didn't seem to care much. She was obviously having a good time just being there.

My burger and onion rings were scrumptious, and it was only when I got up to use the bathroom that anything bad happened. At least, bad to me. As I walked to the back I noticed a very large man bowling on Lane 3. He had just sent a ball crashing into the pins at warp speed, actually sending one of the pins spinning back out of the pit and onto the lane. As he turned back to his team in triumph, his eyes met mine for an instant. It was Joey Bickley. I went into the Women's restroom without any sign of recognition, but when I came back out several minutes later, he was waiting for me by one of the pool tables.

"Fancy meeting you here," he said.

"I don't really have anything to say to you, Joey," I said.

"Yeah, where's Clarence?"

"Find him and ask him," I said.

"Pretty strange that you'd be sitting at that particular table," he said with a grin.

"Those shoes look ridiculous," I told him, staring at the red-and-white striped house shoes that were just a little smaller than boats. "Can't you afford to buy your own?"

"Good friends with Krissy?" he asked. "And dykey Betty?"

When I didn't answer, he went on, "Rivas is okay I guess, but I'm not going to stand at the same row of urinals with that Barney guy. He works for Krissy, so maybe it rubs off, haw haw."

A voice called out, "Joey, come on, you're up on 3!" Joey clomped back to his grou[illegible] I walked slowly back to mine.

Krissy was waiting for me [illegible]w pitcher of Honey Brown, which [illegible]y glass. "I saw you talking to Joe Bi[illegible]

"I don't like that man," I said softly. I *really* don't like him. He scares the shit out of me."

"He's just a hater, darling. Don't pay any attention to him."

"You're not from around here, are you?" I asked.

"I'm from Oswego, Illinois," she smiled. "Home of the annual Drag Strip Festival."

"Sounds like a good reason to leave. Sorry, I'm getting a little drunk."

"No, you're right as you can be. I'm happy here in Forester, even with guys like Joe Bickley around. I saw him looking over here. Did he say anything about me?"

"He . . . no, nothing."

For the rest of the night I paid more attention to Krissy and Betty than I did the others. I watched them look at each other across the table; only brief looks, but I could tell that there was some significance behind them. I watched them high-five each other when they did well at the line—hand slaps, daps, rehearsed moves that sometimes involved crossed arms, touching elbows and even behind-the-back moves. So intricately coordinated and casual that they must have been doing it for years.

I avoided looking in Joey's direction, but I knew that he was looking at me, and I hoped it would spoil his concentration. I played it safe, though, by leaving before any of the teams were finished; I didn't want to be followed home or pulled over for DUI by that bastard.

Despite Joey, it had been an unexpectedly pleasant night; one so full of noise and conversation and beer that I had temporarily been shaken out of my depression. It didn't return until I slid into bed and tried to sleep.

It was still there when I woke up the next morning.

Chapter 25

I knew I had to turn in my rental car soon, especially since I was putting the bill on my expense account, but I had one more trip to make. I got up early, took a very long shower, dresse[illegible] I felt, arranged my new hair, and [illegible], where Maryanne's husband ha[illegible] her papers for me to make copie[illegible] something he would have done f[illegible] *bona fides* were easy enough to check on line. The last time I had Googled myself, links to at least fifty of my newspaper articles had popped up.

I arrived at 10:00 and spent the first hour just going over things with Jim. He had filled a small box with her papers, some photos, and a single cassette tape. I had remembered to dig out an old boombox precursor I had once used in high school—one of those with two cassette windows—try to find one of those in a WalMart today. Using it, we were able to put Maryanne's tape in one side and a blank tape in the other and dub it at a fairly high speed. In all, I made four copies—one for me, one for Creeper, one for Gina, and one for Jim, so that he would always have a backup. I could make more at home, but I wanted to get these copies from the original and not have to go into another generation.

My next task was to take the box of papers to a copy shop. Jim wanted to go with me and help, so we spent the early part of the afternoon in a Kinko's, standing at two different machines, and making copies of Maryanne's lyric sheets, letters, and a couple of entire diaries that she had kept intermittently throughout her life. I also had the photos scanned and reproduced, both in hard copy and on disk.

I didn't learn much from our sporadic conversation. Jim, to be honest, was a fairly boring, nondescript individual. He had spent his whole life in local real estate, his fortunes yo-yoing with the economy. Unlike my mother, Jim had no interests outside his profession; didn't want any. Luckily he had retired before the housing crash, and his wants and needs easily fell within his retirement income. When I asked Jim to tell me a little about Maryanne, he simply described her as "a good agent who could always come up with a sweet-sounding sales pitch." And this is what she had done for the last half of her life. Jim thought in terms of good and bad real estate deals. One memory, in which Maryanne had sold an entire residential block of houses to a religious group, deserved, in his mind, a full chapter in any biography.

And yes, we talked about my doing the biography. When we got through copying the box of papers, he insisted on buying me late lunch (or early dinner) at an Italian restaurant called Mom and Dad's on the east side of town. He said he had worked there as a busboy when he was a student and that, although the original owners had passed on, the cuisine was as excellent as it had been over forty years before. So over an incredible baked dish of what they called Spaghetti a la Bruzzi and a bottle of very dry Chianti (eat your heart out, Jack), we worked out possibilities for the biography. I promised that I would be in touch.

It was only on the way home that my depression set in again. I couldn't help but think of Gina, who was in a parallel situation to the one Mickey and Maryanne had been in. She was one out of how many thousands of singers and musicians who are pulled into the music business by their dreams, then pushed right back out onto the charity of their friends and relatives. Did Gina have the talent that would allow her to make a mark on even a tiny part of her generation? And if so, where would it lead her? And what would be my part in it?

I stopped at a gas station and got a cup of coffee and used it to take one of my thyroid pills. Who knows when I had taken my last one. For the umpteenth time, I resolved to do better. Anxious to see The Creeper, I took out my cell phone and called The Compound to see if Krista would go over and feed my horses. I intended to drive the long way to The Compound and stay the night. Smokey answered on the third ring. "WHEY, here. You say Hi, I say 'Lo."

"Smokey," I said. "Let me speak to Krista."

"Oh, hey, Sue-Ann. Krista's not here."

"Is she at my place?" I asked.

"Naw. Dad bought her a new car and she drove off somewhere. Said she had to go out of town for a couple of days."

"You've got to be kidding me," I muttered, more to myself than to Smokey.

"Anything I can do for you?" he asked. "Or do you want me to transfer you to The Creeper?"

"No, that's all right. But tell him I'm on my way out there to see him and that I'm going to need somebody to open the gate for me because I'm driving. Do you know if he has a cassette pl [illegible]

"Are you kiddin [illegible] he even has an 8-track player."

"I believe it."

So I stopped a [illegible] he horses. I checked the weather radar on line and saw that it was only going into the high 40s so that there was no need for blankets. I had been neglecting them badly, so I took a few minutes to give a little brushdown to Gina's Irene and told her that I hoped her owner would be back to ride her very soon. I clung to Alikki's neck for a while, just breathing in her fabulous warm horsey scent. "Someday," I told her. "Soon, maybe, we can go to a show and see all the other horses. Just walk around the ring for a while and let you get used to things." I told her that I had heard that her mother was working at Prix St. Georges and maybe we'd see her there at the show. And Alikki looked back at me and said with her eyes, That's fahn. And I gave her a half carrot to crunch and let her go into her pasture. And to Enemy Hunter, my half Hanovarian half Quarterhorse, I apologized for neglecting her and letting her run so wild like a child without good parents. And I vowed to do better, to practice loading her on the trailer and teaching her voice commands. "Now go out with your buddies," I told her.

I usually traveled to Torrington on horseback so by the time I finally found the half-hidden road that led into The Compound, darkness had already set in. The thick, forbidding iron gate had been unlocked—and I locked it again after me. A few minutes later I was in Ashley Torrington's private drawing room sitting in one of the red, shell-backed chairs, Maryanne's box of papers in my lap. My coat hung over the back of a second chair. The Creeper sat in his usual place, with the bank of stereo equipment against the wall to his left—his good side.

"We have a lot to talk about," I began.

"Yas?"

"The first thing is bad news. Maryanne Simmons died two years ago."

Ashley Torrington sat up straighter in his chair and leaned forward. "You located her?"

"I located her husband. His name is Jim." And for the next thirty minutes or so, I related to this sad, scarred ex-lieutenant, the story of Maryanne Simmons as I then knew it. From her few years performing with her brother, to her Scientology days in California, to her peaceful life as a real estate agent in Florida's capital city.

I told him how she had continued to write songs until she left California, and even to have recorded some of them with her boyfriend and his friends. I took a cassette tape from the box. "I made this for you," I said.

"It's Maryanne?" It was the only time I have ever seen Ashley befuddled.

"Yes. "Would you like to play it now?"

"Yas, yes, of course." He raised himself to his feet and took the cassette gingerly, like a flower, from my hand and took two limping steps to the stereo system. With his back partially turned to me, I could more clearly see the horrible scar tissue that wound down his scalp like crinkly brown plastic wrap. Here and there a tuft of hair sprang out and drifted down his neck and onto the shoulders of his dressing gown. With his practiced left hand, he turned a couple of dials, pushed the cassette into the player, and hit the Play button. Then, as her voice came, lifelike and breathy, through the excellent speakers, he sank back in his chair and closed his eyelids for a minute or more. The first song was "Pay the Moon," but played starkly, and without the orchestration that had been on the record. In fact, it was similar to the way Gina had played it in Myrtle Beach. When Ashley looked at me again, he said, haltingly, "I, I wanted to believe that she wrote that song, but I never dreamed that she had written others."

"How long have you known it?" I asked.

"Always suspected it. The lines referring to horses must have come from her. And then the whole idea of insanity."

"Which is why you had Smokey play the song along with all those songs about being crazy."

"Yas, but I never really knew for sure. I needed . . ."

"You needed me to prove it. And to do that I had to find her."

"Umm. As you say. And I knew that you were smart enough to figure it out for yourself."

"Gina figured it out, too."

"So you found Gina, too. She thought you might."

"Gina and I had it out about that. But what about Maryanne?" I asked, as the second song began to play; a semi-calypso number. I had heard it once already at Jim Marshall's house, but the change in tempo and subject matter from "Pay the Moon" was still unexpected and fascinating. "If she had turned out to be alive, would you have gotten in touch with her?"

Ashley thought for a moment, then said, "I wanted to know what happened to her, what she had been doing all these years. My curiosity about her has always been great. But, no, I would never have wanted her to see me, never would have contacted her."

"And I think that would have been a great mistake," I told him. "You're a very likeable, a very loveable man. She wrote a song about you, you know."

"Don't joke with an old man."

"No Joke. Here." I handed him the list of songs I had copied off Maryanne's original. "It's the next song."

"Ashley and Me" was a lively song, happy and bright. It was about two people who find themselves out of the world of everyday affairs and in some idyllic wonderland, but only briefly. Part of the bridge went like this;

We rode through the breeze,
Through canopy trees.
Just Ashley and me.

I glanced at Ashley and saw tears streaming down his scarred visage like seepage in a cliff face. I slipped out to the bathroom, wiping my own eyes as I went. I stayed for a few minutes to give Ashley some time alone with Maryanne. When I went back, he had turned the cassette off and seemed to be dreaming in his chair. He knew I was back, though, because he began speaking as soon as I sat down again. "I can't listen to any more now," he began.

"I understand."

"I don't think I have to tell you how grateful I am," he said, and I knew that his voice, like his heart, was close to breaking.

"Shucks," I said, trying to lighten up the mood a little. "That was nothin. In fact, I've got more stuff for you. A whole box full. Maryanne's song lyrics, some photos, and her diary."

"But how did you get all these? Her husband wouldn't . . ."

"I can talk the black off a tire," I said. "Besides, I told him I might like to write her biography."

"Were you serious?" he asked.

"Yeah, sure. But I'm not sure who would publish it. She's not Cindy Lauper or somebody, but it'll give me something to do."

"Yas, but it's odd that she never really went over the edge like her brother or father or even grandfather."

"That was a real puzzle for me, too. I mean, how could she have felt enough of the madness to have written that song? But then I remembered the story you told me about her. She felt that she had the same gene as the rest of her family, that she could feel it inside her like a virus or something."

"Umm."

"She did have it, Ashley," I said. "She didn't escape. It hit her hardest in California, toward the end. When she realized that she was in trouble, she checked herself into a mental facility and got it shocked out of her. It was her choice; she told them to do it—it's all there in her diary. And it worked. For the rest of her life, she was as mentally healthy as you and me."

"Is there a but?"

"Of course. From the time she got out of the hospital in California till the day she died, she never wrote another song or another entry in her diary. It was like she was a completely different person. But I think she was happy, and I think she was content." I put the box of Maryanne's papers on the floor next to him. "I only had time to make one copy, but you can keep these until we get time to make another."

"I don't know what to say," he said.

Well . . ." I said. "You can tell me where Krista's gone off to."

"Krista is out being Krista. Every mynah bird needs to stretch its wings a little, no? She's a grown woman and doesn't need to be caged here for the rest of her life. I prevailed on her father—my well-to-do son—to buy her a new car. Guilt money for sending her and Smokey here instead of coming himself. But it's not his fault; he never knew me. When he was born, I was in the jungles somewhere, getting burned. After that, his mother was always testing the box springs of beds in other men's houses, and I was in a hospital bed, trying to convince myself that I could live a life with only half a face and half a body. She divorced me, and I didn't contest it. I would have divorced me, too."

"I think I know how you feel," I said so softly I wasn't sure he heard me.

"But hormones are not always our enemies," he said. "Without them raging inside me I would have waited for a more appropriate woman to marry, yas I would. But history or fate or bad luck dictated that I would never get that chance. And so my son was born. And so Smokey and Krista were born. And Krista is the same age I was when I went to Vietnam."

"She dropped out of college to come here, didn't she?"

"Umm. Smokey had graduated, so she came with him."

"What was her major?"

"English."

I thought back at some of the poems she had composed and read on the air. "Hmm," was all I could manage.

"She's smarter than she lets on," said Ashley. "She's a great reader and can talk your head off if you get to know her."

"She *is* a mynah bird, isn't she?" I smiled.

"Umm. And a conscientious one. She told me about your sergeant before she left. Are you worried about this Mr. Bickley?"

"Aren't you?"

"We try to always be prepared."

"But you're not going to tie his wrists and drive him to his own police station."

"No, probably not," he smiled. "We all live and learn, yas?"

"But what if—"

"Sue-Ann. What's the worst that can happen?"

"Well, he finds you."

"Yas, and so?"

"What do you mean, so? This place is a secret."

"Yas, we've gone to a lot of trouble to hide ourselves from the world. But we're doing nothing illegal. The property is owned in trust by my family and managed by a caretaker. I'm the caretaker, but Clarence Meekins is my eyes and ears and right hand. Everything is strictly legal; we have a right to be here. We have a right to carry the weapons we have. Our radio station is licensed by the FCC. If Sergeant Bickley finds us, what is he going to do, arrest us? All of us? And for what.? We didn't hurt Cletus Donnelly, we took him to safety."

"But in that case, Ashley, why the secrecy in the first place?"

The Creeper looked at me seriously and said, "Sue-Ann, didn't you ever have a secret? Something important that no one else knows about?"

"Of course. And you know at least one of them."

"Yas, but yours and Gina's are maybe secrets that you wish you could share with others, no?" I nodded. "But the people here in Torrington need to think that it is a place of total safety—somewhere that no one can possibly find them or bother them. And me? Do you think I want people I don't know staring at me or pitying me? I am happy here in my own fashion and happy to be completely forgotten by the outside world, but if Sergeant Bickley finds me, the earth won't explode and the sky won't fall."

"I'm afraid of him," I confessed. "And it's gotten personal."

"Umm?"

"He thinks he knows *my* secret, too, and he's been trying to force me to go out with him."

"And you said no?"

"More than once. But he's so creepy. I don't know why, but I feel that if I ever get in a place where I'm alone with him, he'll hurt me."

"Yas? Well, that changes things. If he threatens or harasses or hurts you in any way, you must believe that we will make sure it is the last time."

"I appreciate that, I do."

"But how did he come to suspect your relationship with Gina?"

"Cletus Donnelly told him on that night I shot him. Cletus saw us together at The Cypress Lake Lodge last year. And I think that's what set him off." I leaned forward and looked straight at him. "I have something else to tell you and I'm not sure you're going to like me much afterward."

"Another secret?"

"It has to do with a young private in Iraq." And I proceeded to tell Ashley about the night Nonnie Gray was killed and the day after, when our convoy was attacked. I told him about Doof and the painstaking letters he had written to his older brother. The fact that I was responsible for Rufus Donnelly's death.

"So that's why Mr. Donnelly wanted to kill you."

"Of course. I don't know why it took him so long to contact me; maybe he needed time to brood about it or plan how he was going to do it. That first phone call must have been totally bogus. He made up the part about his mother and the gasoline and I think he just wanted to lure me to his house that night and kill me. And," I added, "I would have deserved it."

"Stop that kind of talk, Sue-Ann," Ashley said in a firmer voice than he had used all night. "The man was not in his right mind. His clothes and his obsession with weapons—I've seen this every day, here in Torrington."

It wasn't much consolation. "I'm afraid, Ashley," I said. I was starting to sound a little panicky and I knew it. "I'm afraid that I might not be able to live with it. Do you think I could move out here to Torrington? I know I was never a soldier, but I was in the war."

"I think you are a soldier, Sue-Ann. But it won't come to that. What about your horses? Your job?"

"I'll move my horses to your pasture and how can I possibly think about going out and interviewing some of these pompous rednecks when I know I've—"

"What if Gina comes back?"

"She won't come back. How can she when she finds out what I've done? And she's doing so great where she is. You should see her on stage. She's just having so much fun. I—I don't think I want her to come back."

And before I knew it, I was on my knees, sobbing again, my head resting in Ashley Torrington's lap, his hand stroking my hair.

Chapter 26

But The Creeper wouldn't let me stay in Torrington—not even for one night.

"I've stayed before," I complained.

"You were dying," he pointed out.

"I'm dying now."

"You're whining now." After our shared moments of intimacy, those words had struck me like a blow and I stood up and crossed to the middle of the room. I lifted my head. "You're right," I said. "but—"

"No buts. You need to go home and continue living your life. That's what it's for. Sometimes we feel like we've been kicked in the pants, yas, but sometimes . . ." he pointed to the box of Maryanne's documents, "sometimes we get much more than we ask for. And Sue-Ann," he said more softly. "If you ever really need to come here, it will be here for you. And *I* am *always* here for you."

So I went home and rode my horses. I called Linsey and told her I was sick and couldn't come in, then I spent the weekend with my cell phone and computer turned off. I shot hundreds and hundreds of arrows both on and off a horse. I even went to Hi-Score one morning and bowled a couple of games, but I sucked at it.

I had as well as killed Rufus Donnelly, had been at least partially responsible for his brother's going bonkers and being committed. In addition, my girlfriend had left me, and I had to take a thyroid replacement pill every day of my life, preferably at the same time of day. But Alikki and Emmy and Irene treated me just the same as they always had. Irene, who wasn't even my horse, became more affectionate than my own two mares. Sometimes when she saw me leaning against the top rail of the fence, looking out into the field at the three of them, she would saunter over and stand just in front of me. When I put out my hand she would nuzzle it and lick it and I loved her so much that I could hardly bear it.

I dragged myself into the office on Monday morning feeling like I had been stepped on by a giant with dogshit on his hobnailed boots, but it was better than being dead, I thought. I had recovered enough to realize that I was recovering, or, at least, that I was capable of recovering some time in the future. Monday was staff meeting day. Nine sharp, with everybody present. That was the rule. I knew I had some catching up to do (again) so I was a couple of hours early and I hoped I could sneak in before anyone else arrived. No such luck; Cal was waiting for me at the front door with the kind of look that he would have used on someone who had spray-painted graffiti on his office wall.

"Sue-Ann," he said tersely, "Where have you been? I've been trying to get hold of you all weekend. I tried your land phone, your cell, and your email . . ."

Cal followed me into my office, while I turned on the light and put my things away. To my surprise, Cal shut the door and sat down across from my desk. I sat down slowly, contrite. "Cal," I began, "I'm sorry. I was sick. I couldn't talk to anybody. Was there something important I missed?"

"Sue-Ann, if Pine Oak had burned to the ground, you wouldn't have known it!"

"You're right," I said contritely. "I'm sorry I let you down. What do you want to tell me? Are you going to fire me?"

"Fire you? Where did that come from?"

"I haven't been very lucky lately. Bad news on just about every front. Being fired would fit right in."

"No, of course I'm not going to fire you. Just the opposite."

"You're going to hire me?" I have no idea where that little bit of levity came from.

"Just wait for it," he said. "But first I need to know you're all right."

"Yes, sure. I mean, sure."

"I've got some personal news, Sue-Ann."

"Your ex-wife left town already?" I guessed.

He seemed taken aback by that. "Well, yes, she did."

"So how do you feel about that?" I asked.

"I want to be with my kids," he said. "And I found a way to do it."

"You're going to fight for custody?" I asked.

"Hmm? No, I decided not to go that route. Look, for the last couple of months I've been looking around at the job market."

"So that's what you were doing over New Year's."

"Yes. And I've been offered a job in Louisiana. On *The Shreveport Times*."

"When do you have to decide?"

"I've . . . I've already accepted, Sue-Ann. I start tomorrow. It's an online newspaper, so my work will be cut out for me."

I was totally not expecting that. "You . . . you're leaving *The Courier*?"

"I would have left already, but I couldn't go without talking to you."

'But who's . . . are they going to bring someone in or shut down *The Courier* or what?" I was raising my voice a little. "We *need* these jobs, Cal. What are people like Betty and, I don't know, Annie going to do now?"

"They'll be better off, I think."

"How do you figure?"

"I've already discussed my replacement with the owner and he agrees one hundred percent. You're the new editor, Sue-Ann."

"What? Me? You have to be out of your fucking mind, Cal. I'm barely able to get from one day to the next without slitting my wrists. What makes you think that—"

"You don't want the job?" he smiled, "The pay is pretty good, you know."

"Of course I want the job, Cal, what are you, a moron? But what makes you think I'm capable of editing a newspaper?"

"You're the best reporter I've ever known, Sue-Ann. You deserve this job, but it won't be easy."

"You're serious about this?"

"It's a done deal. All of it."

"Are, um, are you going to try to get back with your wife?"

"Huh? Oh, no, no. I think she's serious about this guy she's been writing to. But I'll be there for my kids—for baseball and soccer practice and helping with homework if I can."

I couldn't help but realize the irony of the situation. If I had managed to bring Gina back, Cal may have stayed. Thinking back to some of our earlier conversations, I saw that he had simply been waiting for me to find her to make his decision.

"So, what, you're going to break the news at the staff meeting?" I asked.

"I told the staff late on Friday. This morning it will be *your* staff meeting."

"Mine?"

"I'm out of here."

"But—"

"Good luck, Sue-Ann. If you need anything call or email."

We stood up. He hugged me and kissed me lightly on the cheek. Then he was gone. Wow. I mean, shit. What was I going to do now?

In a few minutes, people started arriving for the staff meeting, putting their things in their cubicles and filing into the conference room. As they passed my office, they looked in and smiled and said, "Congrats, Sue-Ann." and "Good morning, Chief?" and other really stupid things. And when I walked in and took Cal's—my—place at the head of the table, everyone was looking at me, as still and as quiet as statues.

"I guess you've all heard the news," I began. "I'm the new boss, although I can't really believe it yet. Let's just assume that it's true, though, and get down to business. The first thing I want to do is . . . wait a minute, where's Linsey?"

Everyone looked around the table, then back at me. No one knew. "Maybe she's sick," Mark suggested. "I think she might have had an early appointment for an ad," said Annie.

"We'll fill her in later, then. Okay, obviously there have to be a few changes. First, we need to hire another reporter, so if anyone has any suggestions, let me have them in private. My first act is to declare that *The Courier* is going to have an online version, starting as soon as possible. Any reactions? Ideas? Come on, let's have em."

And believe me, they did. And for an idea that I had come up with less than five minutes before, they were as excited as the Bennett sisters at Mr. Bingley's Netherfield ball. I had made a pretty good entrance, I'll admit, and the staff worked steadily through the morning and into the afternoon. When Becky Colley came in after school, I called her into my office—I hadn't yet moved into Cal's larger one.

"I guess you heard the news?"

"About you being the new honcho? Sure." Becky, who had gone from goth to deb only a few months before, was slowly reverting back toward her rebellious inclinations. She wore very tight black denim jeans, low black sneakers like Pepper's, and a voluminous sweatshirt that read, "Take a picture, it'll last longer," that I assumed Jack had sent her for Xmas. Becky's hair was black with blue streaks, cut short.

"Are you okay with it?"

"Yeah, why shouldn't I be?"

I told her the idea about the online newspaper I had in mind. "You're going to have more responsibility," I told her. "If you're interested."

"You mean I can put my photos on line?" she asked.

"Yep. By the way, where's your mother?"

"My mother?" she asked incredulously.

"Linsey, yeah. She works here, remember?"

Becky started laughing. "Looks like the old boss didn't tell the new boss everything."

"What do you mean?"

"Mr. Dent took my mother with him. Don't ask me why; she's kind of a flooze."

"Cal *what*?"

"Mother's going to Shreveport with Mr. Dent. Do I hear the word 'divorce'?"

"Cal took my office manager?" I couldn't believe it, but then, I couldn't believe anything I had heard so far that day.

"Sue-Ann—or should I call you Ms. McKeown now?"

"Sue-Ann."

"Listen," said the girl, "I've been sneaking a look at my mother's cell phone when she's in the shower or sleeping or whatever. She likes to send racy pictures to her boyfriends and I email them to myself so I can blackmail her if I ever need to. A couple of weeks ago, I started finding pictures of her and Mr. Dent. I've got some that show them having sex." She groped in the pocket of her black jeans for her cell phone. "Do you want to see them?"

And here I hadn't thought anything else could surprise me. "Of course not," I told her. But it was too late, she had turned the phone around and I saw Linsey in the midst of an act I had once pictured myself performing. I snatched the phone and snapped shut the cover.

"I can email them to you and you can put them up on your computer screen if you want to,' Becky said.

"Becky, listen to me," I said as sternly as I could. "You are a minor. If the wrong people knew you had gotten pornographic pictures from your mother's phone, she could go to jail. Mr. Dent, too. *I* could go to jail."

"Okay, okay, I'll delete them," she said.

I handed the phone back to Becky and she busied herself with the screen. "Sorry," she said, "I didn't mean to . . . you know. It's just that losing my mother all of a sudden is kind of a big deal for me. Even if I really don't like her much."

"So she's divorcing your dad?" I asked.

"They haven't been getting along very well for ages," she said. "I don't think my dad's got any libido. I mean, I don't think he screws around at all. Guess it's the end of my family, though. Lucky I'm almost old enough to leave home. Legally, I mean."

"I'm sorry, Bec. If there's anything I can do . . ."

"Hey. I have another family now. Right here at the paper."

"Yes, you do," I told her. And so did I.

~ ~ ~

There was a strange car in my driveway when I got home that night, but nobody in sight. My front door was locked, which was a good sign, but I called out before I took a step inside. "Is anybody there?"

I heard a rustling noise, then a mumble, "It's me, Sue-Ann."

No, it wasn't Joey Bickley or Cletus Donnelly or Donny Brassfield or any of those characters. It was Krista, who I found just getting up from my couch, fully dressed in light slacks, a lavender blouse, and rainbow socks.

"God," she yawned. "You're home late tonight."

"It was a weird day," I said. "Is that your new car out front?"

"Yeah, a Toyota RAV4; isn't it cool?" Krista looked even more disheveled than usual. Her blouse and slacks looked like they had been slept in more than once and she was obviously tired. I noticed, though, that her long, strawberry hair had been molded into a kind of soufflé, although one that had gone flat. "I got here a couple of hours ago. Didn't even go home first."

"Don't tell me you went up to Richmond and saw Pepper."

Her grin was right out of a Huckleberry Finn movie. "Yeah, I did."

"And you asked her out?"

"Yeah."

"And so?"

"And so, wow."

"Wow?"

"Yeah. Wow. And you were right: I was really horny. Luckily, so was she. I think she fell in love with me."

"Bullshit, Krista," I said, but I was almost bursting with a kind of childish, girlish, glee. "I can't believe you actually did that."

"I did, though."

I sat down on the chair next to the sofa and crossed one leg over the other, wishing for the hundredth time that I still smoked. "You just walked in and asked her out?"

"Well, first I asked her if she could do anything with my hair. Then when it was all lathered up and everything, I told her I was a friend of yours. And so we started talking. I think at first she was wondering if I was your girlfriend, but I told her wasn't it strange that Sue-Ann was dating a woman now and she said yeah. So we talked some more about this and that and I told her that I had driven up from Florida just to meet her."

"No you didn't!" I squealed.

"Yes I did. Bet you didn't think I had it in me did you?"

"I'll admit it," I said. "But what happened then?"

"We talked some more and I could tell that she was going really slow for a hairdresser that usually needs to get through as many clients as she can. And her hands were about to make me faint."

"I know the feeling."

"So finally I asked if she wanted to have dinner with me that night and she said she didn't think so and I asked her for the next night and she said she didn't think so. I asked if she already had a date and she said yeah, tonight and tomorrow night too and I asked can you break em? And she asked, both of them? and I said yeah, and she said that maybe she would but just because I was Sue-Ann's friend. I told her to choose a nice restaurant and let me pick her up. Jeez, Sue-Ann, what is it about food and sex? I mean, glancing like shy little girls over the soup, smiling a little over the fish, and then, by the time the wine was getting low, staring at each other like two panthers. When we left, I unlocked the car door for her and turned around and suddenly we were kissing like crazy and her hands were in my hair again. I think you know the rest."

"Yeah, I do, and the memory makes me glad and sad at the same time. Are you going to see Pepper again?"

"Probably not. I mean, it was a one-night thing; well, two nights. Two nights and a day. But we're not, you know . . ."

"Not lesbians? Yeah, me neither." We both laughed.

"Well, maybe I'll ask her to come and visit sometime. We're going to write, you know. I have her email address." Krista stretched out her body on the sofa and yawned. "You know, I'm tired, but I'm still so revved up. Tell me about what you've been doing."

"If you want me to talk, you have to give me coffee. Or at least wait until I make some." And as I was pouring out cups for both of us, I told her a few things about finding Maryanne Simmons' husband and giving copies of her papers to The Creeper. And as I was about to go into the part about doing her biography, I had a sudden idea.

"I think I have a job for you," I said. "I need you to do the interviews with Maryanne's husband. We'll write the biography together. Equal credit."

"What makes you think I can write?" she asked.

"I have a feeling you can do anything you want," I told her. "Your grandfather thinks so, too."

"The dear old Zombie. Anyway, why don't you write it yourself?"

"I've . . . I've just been appointed the new editor of *The Courier* and I'll have to be spending a lot more time at work."

"Jeez, Sue-Ann, that's great. What happened to the old editor; did he get fired?"

"He got a job in Louisiana and ran off with our new office manager."

"Wait a minute, wait a minute," Krista said excitedly. "Wasn't that Gina's old boyfriend?"

"She told you about that?" I asked.

"We talked about it the last time she came out. You mean he just changed girlfriends in midstream?"

"Right as a reefer," I said, "and just as goofy."

"What a dickhead," she said, then started giggling much like she did when she was on the radio being Gamma. "So, um, what are you going to do about finding a new office manager?" she asked with a gleam in her eye.

I leaned back and closed my eyes, wondering what Gina was doing in Myrtle Beach and if she missed me as much as I missed her. "Oh, I have someone in mind," I said.

Chapter 27

But the story's not over yet.

About three months later, I was sitting at my round picnic table in the barnyard, drinking a cool glass of Reisling and watching the bats flip and flutter overhead in the late twilight. I had just finished feeding up and was enjoying the warmer weather before I went inside to see if I had anything in the fridge that could pass for dinner. I had the outside radio—set to the pirate station, of course—playing softly. The Creeper had gotten off his craziness kick at last. Instead of laughing maniacs, I now heard the powerful voice of Carolyne Mas, singing,

Still sane;
you may think you're crossing the line
Still sane;
you may think you're losing you're mind
as you stare at their faces
stare at their faces,
stare at their faces.
Ohh, still sane.

Maybe so, Carolyne. It was getting better, anyway.

That morning, I had finished the final draft of my story about Cletus Donnelly. It wasn't the easiest story I had ever worked on; in fact, it had probably taken me longer to write than any other. Still, it wasn't a bad story, although I wish it were better. I wish it had a happier ending.

I kept my word to Cletus. I had written his story. I had personally interviewed his neighbors, some of his co-workers, his teachers, and as many of his schoolmates as I could find. I had even gotten hold of the supersecret psychological reports from Waxahatchee. I felt I knew him better than he did himself, but that wasn't enough.

Thirty days after I had been hired as editor of *The Pine Oak Courier,* Cletus Donnelly died in his room at the hospital. A psychiatric aide doing her usual rounds found hm lying face down and shirtless in his locked room. When he was turned over, the end of a home-made shank was found protruding from his chest. There was a suicide note; I have a copy of that, too.

In my story, I made a point about Cletus' death being the final chapter in the kind of small-town tragedy that might have been written by Tennessee Williams or Clifford Odets. But what happened at Waxahatchee was real, not theater. And it took a lifetime to play out.

Cletus was born on April 1, 1975 in Pine Oak. His father, Albert Donnelly, worked in a hardware store while his mother Betty taught second grade at Pine Oak Elementary. When Cletus was 10 years old, Albert was fired from his job for excessive absences, the absences being caused by alcoholic binges. He then went from job to job, each one a little less well paid than the last. And as his luck changed from bad to worse, he became abusive. In 1986 neighbors called the sheriff's office when they heard a loud argument in the Donnelly home. When officers got there, Albert Donnelly was contrite, but both Cletus and Betty had to be taken to the hospital. Although Albert was arrested, Betty had the charges dropped and Albert went back home, but neighbors heard a lot of less-violent arguments in the years following. No more arrests though, and if there were any further injuries, they weren't reported.

When Cletus was 17 years old, he got his first tattoo—the Marine motto "Semper Fi" inked on his right bicep. His grades, which were always poor, had gotten so bad that he dropped out of high school and tried to join the Marines, not realizing that a high school degree was a requirement. It was a bitter blow to the young man because, according to one of his school councilors, he had been fixated on becoming a soldier. It was a profession in which a common man could become an honored hero.

Maybe as an alternative to the Marines, Cletus developed his interest in martial arts and Eastern weapons, such as the nunchucks, samurai swords, and ninja stars that were found in his apartment after he first attacked me. Although I doubt if he ever took formal lessons, he learned the rudiments of Jeet Kune Do, Bojuka, and Bok Fu from the many books he purchased on the subjects, and which I later saw at Benny's bookstore. He also paid for a dozen more tattoos, all of which had reference to honor or fortitude in battle—an eagle, a *ronin* knight, the Chinese character for "Bravery," and the like.

Around this same time, Betty got pregnant again, and they named the baby Rufus. Everyone I talked to told me that Cletus doted on his younger brother and spent much of his time at home to protect him and his mother from his father's excesses.

In 1994, Albert Donnelly was killed when he tried to cross I-10 at midnight while highly intoxicated. Betty began dating almost immediately, and although Cletus never liked the men Betty brought home, the next few years were relatively stable ones for Cletus. He was able to get a job with the H. A. Hardy Juvenile Center as a guard. Between his salary and his mother's they were able to pay the rent on their house and have a normal life. He often took little Rufus to movies and local sports events.

But his job at Hardy began to wear on Cletus, and I think it was here that Cletus first began to question his sexuality. From his psychological files I found out that Cletus sometimes witnessed homosexual acts by the juvenile offenders and was both repulsed and fascinated by them. Although Cletus was not a virgin, his few sexual experiences were with women who were either very hard up or very drunk—one actually vomited in the bed during intercourse. Sex, to Cletus, was often filthy and unsatisfying, so when he arrived at home one afternoon and found his mother moaning out her enjoyment of a good doggy-style fuck with a stranger, Cletus came to the conclusion that she was being raped and beat her lover—who was hardly in a position to defend himself—senseless.

Although charges against Cletus for battery were never filed, as the man—who was married—did not want his affair to become public, this incident got him committed to Waxahatchee for the first time. There, he was simply diagnosed with a mild case of schizophrenia, given medication, and released after a short stay.

On his release, Cletus applied for and was accepted as a guard at the State Correctional Institution in Forester. What's that you say? How could he have gotten a job in the public safety sector with a stint in a mental hospital? Well, for one thing, there was nothing on the application that asked whether he had or not; and remember that Cletus was never charged for the battery on his mother's boyfriend. For another, information on mental patients in Florida is classified tighter than FBI files. Even if the warden himself had asked—in person—Waxahatchee officials wouldn't have admitted that Cletus had even been admitted.

In 2000, Betty Donnelly died of a sudden stroke, making both Cletus and Rufus orphans. According to one of the men he worked with, Cletus was never able to completely absorb his mother's death, often acting and talking as if she were still alive. He brought up his younger brother singlehandedly, and when Rufus graduated from Pine Oak High School in 2007, Cletus attended his graduation ceremonies with the pride of a parent.

Rufus soon enlisted in the military, a fact that made his older brother happy, but lonely. With Rufus in boot camp, then in Iraq, Cletus began to see his own life with new eyes. He saw corruption and hypocrisy throughout the correctional system that paid his salary; he stared his own loneliness in the face, and became more aware of his homosexual cravings. He hated these feelings—and began go hate himself—knowing that in a small town like Pine Oak, to be different is to be ostracized. It was at this time he first contemplated suicide.

When Cletus got the news that Rufus had been killed in Iraq, he must have felt as if part of his own life was over, too. He had been an odd, but effective "catcher in the rye" for his little brother, but a single sniper's bullet had voided all the care and attention he had put into Rufus' upbringing. Yet Rufus had died the honorable death of a soldier, and that was something to be proud of.

I couldn't find out much about what he did in the year after Rufus' death, although I did learn that he sometimes practiced using his martial arts weapons in the woods near Cypress Lake Lodge. On one of these outings, he must have seem Gina and me together.

He developed a hatred for the press—and for me in particular, the consequences of which you already know about.

When he was transported back to Waxahatchee after his last attack on me and Myra, Cletus started refusing to take his medicine. He was angry and belligerent. He seemed to have given up the idea of ever leaving the hospital. He obtained spending money by selling his books and some of his other possessions, some of which he spent in the hospital canteen. The rest he used to purchase a butter knife that had been honed at the tip into an effective shank. He waited until everyone was asleep, then held the shank to his tattooed breast and sank down to the floor.

Where did he get the shank? Who knows. Probably from another resident. Myra Van Hesse told me that weapons are always being turned up in routine searches. Cletus had worked in a prison so he knew they were somewhere to be had.

And that brings me to Myra, because it was she that accessed Cletus's files and delivered them to me in my office at *The Courier*.

"But Myra," I said when she first handed me the folder. "Didn't you say that anyone who pulled up confidential files tripped some kind of a red light?"

"My land, Sue-Ann," she answered, "when the rumor got out that one of the forensics residents had died, every doctor, WBS, and administrator at Waxahatchee accessed those files. I'll bet at least a hundred red lights went off."

If not for Myra, Cletus' suicide may very well have remained a hospital secret; he would have been buried in a plain grave on hospital grounds—near Mickey Simmons, maybe—with a plastic marker reading CLETUS D. His story may never have been written and his suicide note would have remained unread by everyone but those who failed to help him in his last months and hours and minutes.

It simply said, "I fell on my sword."

A List of the Songs

"Pay the Moon," written by Iza Moreau. Published by Black Bay Music.

"They're Coming to Take Me Away, Ha Ha," written by Jerry Samuels and performed by Napoleon XIV. Published by Print Music.

"Mad John's Escape," written and performed by Donovan Leitch. Published by Donovan Music Ltd.

"Booker T and His Electric Shock," written by Bob Markley and Danny Harris and performed by Markley. Published by Rhombus Music.

"Ashley and Me," written by Iza Moreau. Published by Black Bay Music.

"Stillsane," written and performed by Carolyne Mas. Published by Eggs and Coffee and Music Ltd.

About the Author

Iza Moreau was born and raised in New Mexico, where she was introduced to Arabian horses and to the art of riding them. After a stint in journalism school, she roamed the country for a couple of years before settling down in one of the Southern states, where she has a small farm with a couple of horses. She counts Sarah Waters, Maggie Estep, and the Bronte sisters—Acton, Currer, and Ellis—among her literary influences.

Madness in Small Towns is the second in a series of Small Town novels featuring Sue-Ann McKeown and her friends in Pine Oak, Florida. The first novel in the series, *The News in Small Towns*, was a top-5 finalist in the 2013 Next Generation Indie Book Awards in both Mystery and Regional Fiction, and is available in print and as an e-book. The third novel, *Secrets in Small Towns,* will appear in early 2014.

In addition to the novels, there is a series of Small Town short stories featuring the same characters. Several of these are available at Amazon.com as e-books and will be collected in 2015 under the title *Mysteries in Small Towns.*

You can reach Iza at iza@blackbayfarm.com.

3

24618376R00165

Made in the USA
Charleston, SC
29 November 2013